A RURAL ODYSSEY II

Abilene
Digging Deeper

MARK J. CURRAN

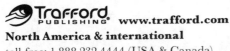

www.trafford.com
North America & international
toll-free: 1 888 232 4444 (USA & Canada)
fax: 812 355 4082

Final Draft in the Time of the Corona Virus
For Family and Friends and Anyone Who Loved Abilene

1

THE VIOLENCE

Abilene, a beautiful historic farm town on the Central Plains of Kansas survived in 1959 its most violent moment since the bloody shootouts on A street south of the Union Pacific tracks in the late 1860s and early 1870s. It was just a coincidence that it was almost 100 years since the founding of the town. In those old days cowboys were bored and celebrating too much after the long trail drives from Texas on the Chisholm Trail, gambling in the bars, and spending their wages on the prostitutes. Hucksters from Chicago and Kansas City knowing there was easy money to be made came to town; it made for a volatile mixture. In 1869 the town tried to fight back. The ladies of the night were told to stay south of the Kansas Pacific tracks. There was a "No Gun" law established. Reports have it that the cowboys ripped down the "No Gun Signs" and basically shot up the town. No less than Joseph McCoy himself (he started the cattle boom) railed against it all. Two peace officers from St. Louis came to town, were accosted in the saloons and got back on the first train heading back east. It was then that "Bear River" Tom Smith, the bare fisted sheriff, brought a semblance of law and order, first taking on the ruffians, reported as riding through town on his horse "Silverheels" and beating into submission any opposition with his fists. This was 1870 and peace reigned for a while. But Sheriff Smith and a deputy went out in the country that Fall to deal with a serious matter, were ambushed, and Smith was killed.

The town did not want to revert to the wild days before Smith, so it looked around and hired a renowned frontier scout and gunslinger to be the next sheriff. It took Wild Bill Hickok and his deputies a few months to settle it all down. There were gun battles, Hickok vanquishing some well-known "varmints and bad hombres" before accidentally killing his own deputy when hearing a noise from behind him after a gunfight. It was reported that after that he never shot a gun in Abilene. The cattle drive days in Abilene were waning, the Chisholm trail cowboys moving on to Ellsworth and later Dodge City. Hickok who had a reputation for spending most of his time in the same saloons as the wild cowboys was made to feel unwelcome as before and moved on to a recent minor gold rush in Deadwood, South Dakota.

This was a young town, only officially founded a few years earlier in 1869. The first settlers had come in 1857. The trail drives, as mentioned, ended just a short time later; some were moved west to Ellsworth, plus there was no need for the Longhorns when quality beef arrived on the rails from the East, via England, the advent of the Shorthorns and White Face Herefords. However, it was common knowledge that farmers and merchants, many Bible Belt Citizens among them, were not crazy about the rowdy trail drives and all the violence that came with them. Cattle were waning and wheat and homesteading were taking their place.

The "moment" in 1959 alluded to was not that momentous in terms of size or stature, but it was the germ of a national phenomenon, much larger, equally violent and downright scary. I'm talking about the existence and actions of the members of the Ku Klux Klan. It was such people who burned down my Dad and Mom's house in 1959, meaning to kill them, and incidentally me too, a teenager and fresh graduate of Abilene High School, soon to be off to college in the big city of Kansas City. They chose us because we were Catholics, Sean and Molly O'Brien and me, son Michael. It wasn't just us. They also ransacked the only Negro church in town, luckily not killing its pastor, Reverend Watson, his wife, Stella, and one of my best friends, their son Jeremiah.

Yet there's more to it, all told in my book "A Rural Odyssey – Living Can Be Dangerous," the result of a senior project at college out just a year ago. If I retell part of it, the reader will have a lot better idea why and how the recent events took place. About six years ago in 1957 through no fault of my own, maybe being in the wrong place at the wrong time, I got in the clutches of three local bank robbers who pulled off a heist at a tiny small town bank in Enterprise, Kansas, just five miles from our farm on old Highway 40 east of Abilene. They tried to kidnap me and use me as a hostage to get away from the police and highway patrol. I was working for my Dad Sean, plowing the wheat stubble in the very southeast corner of our half-section farm on a tiny Ford tractor when it all happened. After swerving around the corner from the highway to the county road on the east side of our farm and screeching to a stop, one of them ran over to the tractor, a pistol in his hand, ordered me off the tractor, grabbed my arms and held them behind my back. He got me into the back seat of their car, one of his buddies up front in the driver's seat, the other in the right front, but now with doors opened and all armed with tommy guns, a shotgun and pistols, ready for the police.

Police cars and highway patrol vehicles had been following them in hot pursuit since Enterprise and were just a minute or two arriving to the same spot. One of the robbers shouted out to the police, "Back off, call your damned friends off. We've got the kid and if you don't cooperate, he gets it. We need us some space to get out of here. I don't wanna see no cop cars behind us when we leave. We'll talk later about the boy." I guess to prove his point and show me to the cops, his buddy in the back seat pulled me out of the car, holding a pistol to my head and yelled, "We mean business."

For whatever reason I can't explain now nor could then, I did a very dumb thing. A skinny guy and not strong even though I had baled a lot of hay for Dad, on an impulse I managed to wiggle loose from his grasp (he was holding a gun in one hand, me in the other), brought my arms down on his gun hand, it went off and I dove for the ditch. Bonnie and Clyde or Al Capone days started all over, shotgun blasts, spurts of bullets from the tommy guns, and return fire from the police. My guy was shot in the leg, the two in the front seat were now hiding behind the big front fenders of the car, one bleeding like a stuck pig in the hand that had his tommy gun. All raised their hands, local sheriff Wiley along with two highway patrol officers came slowly forward with a shotgun in his hand, and said, "Okay, it's all over. Throw any weapons down to the ground, raise your arms. I'm takin' you in. Bank robbery, kidnapping, and attempted murder." Another officer, I think one of the highway patrolmen, ran over to me in the ditch, said, "You are one brave son of a bitch. I take that back; you are one lucky and brave son of a bitch." He literally picked me up, put me in the back seat of the patrol car, and the next thing I knew I was in emergency in the local county hospital.

To make a long story short, I was hailed as a local hero, made it into the paper the "Abilene Reflector Chronicle," not for the last time due to some shenanigans a year after high school, and Dad had me out on the tractor two days later. Dad, Mom, brothers Paul and Joe, sister Caitlin were all up to the hospital when I was still in shock, with a broken arm and bruises but treated to all the ice cream I wanted. Mom said, "We're going to get a St. Christopher's medal for that tractor. No more of this nonsense," all why fingering the ever-present Rosary in her hand.

There's more. I'm not a fighter, never was, but the next school year I got into an altercation with a red neck kid living out west of town, this in the hallway outside the gymnasium in the high school. He called me some names, like "you goddamned mick" and "cat licker," said I was a "nigger lover" (Jeremiah, one of my good friends, one of the few black kids in school, did music with me in the band room and he came out to the farm to play catch sometimes) and took a swing at me. I caught it on the chin but managed to plant one on the side of his head (boxing lessons from brother Joe years earlier did not all go bad), this before the biggest guy in our class, fullback and defensive tackle on the football team, Rip Warner ran up, grabbed the redneck by the arm and said, "Asshole, next time pick on someone your own size." "F*** you, shithead," the redneck said, turned around and ran out the door to the parking lot where he burned rubber getting out of the school lot. My music buddy, Jeremiah, had been in band class the whole time, came running up, saw me and Rip (the football player), me rubbing my chin and with a bloody nose. When he got the story, he said, "Mike, thank you. You are a great friend. I won't be forgetting this. And Rip, thank you, good to know you can be just as mean off the football field when you need to be."

This was all important because it was later in that same senior year when the fire on the farm took place and it was Jeremiah's Dad's church that was ransacked. I'm re-telling all this just to let you know what would happen later. The three bank robbers were sentenced to twenty years in Kansas State Prison in Lansing, told by Sheriff Wiley to never "show their sorry asses" back in Dickinson County, much less Abilene, that is if they ever got out of jail, and there would be no need for a trial. "Shot while trying to escape!" - Sheriff Wiley never minced words, and he got some details wrong sometimes, but punctuated his threat with "I never forget a face, particularly sonofabitches like you, I hope you get my message." There was evidence that whoever burned our house and ransacked Jeremiah's church just a few years later, leaving behind KKK scrawled in red paint on the sidewalk gate post leading to our house and the doorway of the Watson church were cohorts of the same crew that had tried to kidnap me in the wheat field two summers before. In their minds it was revenge. And with some investigating by the sheriff, never one to forget a crime, and lawyers who were friends of Dad's at his local gin rummy games at the local Elks Club, a whole beehive of Ku Klux Klan people were discovered west of town out in the boonies, among them the bank robbers and their families, and incidentally, my red necked "friend" from school among them.

Inexplicably, but maybe not, a whole bunch of those folks west of town moved in a big group up to Idaho shortly thereafter, the word around town being they had joined up with one of those communities out in the woods, "rugged individualists" they called themselves, and avowed complete independence from the local and state police and for that matter, anything to do with government.

The end of all this story, necessary to bring any reader up to date, was that in 1959 my Dad and Mom with insurance money from the burned farmhouse bought a small but pretty house on Rogers Street near Eisenhower Park, and sister Caitlin and husband Ron bought the arable land from Dad's old farm and built a new house. Ron and his brother would farm that land and much more in the area in the ensuing years. I was off to college in Kansas City with big plans for the future. It was a new life starting.

2

THE KLAN

The Ku Klux Klan was still a national organization in 1959, the year I went off to college, albeit not like the halcyon years before. It had existed in three phases, of white nationalism, anti-immigration, and anti-Catholicism. It used physical assault and even murder in the first phase of the 1860s against blacks and their allies in the South. The Klan was especially powerful then, opposed to the Republicans in government, many blacks among them since the Civil War. Each Klan group was local and autonomous. Membership was secret and they wore robes, masks and conical hats, all to scare their opponents and victims. Huge bonfires, marching and the burning of crosses marked many meetings. It was finally suppressed about 1872. The second phase started in Georgia in the 1920s, but grew to be nationwide, even in the Midwest and West. Rooted in local Protestant communities, it wanted white supremacy, was pro-Prohibition and opposed Catholics and Jews (the main source of immigration in the times). It was especially against the Pope and his power and the Catholic Church. The third phase after 1950 centered on opposition to the Civil Rights Movement. Classified as a hate group by the Anti-Defamation League, it supported "Anglo-Saxon blood" and swore to uphold Christian morality. But it was denounced by virtually every Christian denomination.

The Klan was especially strong in Kansas in the 1920s, estimated to have up to 60,000 members. A famous Kansas journalist, William Allen

White, battled against the Klan in his newspaper *The Emporia Gazette*. A candidate for governor in 1924, he lost the election perhaps in some part due to his own opposition to the Klan, reportedly with 10,000 members in and around Emporia, including the chief of police and most of his men. However, the Klan was opposed by many and the State Legislature the next year outlawed Klan business activity and its popularity was on the wane. The Klan was finally outlawed, however in 1925 by the state legislature. Its members had been particularly successful in Kansas City, Kansas in the early 1920s with a membership in the thousands, and parades when hundreds paraded on horseback with Klan robes.

It was all this that caused my grandmother and her husband to sell their farm west of Solomon, Kansas, in fear of the Klan with its threats to Catholics. It was then that they moved to Abilene and bought the farm I grew up on east of town.

Why do I write all about this, dredging up memories of my grandmother and even the fire four years ago?

Nobody knows what strings were pulled, or what squeaky hinges were oiled (I mean bribes), but there was some astounding news from home and Abilene four years later in 1963. The criminals sentenced to twenty years in Lansing were released "on good behavior" and word had it they joined their own old friends and cohorts up in the woods in Idaho. Maybe afraid of the threat of Sheriff Wiley, reelected in the interim and pretty much the "permanent sheriff" in Abilene (there were no rules against re-election), they didn't show their faces anywhere in Dickinson County. Or at least that was what people thought.

3

BACK HOME TO ABILENE

Anyway, I was now out of college in Kansas City, a B.S.B.A. degree in Business Management and a minor in Spanish. I had done summer school in Mexico City in 1962 and was offered a job in Guatemala City in a pharmaceutical firm owned by a good Latino buddy's family from there. The buddy was from college days in Kansas City. I was pondering the offer, unsure if I could get used to the idea of actually living in another country or even making a living there. In spite of my love for Spanish and the great experience in Mexico and Guatemala, I was still a red-blooded patriot and tied to family, friends and just living in Kansas.

It was then that a big break came, one of those things that can change your whole life. Abilene had been chosen as a site for a new junior college, called Dwight D. Eisenhower Dickinson County Community College, this back in 1960. It was probably because of the good word, influence and political sway of President Eisenhower himself. He was our home-grown hero, Commanding General of the Armed Forces for the battles in North Africa against the Axis Powers and the Landing at Normandy and battle to defeat Hitler and Germany, then President of Columbia University in New York and finally President of the United States. All that got us in Abilene the designation for the college. The town was only 7000 in population, but much larger in reputation and importance in the whole state.

Even though I just had a Bachelor's degree, and Spanish just a minor, a good word from my Abilene High School Spanish and Latin mentor, Miss Stromberg, and my undergraduate Spanish teacher, Mr. Short from New Orleans and Louisiana State University in Baton Rouge, was enough to get me a full-time job as teacher on the junior college level with the proviso I would add a Master's Degree in coming years. It did not hurt that my undergraduate Jesuit Education at a good Liberal Arts College and the studies in Mexico City prepared me for teaching. I would teach U.S. History as well (after great training at college) and promised that I might be able to teach a Latin American History course to high level students once in a while.

When I had left Abilene in 1959, I was ready to leave behind the farm and small-town life for the big city, Kansas City, Missouri in this instance. The next four years I would thoroughly enjoy the city with its famous downtown "12th and Vine," the Muelbach Hotel, and the sports scene with a minor league professional basketball team and of course the Kansas City Athletics fresh from Philadelphia – real major league baseball! (I grew up for ten years playing sandlot baseball in Abilene, collecting baseball cards and listening to the Game of the Week with Pee Wee Reese and Dizzy Dean announcing, usually the Yankees and my hero Mickey Mantle.) Not to ignore were the great basketball games on the NAIA level at my small college. And more important, there were chances for classic guitar concerts in Kansas City, my main non-academic interest. I figured I was heading for some kind of a career involving Spanish, maybe business in Latin America or if I could pass the damned Foreign Service Exam, maybe the State Department.

All that seems pretty "high falutin'" as I think about it now in 1963. But I'm only 22 and can always change my mind about being in Abilene. There were a lot of other reasons to come back – my immediate family still lives there except for brother Joe who is off in the Navy in the Pacific, and I am very close to Mom and Dad, living their retired life out on Rogers Street. My sister Caitlin is married to Ron Schmidt and they have built a new house and are farming the land on Dad's old farm, and that is going well. A few good high school buddies are still around town, either farming or in the case of good friend Jeremiah Watson of high school music days and the KKK actions, working at jobs at Deershon Mfg. in Enterprise, and we can drink beer down at Frank's Friendly Tavern on 3rd street, although draft beer, that old Kansas 3.2 Coors, has gone up to 25 cents a glass. What is lacking at the moment is any prospect of a love life. All the former high school girl friends are either married after their own college days or engaged to be married. This will turn out all right when I discover there are two eligible young ladies starting out like me in a teaching career at the junior college. And for that matter, it is only an hour's drive to Manhattan and the coeds at K-State or back to Kansas City and a smattering of the Catholic girls from the sister school of my Jesuit college.

So after teaching English to students from Latin America at my alma mater in Kansas City in early summer 1963, a six week job, and playing music in a bar in Kansas City, Missouri the rest of the summer, I moved back "home" to Abilene to start at the Junior College in mid-September. It was really with mixed feelings – not taking the job in Guatemala and being in a new country I loved and a totally different life or being back home but challenged to do what I thought had a talent for and loved – teaching Spanish and some basic culture courses and a bit of history.

4

SETTLING IN AND A PREMONITION

It was quite a change moving back to a farm town of 7000 after those four years in Kansas City, Missouri but there were all the good reasons for it I've already mentioned. The Junior College, I'll just call it the Juco from now on, had been started in 1960, and was very small. There were three buildings, all located on the big empty lot north of 14th street just across from the old high school, this because the Garden Nursery had gone out of business, the children of the family I knew in high school not wanting to carry on the business. It turned out well – fifteen acres of space and three buildings were in place by 1963, an administration building with faculty offices, a classroom building which had a cafeteria and book store on one level and classrooms on the three top levels and a large co-ed dormitory, girls on one side, boys on the other. There were no sports teams, at least not yet, and it was really all set up as kind of a building block for kids not quite ready for K-State or KU or Emporia State, but with a dream of getting their AA degree and moving on to one of the "big schools." I arrived early September and checked in with Professor Halderson my boss. He seemed happy to have an Abilene resident familiar with town and families on the faculty and particularly with the teachers at Abilene High School, thinking maybe that link would be an avenue for shifting AHS students on over to the juco. We promised a conversation, but I had to get settled into temporary living quarters in Mom and Dad's upstairs bedroom and tiny bath first.

I'm not sure of their reaction to events. There could be no link to the old farm; those days were gone for Dad except the big vegetable garden on the northeast corner of the remaining acreage of the north 40, the horse shed and small corral he built to board town kids' horses, and me with no aptitude for farming anyway. Dad never said much, but Mom probably had higher aspirations for me than teaching at a Juco back home. On the other hand, they never put their views in opposition to mine and maybe having me at home or at least in Abilene would be good for their senior years. We had a wonderful reunion, lot of hugs and kisses and talk about college days, and them catching me up on events in Abilene. That didn't take long. I assured them the upstairs would be short term maybe for only a week. I had pretty insignificant savings from school, but did have enough for a month's rent somewhere in town, and that was the idea; I would be counting the days until the first juco paycheck. Brother Joe was out in the Pacific on a Navy destroyer and brother Paul up in the Dakotas as an estimator for a big construction site, so that left Caitlin and Ron at home on the old farm, Caitlin now with two tiny tots and another on the way. So maybe having me around was okay. I would not hang out at their house every day, but did call and check in at least once a week.

I found a reasonable two-bedroom apartment with bath, living room and small kitchen in one of those two - story Victorians on north Buckeye. I could use one of the bedrooms for an office. There was room in back to park the old rattle trap Dodge left over from junior and senior year days in college in Kansas City, and in fact I could actually walk to the Juco if need be. We hooked up the phone right away, I bought a small color TV at the Appliance Store downtown and was off and running. I could prepare a light breakfast and coffee at home, generally ate lunch at the Juco cafeteria with colleagues or students, and availed myself of Abilene's south side café (where I ate lunch with Grady Zimmerman when I helped him farm during one of my summers at college) and the only two real restaurants in Abilene, the old Lena's out on the highway 40 curve west of town and the Brookville Café of fried chicken fame for dinner. That is, most days, Mom cooked homecooked meals once a week, and I would go out to the old farm to have dinner with Caitlin and Ron once in a while; it was an honor to become a godfather to one of their daughters. Dinner invitations from a young lady at the Juco would come later.

So this story actually starts in mid-September 1963. Before I get on with it, there's a somber note. Some strange things happened during that first year back in Abilene, and I had a flashback one year earlier earlier. During college I had visited Mom and Dad at home in Abilene whenever I could and had unwavering correspondence, Mom's letter to me and my weekly letter back, a thing started four years before when I left Abilene for Kansas City. It was almost casually that she wrote in September 1962 that the local paper reported a rock thrown through the window of the jail down at the country courthouse. A letter was taped to it. She included the local newspaper clipping which is pretty scary:

> "To All the Shitheads in Abilene: There's going to be hell to pay. We'll be getting even for all the misery yur righteous, hypocritical, son of a bitch, shit eating town and county put our friends through. We got a long list. Cat lickers, those lazy micks who ruined our town, and the blacks who are ruining our country. And that fat slob piss ant sheriff who caused us all the trouble. He's a "cat licker" too. Ain't no one going to be spared. You're put on notice."

> Time passed and no more such incidents took place, all this before I moved back home.

5

HIGH HOPES FOR HUMBLE STUDENTS

I guess I need to talk about the job first because things seemed to flow from that. That first September and Fall Term I had two Spanish classes, a beginning and an intermediate, and one class in U.S. History. Enrollment was small, but in a sense that was good, twenty students in the SPA 101 and fifteen in the Spanish 201 Intermediate. The students at the Juco were not unintelligent; in fact, a few could have gone to school anywhere. Most however certainly were not those high school high achievers who had the grades and brains to at least allow them partial scholarships to the "big schools" already mentioned, or those with family money. There were a lot of wealthy farmers around Abilene, and the sons and daughters of the merchant business and "government" class - their parents owning the businesses in town or being part of the courthouse crowd of lawyers, county and state administrators and the like. Their kids were in Manhattan, Lawrence, Emporia or maybe Washburn in Topeka; or in the case of Catholics, at schools in Atchison (St. Benedict's) or Kansas City (Rockhurst) or even Salina (Marymount). And a smattering of kids went to the small Protestant Liberal Arts colleges scattered all over Kansas, depending on what type of religion they had at home.

The main common denominator of my kids was economic; their families were just getting by and the kids did not have high enough grades for scholarships to the big schools. But college of some kind, even two years and an AA degree was a way out. Tuition, it seemed to me, was quite reasonable, $10 dollars per credit hour, so about $150 dollars per semester, plus perhaps $50 for books. Most all lived at home, but there were some who could afford the dorms and three meals, maybe another $100 per month. Still, when added up, it was a lot of money. There were no fraternities or sororities and few "clubs" or "activities." It was come to class, do your work, pass the tests and in two years earn an AA degree qualifying you to apply to one of the big schools, and if you had good grades, maybe get some kind of financial help.

Incidentally, what was not present, and I and most of my colleagues really believed in it, was a Juco Industrial Arts preparation; the main reason was because there was already such a school in Salina just twenty-five miles away. I had learned a long time ago, meaning the week before classes in my freshman year of college, that there are different kinds of intelligence. If I had not luckily talked to a Biology Liberal Arts major and seen the advanced math and science requirements for the B.A. degree and weaseled out of them after a tense interview with a wily Jesuit dean, I would surely have flunked out of college. I switched to general business with a basic math requirement, no science, but lots of Spanish, History, and a smattering of English and a B.S.B.A. degree. What I'm saying is that those industrial arts (auto mechanics, plumbing, electricians, agriculture and the rest) students might be geniuses in their own right and do a helluva lot better in the real world than language majors and were in no way inferior to them – just different!

So, you might imagine in Central Kansas, most of the kids in my classes in the Juco were what we called "Anglos" in those days, and many aspired to that jump to a "real" college where a foreign language was a requirement for graduation. Spanish had a reputation for being the easiest to learn, a widely held opinion but greatly exaggerated. The DDE Junior

College or just the "Juco" also offered French with an enrollment just slightly below Spanish. It was still widely held by the general public that it was the language of diplomacy and also a couple of notches up from Spanish, more sophisticated, how can I say it best, "snootier." Interestingly enough there was a smattering of what we called "Hispanic" students, mainly whose parents and grandparents had come from Mexico. Racists in the region still called them "spics," just a notch or two up from the Negro minority in town. I naturally had a warm place in my heart for them, dating from working at the old Abilene Ice Plant in the summer between high school and college and after freshman year. Some of the happiest times of my young life were the chatter and laughter and beginning efforts of talking Spanish to them, and being accepted by their families for an introduction to spicy Mexican food. Most had relatives who came to Abilene to work on one of the three major railroads, laying the wooden ties and making the roadbeds with picks and shovels. And of course, being a minor in Spanish and with that study experience in Mexico and Guatemala, plus the huge effort to learn Spanish from Latin Americans at college, I had no prejudice against them at all, in fact was happy and proud to know them and their parents.

But, hey, I was also one of those "Anglos" from an Irish American family, a farm kid who did well at Abilene High School, mainly because of some terrific teachers of English, Debate, Latin and Spanish and American History. So, if an "Anglo" kid at the Juco showed interest, enthusiasm and was a hard worker, he or she got an extra "push" or bit of encouragement.

The Juco was so tiny that I was the only one teaching Spanish, and maybe "cheap help" at that. I brought good, proved methods of learning from that Jesuit School in Kansas City, and insisted on a balanced approach of grammar, structure, oral practice and something I think I was a pioneer of in those days, "culture day" with music, travel slides and the rest. And a lot of enthusiasm. There's more to be said as we move along in the story. Friendships with the students and their families came easily in a small town. And liaison with the former Spanish teacher – "school - marm" of old Abilene High School and her successor, a fellow student in Spanish with me at AHS had a lot to do with what would happen.

Maybe more interesting and even surprising was what happened with my single course in American History. Even though I was honestly weaker in History than Spanish, the courses in college were terrific, I did well, and adopted many of those teaching techniques. Included were a good textbook, burning the mid-night oil each night to "bone up" on what I did not know or knew pretty superficially, to have a good lecture the next day. But as the days, weeks and first months went by and I became really immersed in Abilene's life, a light bulb went on with a bright idea: what a terrific place to study history right at home, what a place to write a small book – the History of Abilene and Dickinson Country – and maybe all in an early preparation for graduate school courses the Juco demanded of me, now just with a bachelor's degree.

One of the ingredients in the pie was the new Eisenhower Presidential Museum, the on-going construction of the Eisenhower Library to house Ike's World War II and Presidential Papers, plus the colorful, fascinating history of Abilene itself. I would spend a lot of spare time down at the museum and a whole lot more at the library when it was finished, a guest "researcher" pass because of the Juco job. It was probably two thirds through the first year at the Juco that I seriously started my amateur "History of Abilene and Dickinson County" which I'm leaning on to tell this story. A good deal of it would come from just "leg work" around town, seeing the old places that were unimportant as a boy growing up.

School started and I discovered how incredibly busy I would be, getting to know the students in the classes, office hours to answer their questions, but really basic daily preparation – grammar explanations and drill sheets for the language classes, grading of homework, quizzes and major exams every three weeks, but a close reading of the text and preparation of lecture notes for the daily lectures in the history class where I basically found out how much I did not know. It was a small place and being a bachelor, I was keeping my eyes open for any young coeds starting out like me. Turns out there were two, Mariah Palafox teaching basic English and Jenny Winthrop doubling in geography and Kansas History. Both were fresh out of college, Mariah like me in her first year at the Juco, from K.U. and Jenny in her second year, from Emporia State.

6

PRECAUTIONS IN
THE BIBLE BELT

There was more to the time back home than teaching. My sister Caitlin, teaching English part-time in the high school and a real veteran of small-town teaching in the entire area, clued me in on some do's and don'ts. First of all, it's a small town and there are busybodies and gossips, and everybody knows everybody else's business. When she and Ron dated, most of the dates were in Salina, Kansas twenty-five miles away and about 30,000 people; even then it was the movies or what they called a "supper club" in those days where you could have dinner and dance. There were no theaters for plays and the like, but the high school plays and forays down to Manhattan or even Lawrence could provide a little "culture" if so needed.

More important was the whole idea of drinking and alcohol, something most of us did in college. Kansas was a semi- "dry" state, semi because it had evolved to the point where you could buy a bottle of booze or wine at a liquor store and take it to the local private "club" attached to a motel on North Buckeye near the interstate and buy set-ups for 35 cents. Only thing there was that you could be sure to meet locals and bar-flies, and everyone would know you were out and about. Kansas, including Abilene, allowed 3.2 beer joints, package liquor stores and the private "clubs" just mentioned; that's all. I would meet and date particularly one of my colleagues from the Juco that first year.

Everyone in town expected the teachers to hold unrealistically high moral standards of behavior, but in spite of it I did continue in moderation one "no-no" I suppose carrying over from summers between college years – drinking beer at Frank's Friendly Tavern down on 3rd street once a week, but carefully driving home that evening after the 25-cent draft beer. There were a couple of good reasons to still hang out at Frank's – first a few high school buddies were still in the area as well as a music connection. Jeremiah of high school music days (I talked a lot about him and his family in "Rural Odyssey"), and Loren Beasely, a bongo playing drummer, was a teacher himself in a high school just a few miles from Abilene, but generally home on the weekends in his snazzy, new, red Buick.

The other reason for Frank's turned out to be more important for my research on Abilene and Kansas History; the tavern had among its regulars Wally Galatin the local photographer who knew everybody and everything going on in town. He was an absolute treasure trove of local history with his family going back three generations and taking any photos (the only photography shop in town) of any event from 50th anniversaries to junior high and high school team photos, dances, weddings and the like. But most important, he and his dad before him were the main chroniclers of the whole Dwight D. Eisenhower story, past and present, in Abilene. We sat at that bar at least once or twice a month and he, knowing I was teaching U.S. History and very interested in Abilene, basically told me most all he knew (at least the publicly presentable parts) about the town. I think there was plenty more he didn't tell me, but would make hints about local amorous and other perhaps salacious events. I told him I just wanted the facts and those on local history. He said one night, "You are going to write one hell of a boring, dull history book if you stick to History." I soon discovered that from the very beginning with that wild cowboy and prostitute life down on A street there were times to get away from dry facts. Amazingly enough at that time there was no "big book" on Abilene history, but many newspaper sources and clippings and a massive number of articles in magazines. I would end up quoting Wally frequently in the rough manuscript I would come up with in the next two years. But this is getting ahead of those first days in town.

7

❖❖❖

BEGINNING TO UNDERSTAND LOCAL HISTORY

I found out that my students expected me to know a lot more about Abilene than I already knew. There would be lots of ways to bone up on all that including a lot of driving around town and even the whole county looking up places I had not had any interest in seeing when I grew up, other priorities then. The first was the Abilene Cemetery, the Protestant one; being Catholic I guess about fifteen years of funerals and Memorial Day Services at the Catholic Cemetery had made me familiar with those families. They were not among the real old timers in town. (It took me a while to figure out why. It was almost all Protestants who came first to Abilene. The Catholics only came later after the Homestead Act and when farm land became available.) So I drove out to the Protestant Cemetery, just spitting distance from the Juco and started to familiarize myself with tombstones and names, having to go back into town to the Library to check them out.

One of the oldest and largest stones simply said "Brown." It didn't even register with me at first, but this was the name for Brown's Park outside of town on the south side of the Smokey Hill River. That park for me, growing up, was not too familiar, just remembering drives out through the old Girl Scouts' Camp thick with trees and a lot of mosquitoes. Caitlin my sis was never in the scouts, just 4-H, so the State 4-H Camp at Rock Springs was far more important to us. I remember people talked about going snipe hunting out at Brown's Park, and I think I got suckered into that once by my bongo playing high school buddy. Ha. Once I started digging in the history books and even newspaper clippings in the city library it became clear that Brown indeed was one of the first names about local history you needed to know about. I guess I had not been a very good citizen about all that, but hell, like I said, there were other priorities growing up and living on the farm and being a "normal" kid in Abilene schools and such.

It turns out C. L. Brown was really instrumental in the development of the whole town. Born in Pennsylvania in 1872 and deceased in 1935, he started with a grist mill and wood lumbering mill out of town south of the river. The story is amazing: from the grist mill it evolved to the Abilene Electric Light Works providing power to the town. That idea evolved to a telephone company in1902; that evolved to the sale of the property to what eventually would become Southwestern Bell Telephone Company, a giant in the field. With the spinoff money he really established an empire in Abilene, responsible for the Sunflower Hotel, and the banking, insurance, investment trust called United Trust. At the height of his business days there were 85 companies, among them the grocery chain to become famous in the South, the Piggly-Wiggly Stores. Sources have it that in spite of the great Depression of 1929 he continued in expansion mode and eventually just plain ran out of money, dying bankrupt in 1935. But this was not before he had generously made significant gifts to the town – the Brown Memorial Park, amazing in its day and the Brown Memorial Home for the old and ailing (we sang Christmas carols there at Christmas Time) and many other gifts. The huge cemetery stone and marker I saw in Abilene simply saying "Brown" was done by him in dedication to his father, yet today the largest such stone in town. This was just one of the historic jewels one could dig up in Abilene history. There are a dozen others, but like I told the students, "You've got to start somewhere."

The other old stone I recall (other than those of Ike Eisenhower's parents) simply said "Duckwall." It was the Duckwall family monument, recalling an important part of Kansas and even national history – the "5 and Dime Store." Its motto was "A Little of Everything," and it was started in the very early days of Abilene in 1901. Alva Duckwall who started with a bicycle shop in Greenleaf, Kansas, came to Abilene and bought the old "Racket Store" across the street, a variety story for common, usable and reasonable household goods. The concept of the "5 and Dimes" started back east in the late 1870s and evolved to the big Woolworth chain in 1911. Duckwall added stores, up to 30 all over Kansas by his death in 1937. The forte was the small, inexpensive item for daily use, including candy, but with school supplies, note books, pens and pencils, and today what we called "stuff." The lunch counter was a mainstay with quite reasonable and simple fare. For kids there was a huge toy selection as well. An interesting anecdote of the very early days was that Duckwall himself would get in a horse and buggy and go out into the country to the farms, along with a paint brush and a can of paint, and ask farmers if he could paint the name of his store on the barn roof. Those thirty stores and the pioneering one in Abilene along with its warehouse were major contributors to the commerce of Abilene. Its executives, all in Abilene, were the mainstays of the country club set as well.

He was just one of the persons old Wally and I talked about in Frank's Friendly Tavern over beers. There would be more to come. That first Fall in town was extremely busy. I was up to my neck in school work and class preparation, starting the historical research, and just trying to be a good citizen. There were the once a week visits to Mom and Dad's out on Rogers and a good home-cooked meal along with it – fried chicken from farm days was still my favorite, and Mom's goulash. She was busy with lady friends, the D of I's down at St. Andrew's Church and a bridge club, plus her large flower and vegetable garden back of the house in Abilene. Dad was out to the farm during good weather either preparing a huge vegetable garden or weeding and watering it with buckets of water from the well, maintaining a small stable and barn, both to hold the horses he boarded for kids from town, volunteering down at St. Andrew's with the Knights of Columbus (carpentry work and pall bearer at funerals) and his one outside relaxation – the Gin Rummy games on Sunday afternoon at the Elks Club.

And I tried to get out to Caitlin and Ron's place on the old farm, but maybe not as often. Caitlin was teaching part time and Ron was farming a couple of thousand acres all around Dickinson County with his brother, plus running a small feed lot for cattle on the home farm. I was of no use as help but enjoyed seeing it all and how he and Caitlin would really spruce up the old place with new buildings and farm house, although they could never replace in my memory the original place I grew up on, all described as I said in that book I wrote when I was eighteen, "A Rural Odyssey – Living Can Be Dangerous."

8

A YOUNG MAN CAN GET LONELY

There was a beginning of a love life, or at least a smattering of one. I met Mariah Palafox, a young vibrant English teacher at the Juco and for a while we went out about once a week, burning a lot of gasoline in my own worn car going over to Salina to the places I already mentioned. Everyone in town, including everybody at the Juco knew about it, and there were no rules against dating a colleague, but I suppose there was a lot of gossip. Mariah was a Kansas City girl, her family pretty well off since her Dad was an M.D. with a general practice in Overland Park. She went to K.U., the respectable place for a good degree in English, did the sorority bit, got engaged to a playboy but soon broke it off when she found out he was doing a lot of extra-curricular playing around. The rub was, well, she was Jewish. There were no, zero, Jews in Abilene, and relatively few in the whole state, any significant number in the cities like Kansas City, Topeka and Wichita. The Jewish people were not known to be farmers in the U.S., and there was just one well-known experiment in Kansas called Beersheba. Their heritage in the U.S. was big city, especially New York, with a strong connection to Medicine, Law, Business and of course Entertainment. You would have to be a little crazy to move to a Bible Belt town like Abilene

27

with twenty-seven churches, one Catholic, the rest Protestant. There was no anti-Jewish sentiment, but just a more basic lack of knowledge about Jews and Judaism.

It turned out however there was a connection to Spanish. I scarcely knew about it, but had been introduced to it in a Survey of Spanish Literature in College – I mean the Sephardic Jewish tradition in old Spain and their literature. Mariah knew all her heritage, and really unrelated, spoke beautiful Spanish and even a bit of Ladino the old Sephardic language from the 16th century, but this due to her centuries later connection to that branch of Judaism. And even though her family went way back to Sephardic traditions, she was quite familiar with the major Jewish ethnicity of Ashkenazi Jews and their language Yiddish. The family surname was as I said earlier, Palafox, and she told me the name went back in Spain but not necessarily to the Sephardic Jews. A basic historic fact about Spain was that the Jews were either forced to leave or forced to convert to Catholicism in 1492, the latter known as "conversos" [converts]. Many also took on family names in Spanish. Mariah's family had relatives in Mexico and its historically important Jewish colony. I doubt that anyone in Abilene even knew she was Jewish (history and recent history, i.e. Hitler and Germany, had taught most Jewish families to keep it low key), just a Kansas City girl. And her KU connection was well looked upon. But all that plus her Spanish gave us both some extra motivation and fun in the dating.

Mariah said she's had to deal with nicknames all her adult life, being called "foxy" or "the fox." I didn't doubt her capacity to be clever like a fox and told her with her good looks and build she was plenty "foxy" for me. I wondered if it was just a coincidence and where "foxy" came from.

9

A PAUSE AND A CAUSE FOR CONCERN AND PRECAUTION

Amidst all the above something was in the back of my mind and bothering me, that old clipping Mom had sent me in college about the vandalism at the Abilene Courthouse and jail. I drove down to the sheriff's office (same building as the jail) one free day from school and re-introduced myself to Sheriff Wiley. He looked much the same, maybe a little more weight and a bigger waistline, but the same smile. He said, "Mick, I remember you well and personally am really happy you're back in town up at the Juco. I remember your altar boy days from church, and I know your parents well from church, especially your Dad through the Knights of Columbus; both Sean and Molly still contribute much to the parish and Caitlin and Ron as well. If you've got time, let's have a cup of coffee and I'll talk about that incident back from 1962. We haven't stood still and we've followed up on it. There's a lot to add, most we don't make public but, in your case, I make an exception. It all started with the Enterprise Bank Robbery and the attempted kidnapping back out at the farm in 1957 and you were a major participant, that's why I'm cluing you in."

He shuffled through a big drawer in a file cabinet in his desk and pulled out a manilla file folder, and inside of it was the original scribbled note on yellowed notebook paper like the old lined notebooks we used in grade school, but encased in a plastic liner. "Mike, why don't you read it and then we'll talk."

> "To All the Shitheads in Abilene: There's going to be hell to pay. We'll be getting even for all the misery yur righteous, hypocritical, son of a bitch, shit eating town and county put our friends through. We got a long list. Cat lickers, those lazy micks who ruined our town, and the blacks who are ruining our country. And that fat slob piss ant sheriff who caused us all the trouble. He's a "cat licker" too. Ain't no one going to be spared. You're put on notice."

"Mike, this note was attached to the rock they threw through the jail window in 1962, breaking the glass and landing in one of the cells. We've tried to trace the writing but records are really lacking. There are no samples of writing from the original three men arrested back in 1959. And I'm not sure this was written by one of them. You know I guess of their release from Lansing on so-called 'good behavior.' I'd like to know the whole story on how that happened. Some of the people on the outside, including the guards, ought to be on the inside. Somewhere along the line money was exchanged I'm positive about that, but we can't prove it. The final decision had to come from the warden and he's his own boss, a whole story that in itself.

"It's the threat that bothers us. Not me personally, I'm used to all this, but to the town. Our responsibility is to the entire county and there are some strange goings on up on our north boundary with Clay County we are keeping an eye on. The state keeps surveillance on anyone in the prisons, especially after their early release, but there's not enough money in the budget for a day-to-day checking. Released prisoners do have to check in once a week to their parole officers, and we get reports (Lansing sends them on to me in this case). The three are currently living in a compound up in Idaho, near Coeur de Lane, working at menial jobs but also evidently supported in part by friends, all of that rugged individualist type, but with connections to the old KKK. But the tentaclcs of the Klan are pretty far-reaching.

"I've got some advice for you however, and for your friend Jeremiah Watson. He's still around, working at the foundry over in Deershon Mfg. in Enterprise; I expect he's waiting to hook up with you, lots to talk about. I'm recommending, and I don't say this lightly, that you be vigilant. Are you armed by the way?"

"Hell no. I'm a lover not a fighter. I hunted a lot when we lived on the old farm, but it was a single shot 22 rifle and the 22 Special. What are you getting at?"

"Mike, I'd like you to purchase a pistol and get training. We can in fact handle the whole thing right here. Under the circumstances, thinking it over, it might be better if you don't buy a gun; I'll arrange for you to get "hand me down" from the office. No records kept on that, but we'll get you the license form, help you fill it out, send it in to the state firearms agency, and teach you how to use it. I don't want to scare you, but these folks seem to have long memories, and that includes your involvement in catching and arresting them that day of the bank robbery. I'd like to assure you that half the men in Dickinson county have guns, most all for hunting, so maybe you'd like to go out rabbit hunting or for that matter quail or pheasant hunting with someone. I know Ron your brother in law and his brother Stan are avid hunters. And maybe taking part in the Turkey Shoot by the Knights of Columbus out at the old Wassman farm along the river this Thanksgiving would not be a bad idea. The idea is to make you just 'one of the guys with firearms.'

I stammered that I was not sure about all this, but he patted me on the shoulder and assured me it would all work out okay. Before I left the office, he handed me a gun in a leather holster, a Smith and Wesson 357 magnum, 2 ½ inch barrel, saying, "This is what me and my deputies carry. We've got a lot heavier stuff when there's a call for it, but you'll see this pistol in our gun belts. You're probably a little overwhelmed right now, but I personally will get you used to the idea and get you some practice. You can keep it in the glove compartment of your car; no open carrying is allowed in Kansas, or maybe in a drawer in your bedside table. Oh, yeah, here's a box of shells as well. I'm not thinking you will need to use this, but I'll feel better if you have it for an emergency. I don't think your apartment up on Buckeye has rats, but it will blast one of them across the room if you want. Ha ha."

I guess I was glad I went to see the sheriff, but was just as glad to be distracted from all that afterwards.

10

LOCAL DISCOVERIES WITH MARIAH

The distraction was teaching, and, uh, Mariah. We had an agreement that if anybody asked, I would just say, "She's that cute new English teacher at the Juco from Kansas City." She would say, "Mike being a local boy has volunteered to show me around town, and we get to practice Spanish, and besides, his writing in English needs some work, punctuation and grammar and all that. Ha."

She made a couple of trips out to the cemetery with me to check out all those old stones, both the Catholic and the Protestant being a bit of a revelation to her. She said, "Mike, I don't see any 'converso' [Sephardic Jews forcibly converted to Catholicism in Spain from 1492 on] names here. Lots of us changed our names, or anglicized them. I showed her the Catholic cemetery first and we walked (it's small) each row of graves with me giving comments, sometimes ribald, of the folks beneath the stones. I knew lots of stories, some related to my altar boy days and serving at the weddings or funerals of several families, others based on gossip from the old days. Mariah did wonder why Dad and Mom's funeral lot was so close to the old stone altar and cross at the entryway, "Were they big shots or something?" I said, "Big shots, no. Dad was an early member of Knights of Columbus ("What's that?") Maybe that's how they got the lot. They had a stone with their names, date of birth, and of course no date of death. But there was a simple marker, not even a stone, for my twin brother who died one day after our birth, August 31, 1941. When we saw that, I think that's when I really began to like Mariah: she looked deep into my eyes, hugged me and said, "I guess we all have our stories. You haven't told me about your twin brother yet." She wasn't pushy or demanding, but left it up to me what to say or not say.

I kept it simple: "We were both incubator babies, my mother being 41 years of age, and I was told we weighed in at about 3 pounds each. John died the next day, August 31st. Mom said much later, in fact on one of my visits from college days, 'It was just a tiny, country hospital. They did the best they could.' For me, you can't help but wonder if we had traded places, what would he have been like? But I don't allow myself to think about it often. Hey there's more to investigate; we better get going."

Mariah leaned over in the car and hugged me, kissed my cheek and said, "Wait for just a moment. Thank you. I'm glad Mr. Mick made it and is here with me. I will see you now with a little different eye, and your Mom too."

The Protestant cemetery just to the south had more old graves and markers, and I figured it would take several visits to come up with ones necessary for that possible history of Abilene. It turned out though that a lot more information was going through dusty old records in the Abilene Public Library. I read there about the early history of the town and its founders Timothy and Eliza Hersey. They were the first settlers in Abilene in 1857 and Eliza is credited with giving it its name, "City of the Plains" from Luke's Gospel in the Bible. Their first home was a stone dugout on the west bank of Mud Creek which runs through town (this is the same nondescript meandering stream that I wrote about in the "Flood of '51" in "Rural Odyssey – Living Can Be Dangerous"). Hersey made his money providing food for passengers and employees of the Butterfield Overland Stage Line. And one thing leads to another, that stone dugout became the stone foundation for the tower in the famous Lebold Mansion out on

Vine Street west of Mud Creek. I drove Mariah by that old place after the cemetery; she couldn't believe Abilene had such places, but we together delved into the places about town, it became a regular "dating" event. Only thing to add at this point was that same glorious mansion in my days growing up was a run down, beat up apartment building considered to be in the "bad" part of town. And maybe haunted at that! What I did learn after many visits to the Library was that there were snippets and pieces of the town's wonderful and exciting history, mainly in old, yellowed newspaper articles or magazine articles but no "big" book. That was kind of amazing and whetted my appetite for staying in town for the near future to see if I could come up with something more substantial.

That year was spent teaching, going to the "obligatory" Abilene High School football and basketball games, high school plays and such. You might figure, as Mariah and I got to know each other more, there were some pretty "hot" dates, hormones acting up at the drive-in movies, but for the reasons already stated, nothing beyond that. She did visit my apartment and I hers, just down the street in another Victorian close to the old Seelye Mansion on Buckeye (more on that later), but never spent the night. At least not then. We did have a heck of a lot of fun, and were good company for each other, once again the Spanish connection adding spice to it all. It got to the point Mariah suggested we do a long weekend in Kansas City, including, gulp, introducing me to her family. In my day that was a very big deal, a boy friend from out of town, and hinted at bigger things. I'll tell about it in a moment, but something came up that jolted our reality and really the whole town's later that first year, in March I think it was.

11

JUST A TRIFLE OF NEWS OR WHAT?

It was mid-week and I was having early morning coffee at home and picked up the daily "Abilene Reflector Chronicle" outside the doorstep of the apartment. There was a one-inch headline and large picture below:

HISTORIC STAINED-GLASS WINDOWS AT ST. ANDREW'S IN ABILENE BROKEN AND SMASHED SOMETIME LAST NIGHT

The front-page article filling both columns below the photo basically said it all: "There were three windows broken, all on the north side of the church, the side facing the church parking lot. The bottom portions of the windows were smashed, but because the windows are so tall, the top portions remained intact. The windows according to Msgr. Fahey are priceless and cannot be replaced. 'They can be replicated, but that original style dating from 1913 is no longer available; the artisans who designed them are deceased. We have insurance and there are artists today who can do religious themes on stained glass'." When queried more, the long-time pastor and now Monsignor said, "At St. Andrew's the windows were done with donations from the old families in the church, dating back to its founding. You can be sure we will replace them, but it's not the same. It's part of our history and the love families had for us."

"The police were called as soon as the damage was discovered, this early in the morning by Msgr. Fahey and his housekeeper Josephine who heard the sound of breaking glass on the other side of the church from the rectory. By the time they dressed and ran out to the parking lot, a good way from the parsonage on the south side of the church, this about 5:00 a.m., there was no sign of people or vehicles. Police Chief Earl Sampson said he would guess the culprits used a long-handled ax to break the windows, but there was no evidence left at the scene. There were tire tracks but not like from burned rubber in a quick getaway, so really indistinguishable from any other cars in and out of the parking lot on a regular basis. The police and the sheriff's department are continuing to work at the crime scene. It appears to be simple vandalism at this point.

"We at the 'Chronicle' have long memories, and those of us reporting in 1962 recall the rock-throwing and window breaking incident at the county jail and we cannot help wondering if these events are related. No other such incidents have been reported, but this seems too much of a coincidence to be ignored. The 'Chronicle' implores local and if need be state law enforcement agencies to continue with all due diligence on the case. Abilene takes great pride in the peace and quiet of our historic town."

I was teaching that day but after classes were out, I drove down to the courthouse with attached sheriff's office to talk privately with Sheriff Wiley. He said, "Hi Mick, I'm not surprised to see you. I know what your

and he's sharing any information. So far it's a local matter, no KBI folks involved. This hits close to home doesn't it, both our families being long time members of St. Andrew's. I doubt it's anything as personal as that, but I've got my hunches. Off the record, and I know I can trust you, I'm pretty sure it's related to the jail windows incident last year. The Klan never liked Catholics, and maybe it's just a coincidence; they were after you because of the Enterprise affair. But I'm thinking now they're up to this vandalism because of the religion angle. I'm just thinking back to that message tied to the rock."

"I've got that memorized, Sheriff. Am I right though that there are no clues at all at St. Andrew's? I know you guys can trace tire marks and the paper said there were some near the windows in the parking lot. I'm with you thinking it's the Klan. Can you tell me any more about what's going on up north near Clay County?"

"Mick, it's pretty involved and pretty sketchy yet. Are you sure you can keep your mouth closed? I know you're nosing around at the cemetery and the library on that Abilene History stuff (I had told the sheriff about my history project). And it's time you got that pistol practice I talked about. We can do it out at the Wassman farm down by the river, just telling them you're getting ready for the Turkey Shoot. I'll bring a shotgun and shells to cover our story.

"Back to your question. It's pretty involved. Mick, you know there have been about a dozen forced sales on farms here in the county, all because of the lousy economy, and maybe the changing economy. Let's face it, farming is not as big a hunk of the national economy as it used to be. And besides that, corporations or corporate farms are buying out the little guys. If it had not been for Ron and his brother the same thing might have happened to your Dad's half-section. We think there is a corporate 'front' organization buying some of these farms. It's all legit, but incorporated in the State of Idaho; that's a red flag for us. The name is IFI, Independent Farming Industries; they have purchased thousand of acres mainly in Nebraska, Kansas and Oklahoma. Three or four are up north of Talmage near old Highway 24. The deeds and property taxes are listed under IFI, but there are people living in the old farm houses and operating much like any other farmers in the county. We've talked to a few and they all say the same thing, they are leasing with rights to buy after five years. They shop and do all their business in Abilene and the kids are bused into the Abilene schools, nothing suspicious at all. But we've checked with the corporation commission and they have access to at least names of corporations all over the country. IFI has some threads going back to the Klan, but that's not illegal. It's a free country yet as far as I know. But a word to the wise, don't go nosing around up there. It's easy enough to identify your old car and get a license number. No problem going up to the lake though (Milford Lake just across the line into Geary country was started a year ago in 1962. When full they claimed it would be the biggest lake in Kansas. Abilene residents boated, water skied and fished there ever since.)"

I said, "Thanks Sheriff, that's a lot more than I knew before, and you can be sure I'll not forget your warning. I never have owned a boat and the only fishing I did growing up was a in the muddy water of Dad's farm pond. It might be fun to wet a line some time up there. But it's still way too cold now. Maybe next summer."

12

CITY GIRL MEETS COUNTRY BOY'S FAMILY AND QUESTIONS

Not mentioned, not for any good reason or on purpose, but that first Fall in Abilene I did take Mariah out to visit Mom and Dad a couple of times, and even out to Caitlin and Ron's once. I knew Caitlin had told Mom and Dad we were dating, so no since hiding it. We did however decide to keep her Jewish background to ourselves, no point stirring up Mom – she is a notorious worry wart! She still figured I'd find a nice Catholic girl. Mariah is so darned wise and aware, and natural, not a phony thing about her, that she was relaxed as can be when we went on a Sunday for Mom's fried chicken. She in a few words charmed the heck out of them both. How do I know? Mom pulled me aside in the kitchen and whispered, "She's wonderful. Mick, don't let her get away!" I said, "Hey Mom I'm just 23 and she's the same age. Let's not rush anything. But if it means anything to you, we will go to Kansas City one of these times, and I'll meet her parents. Her Dad's an M.D. and she says they have a big house out in Overland Park, but she says 'Mom and Dad are pretty down to earth,' so we'll see." Dad just smiled and agreed that he would take us all out to the big garden he was planting north of the pond on the old farm, I'll tell about that later. Turns out Mariah has a green thumb.

I haven't talked about her looks yet, maybe you'd be interested. About five foot seven, don't know her weight, but a really nice figure, curved in all the right places. So far I haven't had a chance to investigate much but can say she's all real. Close slow dances at the dinner club in Salina and front seat shenanigans at the drive-in movie revealed all that. Dark brown hair, green eyes, a sparkling personality, smarts and a whole lot of common sense. What more could a guy want? Oh yeah, and a new Mustang and a nicer apartment in town than mine. It couldn't have been the salary at the Juco; must have been a little help from her Mom and Dad, but she was low key about all that, saying they didn't want her to have a breakdown driving all the way out to Abilene, and wanted her in a nice, clean, safe place to live. Ha. Damn! Do I sound like I'm in love? Whoa.

She wondered how and why I ended up teaching Spanish, a "goy" [gentile] farm boy. The explanation was simple: absolutely no mechanical inclination, no idea how to run a farm, lousy in science and math, but weirdly good in languages, history, public speaking and the like. Mariah said, "In my house that means a Liberal Arts Degree and Law School." I said, "At least I did the Business Management Degree (your family should appreciate that) but no aptitude or interest in that either, and I almost flunked out from a Business Law class." She said, "What a loser! Oh well, there's always education, you know, 'Those that can't do, teach.' Hee hee. I guess that makes two of us. For now, I won't accept all those calls and local studs hitting on me, Mick, maybe we can end up on a beach in Mexico."

There were actually two visits to the farm for the city girl. The first was out to the pond later that spring. During retirement Dad had a garden tractor he rented once a year and put in, jeeze, it must have been a half-acre vegetable garden. He said, "Wear work clothes, shoes you're not afraid of muddying up, and take some work gloves and mosquito repellant." We met Mom and Dad up at the horse shed at the northeast corner of the 80, next to the gravel county road, this because Dad had his green Dodge full of garden stuff, and only the front seat was fairly clean. The pond which was famous in local history when I was in high school – beer blasts for the football team with beer from the local pool hall my brother Paul once owned – was all overgrown. Dad now in his 70s just couldn't keep up with what he had planted over the last twenty-some years. It was a forest of trees, most I didn't know, but maybe Mulberry, Oak, Elm and his pride and joy – Black Walnut trees for what else but black walnut fudge and mostly for the squirrels. I told Mariah you practically had to have a sledge hammer to open the black walnuts, not too big an exaggeration.

She was amazed at the whole place – trees, water and birds we saw – saying she had been down to the Lake of the Ozarks but that was a lot different. She was full of questions: What are you planting? How do you decide what and in which rows? And most important, "How can I help?" That made Dad's decision. He said, "Mariah, I wish I could have got your enthusiasm and curiosity and desire to do this in Mick fifteen years ago. I'll give him credit, he did help, but still couldn't hoe a straight row." Mom just listened and laughed. Mariah wasn't bullshitting; she had no reason to. I think she was a very happy girl with this change in routine from teaching English grammar and smidgens of English and American Literature. I could not help but brag: "Mariah, most all those trees you saw were planted by hand by Dad, digging the hole, planting and mainly carrying the water in a 50 gallon barrel on the back of our little Ford tractor and then one bucket at a time to get them started. And he's doing the same thing to get water to the garden. Otherwise it's rain in a good year. I don't know what you're going to be doing this summer, but if you're here we can have a garden party picking all this stuff. Great tomatoes, green beans, peas, onions and my favorite, sweet corn!"

The repellant kept most of the bugs off, but she was a sight to see with muddy jeans, boots and mud on her arms and even cheeks. We left a bit later saying we'd see them next time in town. I dropped her off to clean up, me too and then both of us had work to do for school. That night was the first time I took her to Lena's the locally famous "home cooking" restaurant out west of town. It's worth telling about. It's what we all used to call "family style." That means all the main dishes are served on huge platters or bowls, the specialty being fried chicken, the sides huge mounds of mashed potatoes with chicken gravy and green bean casserole with bacon on the top. I still don't think anyone in Abilene topped Mom's fried chicken (we ate it every Sunday in the summertime for years while growing up on the farm), but this was close. Good ole' Mariah – she made some brownie points – told me the same thing, "Yummy good but not as good as your Mom's." Kansas being that semi-dry state, we bought a bottle of wine at the local liquor store and took it to Lena's where they were glad to open and serve it.

I didn't see many people we knew that night but did say hello to Mr. William Donaldson the editor of the local newspaper the "Abilene Reflector Chronicle." He remembered me, just slightly, from high school days, but we had never actually met. He said, "I'm a good friend of Carleton Stone your old English and Debate teacher, and he waxed euphoric on that 1959 Debate team when you won state for Abilene. Last time it's been done. Your name came up a lot. Carleton and I were buddies at K.U. By the way I'm glad to see one of the locals come back home. We lose too many of you." I told him I saw the article on St. Andrew's and thanked him for it; his only response was, "I'm a Methodist and we've never seen eye to eye with the Pope in Rome, but we sure as hell can support good Catholic Christians and protect all our churches. There are at least a half dozen in town with those stained glass windows, so you don't know who is going to be next. I'm in touch every day with the sheriff's office, anything new you'll hear about it."

13

BACK TO ABILENE – HOW THE TOWN STARTED

The next day there some free time, so I was down at the city library checking out more local history. There was a very important person I should have mentioned earlier, but guess I didn't because he wasn't actually buried in the Abilene Cemetery. I'm talking about Joseph McCoy the man who brought cattle and made history in Abilene. There was a two-part series on him in an old issue of the same "Abilene Reflector Chronicle" and I got my information from that article. He was from Illinois, born in 1837, was active in the cattle business in that state, but after the Civil War he became aware of an increasing cattle market and the good land, soil and conditions "out west." He learned about the Longhorns in Texas, and figured there had to be some way to get them to the eastern markets.

McCoy landed in Abilene in 1867 because of the aforementioned good soil, plentiful water and proximity to the recently constructed Kansas Pacific Railroad (eventually to become the Union Pacific clear across the country when it met the Central Pacific coming from California at Promontory Point in Utah in 1869) perfect to ship the cattle back East. He bought 250 acres on the outskirts of Abilene and built a feedlot and the later famous Drovers' Cottage, a rough, spartan hotel for the cowboys coming up the Chisholm Trail from Texas. The first year 35,000 cattle came to the railyard; in 1871 when it all faded, there were by some estimates a total of 600,000 that had passed through Abilene! By then the whole thing had been controversial - "We got trouble in River City!" - and McCoy left town, even after serving a term as mayor, and went broke as the cattle trail ended. He moved on to Kansas City and Wichita where he died. It wasn't just him but what the town had become in the Chisholm Trail days.

My thinking is Abilene owes the man most of its 19th century history! It doesn't hurt to repeat a little of what came before in these pages. The drives had always been unpopular with some, first of all because Texas Longhorns were reputed to carry a tick which was harmful to the Shorthorns already in the Abilene area. Rowdy cowboys, violence south of the tracks, prostitution and rough living got on the nerves of the local right-living farmers and other Bible Belt citizens, and they called for an end to the cattle drives. These moved west to Ellsworth and especially to a "golden age" of ten years in Dodge City (shades of TV's "Gunsmoke," Marshall Dillon and that fiction) before fear of hoof and mouth disease brought that to a close. However, the halcyon days of Sheriff Tom Smith, brought into town in 1870 to quell the violence and disorder, and after his untimely and bloodcurdling vicious death, the relatively short reign of Wild Bill Hickok followed. Hickok did rid the town of a few sidewinders, but spent a good deal of time in the same saloons as the cowboys, seemed to like gambling and the ladies of the night and did relatively little to advance peace and progress later on. Abilene just got fed up, dismissed him and outlawed the cattle drives. It gradually evolved later to the so-called peaceful and right-living town it is, mostly, today.

One personal note: that old Drover's Cottage of McCoy's and its successor south of the tracks was turned into a creamery and icehouse after cowboy days. Dwight D. Eisenhower worked there as a young man, and by an unlikely act of circumstance, so did I, one summer while still in high school and another between freshman and sophomore years in college. I always wondered if the ancient ice tongs I used every day might have once been in Ike's hand. When I told Mariah this she howled and made me drive her by the ice plant and ask Paul Murchison for a tour. It was like going back to the 19th century for her; she said she had never seen anything like it, just remembering James Dean in an ice house scene in "East of Eden," a film shown during those days in the Plaza movie theater in Abilene. Paul remembered me, even went with us on the tour and offered us ice cream from the freezer after the tour.

I was beginning to get quite a stack of notes for local history in my handwritten notebooks.

14

THE K.U. RELAYS – A REPRISE AND MORE

There's always more to tell as this story continues. Spring was getting along, welcome to me after a cold Kansas winter with snow a few times along with horrendous wind, blizzard conditions in western Kansas and not far from it in Abilene. You could actually see yellow daffodils blooming through an inch or two of snow still on the ground and the tulips ready to come out. For an old half-miler in track and field, the still cold wind of spring would remind me of track in high school, but alternated with a few better sunny days. The adage "March comes in like a lion" was sure true in Kansas. As time went along it was time for a big spring event in our state – the K.U. Relays. A bunch of my friends in high school had made the drive down to Lawrence in April of 1959 to what seemed like a runner's heaven. There were the gazelles from Texas Southern along with Big – 8 runners from all the plains' states schools – Oklahoma, Kansas, Nebraska, Missouri present in that great oval in the football stadium at K.U. And Kansas was famous for its stable of mile runners; Jim Ryan, the one that year went on to the Olympics. What was most exciting was hanging out in the KU student union before the track meet and seeing no less than Wilt Chamberlain, all 7 feet of him, bending over to aim his pool cue for another shot. And then seeing him in a KU track outfit, complete with Irish cap, warming up for the high jump (this was before the Fosbury Flop, Wilt went over the bar above six feet side-hurdling style).

I asked Mariah if she would like to go back to her old haunt at K.U., and she jumped at the chance. She would be my guide after the relays. And then came a surprise invitation, "Why don't we bop on over to Overland Park and see Mom and Dad? I'm thinking Sunday for lunch or brunch or whatever. You know it had to happen sooner or later, what do you say?" "No harm I guess; they say if you want to know what your girl friend will be like 40 years later, look at her Mom. If she is anything like you, she'll be a knock out! I assume you've not told them you are seeing a cradle Catholic, but maybe not a regular church-goer. And I have never, not once, been in a Jewish family's house. I won't really know how to act." Mariah said, "You are correct about the religious part, but they do know you teach Spanish and have studied at the National University in Mexico City. It's okay. I'll coach you. Here's an idea, if it's any easier we won't have to go to the house. I'll drive down to Overland Park Friday night, spend the night with them for the Shabbat preparation services, meet you in the student union at K.U. Saturday morning we'll go to the Relays, then go out on the town to some of my old haunts Saturday night and drive into Overland Park Sunday morning. We can meet Mom and Dad for a great lunch (Dad will want to take us out to that famous Kansas City steakhouse near them), and drive home Sunday afternoon. But Mick there's nothing to scare you at our house. We're not Orthodox, far from it, and Dad's a huge sports fan and a bit of a bibliophile. He would want you to see his Sephardim Library; some of it is really rare. I learned to read Castilian and Ladino in the old "romances" from books in that Library. Depending on how it goes, maybe we can just go over to the house for an hour or two after lunch."

I didn't say before that since we had just started dating toward the end of September, Mariah had spent the Thanksgiving break and two weeks off at Christmas with her family in Overland Park, doing the family Hanukah celebration (and I didn't know if seeing any previous boyfriends). I was at Mom and Dad's house for Thanksgiving and we all were out at Caitlin's for Christmas dinner. Paul was home, so Christmas gifts and all were out at Mom and Dad's house. Mariah had been for dinner like I said before; Mom had hinted about her coming for Christmas, and we could all go to Mass and all. I had said it was a bit soon for all that and besides Mariah hadn't been to see her family much since the move to Abilene.

So the KU-KC weekend was planned. Oh, a one-time-in-your-life event had unexpectedly happened in February. My favorite Uncle married to one of my Dad's sisters and living in Western Kansas died after a very short illness. I don't know any of the details, but evidently he had more than enough fortune to spread around with only two kids, and willed me $25,000. That was like a million dollars to me. We had visited the farm when I was a tot and I had ridden on the John Deere tractor, must have made a positive impression. He only said in the will that he wanted to make sure I had a chance for a good education. So that money was earmarked for the graduate courses the Juco wanted. I was thinking of doing a two-night per week commute to Manhattan and K-State starting that next fall. But there was enough extra so that I could finally replace the old junker Dodge from college days with a new, but stripped down, Chevy. Long story short – I had new "wheels" for Lawrence and Kansas City. Oh yeah, I bought two nice suits from the men's' apparel store in Abilene, the one we could never afford while on the farm, but nice clothes and nice employees. It was time.

As planned, Mariah left after early Friday afternoon classes for home, I got up at the crack of dawn on Saturday, drove to Lawrence, figured out a safe place to park on campus, and waited at a pre-arranged place in the union for Mariah. She showed up pretty as ever and with a wind breaker and a hood (with KU Jayhawker logo) and pronounced herself ready for the relays. We probably sat on those cold metal seats for five hours, but it was worth every minute. The mile relay team from Texas Southern was still there, each long-legged guy running about a 48 second quarter-mile, and the traditional good milers from Kansas and the Midwest were in good form, one guy running a 3.59, still a rarity in the world of track and field.

But no Wilt Chamberlain. Mariah knew very little about track and field so I got to play the big shot role explaining ins and outs of every event. But the day grew later and we baled out about 4 p.m.

Now it was her turn. I haven't said - she was bunking at her old sorority house and had a place for me at the Sigma-Chi house. I told her I'd rather be in a Motel 6 with her and would not be comfortable with the frat boys. There were no fraternities at the Liberal Arts Jesuit school, and besides, I had a bit of prejudice against the "Greek life" from all the stories of Abilene High School kids who either were ecstatic or absolutely miserable when not pledged. It all reeked of a class system to me. Mariah convinced me saying it was just one night. It turned out all right, after all I was just almost one year out of school, so age was not a problem. Mariah's sorority friends seemed ecstatic to she her again and there was a lot of what I would call giggling and girly stuff. We repaired to one of the student hangouts down on Massachusetts's street where most of the water holes were for K.U., four girls and four guys including me. I don't recall how many pitchers of that Kansas 3.2 "panther piss" we downed, but the night was full of laughter and Mariah and I danced to some local band "brought from the city," a pretty big deal. We said goodnight outside the bar, she saying, "Mick, you are in good hands. I dated Sigma-Chi guys and they will be sure you get "home" safely and tucked in. It was later that night, sharing a dorm room with about six of them, still drinking bottles of Coors from the tavern that one drew me aside and said, "Do you know what a prize you've got in that girl? All the upperclassmen from the last two years lusted after her. And her Dad's loaded. I can't figure what she sees in a Kansas hayseed, but congratulations are in order. Have you screwed her yet?" "None of your damned business; we're just friends." He laughed and laughed and said, "I thought you farm boys knew what it was all about, I mean stallions and the mares, the bulls and the heifers. Get on it man! We actually had a lottery here last year wondering who would win the prize." I said, "Thanks for the big city advice. I'll check it out," and crawled into one of the bunk beds and was out like a light.

Revived by about three strong cups of coffee, but showered and shaved and in my "casual" best, I left Lawrence at about ten o'clock, walked into the Stockyards Steak house in old downtown Kansas City, Kansas, and was ushered to a comfortable, leather lined booth to a radiant Mariah and well, two proud parents. Mariah stood up, held my hand, and said, "Mom and Dad this is the 'goy.' Habla major que yo un castellano limpio y ya unas frases hasta en Ladino." Mr. Palafox stood up, saying "El placer es nuestro Miguel. Realmente. Mucho gusto," and he gave me a firm handshake. Ariel her mom was a little less out-going but offered her hand which I took and said, "Now I know where Mariah got her good looks! Oh, pardon me for saying that." She answered, "How did you like that K.U. scene? Mariah doesn't invite just anybody to meet her friends. She has been mentioning you a lot in our phone calls. It's like an Irish Messiah saving her soul out in that leaded Bible Belt! Sorry, I didn't mean to say that. It slipped out; we weren't crazy about her job in the great outback." She laughed. "I hope you are hungry because Benjamin thinks you can handle the big T-bone."

Lucky I was ravenous, the steak was terrific as well as the loaded baked potato, and Benjamin said we could handle either Mimosas or Bloody Mary's to wash it down. It turns out everyone joined him and conversation was flowing like the bubbly. Mariah did most of the talking, maybe sugar coating a little the work experience at the Juco, but going on about how Abilene was so historic and had these beautiful Victorian mansions to prove it. I added, "And a lot of tractors, wheat harvesters, and alfalfa and cattle and sheep." They were curious about my family, how they ended up in Kansas and I gave them the short version – a 100 per cent Irish background dating from great grandparents immigrating from Ireland, working in the coal mines in Ohio, then a chance to return to farming in Nebraska and finally, a new start with the same at Abilene in Kansas. But I tried to say more about my experience at the National University in Mexico City and the "Industria Farmacéutica" and the Meier family in Guatemala City who hosted me and offered me a job back in 1962. And telling the truth, I told them my tenure at the Juco was just a first step, thinking more of graduate work and who knows what, maybe a Ph.D. in Spanish and Latin American Studies. I also mentioned that I tabled a grant application for the same under the NDEA program, but still had it in mind. If I had done that I would have never met Mariah. This seemed for them to give pause.

Mr. Palafox said his own family had antecedents in Mexico, migrating from Amsterdam after the diaspora from Spain and Portugal in the late 15ᵗʰ century. He said, "Mike, how much do you know about all that? And more importantly being Irish and Catholic what do you think of it?" Mariah turned red, and said, "Dad, that's unfair. Mike is only 23 years old like me, and I'm sure they don't talk much about the 1492 Edict by Fernando and Isabella in Abilene!" I countered, but humbly, "Mr. Palafox I had terrific training in Spanish and Spanish Literature if you can believe it at a Catholic and Jesuit school. My first Spanish teacher was Jewish I suspect, but he never said it, but was really happy introducing us to the "muwassahas" and "jarchas," the lyric poetry in Andalucía in the 11ᵗʰ century. We learned of the Arabic and Hebrew verses from the period. Other than that, you are correct, I don't know much."

"Well," said Mr. Palafox, "that already puts you into the one tenth of one percentile of folks here in the U.S. who know about it. I'll drink to that that!" "Enough for now, we've truly been pleased to meet you and I am making you an offer you can't refuse – to see my library, blow the dust off some ancient volumes and see what we "Sefardi" contributed to Spain before it was Spain, just "Hispania" and "Al-Andaluz.""

Mariah cut in, "Dad, that sounds great, but we both have early morning classes tomorrow, and class prep and papers to grade, right Mike? (She nudged my knee under the table.) It's a three-hour drive home and already one o'clock."

Mr. Palafox acquiesced and said, "Oh, one final thing. Mike I think I've heard about that drug manufacturing company in Guatemala. The Meier family if I'm not mistaken also had their roots in Spain and England (their anglicized name was Meier). We might have a lot to talk about if we ever met. I'm a bit sorry you didn't take their offer; it's a growing industry with a big future. But that's none of my business, just an M.D.'s murmurings. And right, Mariah was not hanging out down there! (A belly laugh) We'll take a rain check. Thanks again for helping our daughter keep interested and safe in the land of the cowboys and Indians. She says by the way you are a "mensch" [Jewish slang for a person of integrity and honor] if there ever was one." Mrs. Palafox (Ariel) once again was quiet, but I could tell she did not miss a word, maybe a small calculator in her brain conjuring up possibilities. Who knows? She stood up when we were ready to leave and said, "Miguel, we give big embraces to loved ones and friends in our family. May I give you a hug?" My time to turn red. "Claro, señora, es un obsequio que no olvidaré." Benjamin followed suit, they hugged and kissed Mariah with her promise to call when she got "home" to Abilene and keep them posted. Not too many weeks until the end of spring term and seeing them in the summer.

Out in the parking lot Mariah was a'glow. "Mike, never but never could I have imagined that last hour. You were terrific. I'll tell you the rest when you come over this evening for a quick drink before we have to get to work. I am so excited I'm ready to burst my buttons." She gave me a big hug, a warm kiss to the lips and said "My Mustang beats your Chevy home!"

15

ABILENE – THE MEXICAN CONNECTION

We met at Mariah's apartment and she said "This calls for a celebration!" She got a bottle of champagne out of the frig which she expertly opened and poured into wine glasses the likes I had never seen. "From my grandmother. Let's toast to your making it through the entire weekend, I mean the sorority and fraternity scene, and then impressing my Mom and Dad. I know you were not comfortable with that crew in Lawrence, but I really had a good reunion with my girlfriends who by the way told me if we break up, they want to be next in line. (Laughter) You did get yourself into a bit of a pickle – there will have to be a second trip, this time to the house and Dad's library. We won't worry about that for now, but I'm thinking maybe before school is out in late May. But I want to thank you now."

There was a good amount of kissing and I dare say, close hugging, but then both of us took a deep breath agreeing that now was not the time. I left her place walking on clouds and headed home to a drafty, cold apartment which took a while to warm up and then was greeted by papers to grade and class prep for just a few hours away. It was back to more work as well on the Abilene project. There were about a half-dozen students in Spanish class really doing well and showing promise. I didn't mind extra time with them getting them ready for final exams coming up; if they did well there would be a good chance to get at least tuition help from K-State or K.U. The problem was these kids could not afford the board and room, so I and the guidance counselor were pouring through the files of scholarships available, and from any source. There were some possibilities; a student needed about $100 per month for board and room. And I began canvasing local merchants and banks to sponsor them. The problem was most of them were not interested in Spanish majors; they needed Business Administration, like Accounting or the like, or Business Management or even Livestock Milling, majors more likely to bring young folks back to work in Abilene. I explained that Spanish was mainly to satisfy the college language requirement, and the kids would almost always major in something else. A fun thing involving Spanish did happen the next week.

I may have mentioned or not that as a farm boy in Abilene my first practice in Spanish came with co-workers in the Belle Springs Creamery and Ice Plant during the two summers I worked there. I was still in touch with Ernie and Maria Gómez and in fact two of their kids were at the Juco in Spanish class. They said that the school Spanish was a lot different from what they heard at home, and when "cornered" by me one day admitted that they were not encouraged to really learn Spanish, that English was the only way to bettering their lives. As good fortune would have it, both were in Mariah's English 101, struggling a bit to compete with the "Anglos" but loving her as a teacher. After I stopped by one afternoon after class to check their homework, Mrs. Gómez said we needed to do another real Mexican dinner. And she remembered I played the guitar and knew a half dozen Mexican songs. Ernie (Ernesto) said, "I can get some Dos Equis and good tequila and we'll make a night of it." I said, "I've got a girl friend who knows Spanish, has been to Mexico. It's Mariah Palafox up at school and Timmy and Mariela are in her class. Can I bring her along?" Mrs. Gómez winked at me, had a big smile on her face and said, "Hombre, para qué son los amigos? Seguro que sí. Tú mereces enamorar a una buena chamaca! If Mariela was old enough, I'd have her after you as well."

Mariah was happy to join me, no stranger to Mexican ways but much more accustomed to sophisticated big city people. But she as I've said is smart, has a big heart, and a lot of common sense, no worries she would act snobbish. As it turned out, it cemented our relationship even more. That Friday night, incidentally during Lent, a no-meat day for Catholics, created a bit of a problem. I actually called the young assistant pastor at St. Andrew's (not the stiff old monsignor - pastor) and explained the invitation and he said, "Mick it's worth a dispensation. Maybe you can get more of that crowd to church on Sunday. I remember you from altar boy days. I guess it's a little late now to get you to seminary." We both laughed and I said, "No promises, but thank you for the dispensation." Why? María was preparing the whole shebang – tacos, tostadas, rice and beans, her own special salsa (look out!) of "pico de gallo" and I knew Ernesto would have lots for everybody to drink. She offered the "mole poblano" from last time, but I said, why not something new?" She laughed, saying, "No aguantaste los chiles, verdad?"

Start and end of story – that Friday night we were celebrating until 2:00 a.m. an ungodly hour in Abilene. There was a big crowd at the Gómez house, most everyone from the tiny Mexican community in town. I knew almost everybody including the guys I had played summer baseball with years ago. Ernesto broke out the Dos Equis and everyone wanted to know about how I had learned so much Spanish. I think they were most interested in Mariah, her dark hair and green eyes and good looks could have been Mexican. Me, I was the "guero" or "Anglo Gringo" guy. Mariah made an immediate connection explaining that "Mariah" was just another version (she didn't say which) of a name related to Mary or María. I broke out the guitar and did those ole' corny Mexican songs – "Las Mañanitas," "Cielito Lindo," "Adelita," "Guantanamera" from Harry Belafonte and Cuban music, and a couple of new ones I had learned in Mexico City from the Trío Los Panchos: "Peregrina" and "La Barca de Guaymas."

Ernesto but mainly David García got oiled up and began to sing more Mexican love songs, "Tierra del Sol" and "Guadalajara" just some of them. María came in, banged a spoon against an iron pot and said, "Basta! Vamos a comer." So for the next hour we gorged ourselves on incredibly tasty, but a bit hot as well, Gómez' specialties. María even had sopapillas for dessert.

What followed had not been planned but ended up being another important "chapter" for my Abilene history book. It all started when I asked Ernesto, pretty much the spokesman for his family and friends, to tell me again how he and María met, how they arrived in Abilene and really how they were getting along. What I got I think was the story of an entire generation of Mexican immigrants, then migrants with green cards and now all U.S. citizens.

They smiled at each other and Ernesto started, "My people were from Chihuahua State in north central Mexico. Life during and after the Mexican Revolution was really difficult there; many people of all social classes had died fighting in that ten-year disaster. Supposedly the ideals of the Revolution would favor the poor but it wasn't working out; really it just upturned all – a new ruling class, new landholders but still no real way for us to better our lives. I think in the big cities there were better chances, the Labor Unions were a big part of post-Mexico revolutionary days and the Mexican Railway Workers' Union ("Los Rieleros") was one of them. The British and the old Porfirio Diaz regime had extended the railroads all the way to the U.S. border to help out on international trade. At the same time, that was when we heard of temporary visas for anyone willing to do stoop labor on the farms in California and even in Texas. Texas was closer to home so my Dad and his two brothers crossed over and worked the cotton fields down there. It wasn't much better than back home but at least people were not shooting at you. It was then we got a break, or at least it seemed like it. The railroads were expanding all over the western U.S. and there was a shortage of people willing to do that hard work putting down the ties and rails. And there was a call just for maintenance; wooden ties would rot and wear out under all that weight from the engines and box cars and the roadbeds would deteriorate. That's when Dad and some others got jobs on the Santa Fe up toward Abilene. They called them the "traqueros" - "the track guys." But, hey, the old timers told stories of Mexican cowboys in the old cattle drives on the Chisholm Trail to Abilene, so some of us go way back!"

María chimed in, "It was in the early 40s when Ernie and I met; his Dad knew my Dad from work on the railroad and both our families had settled in Abilene in the late 1930s. We lived in a small part of town south of the tracks on the west side, and I can remember some folks living in boxcars. Life was not easy, no extra money but we shopped for food at the Catholic grocery store south of the UP track, Zane's, and they offered us credit. We always but always paid those bills at the end of the month. I think we were lucky in a way; lots of Mexicans ended up in the meat packing plants in Kansas City and Wichita, and a lot in those filthy sugar beet mills out west near Colby and Goodland. Abilene seemed like a good place to be. There were only three families at first and most of us in Abilene are part of them, the Gomezes, the Garcías and the Gonzalezes (we called them the three G's). So you might figure, we married each other, and even the kids are doing the same.

Ernie broke in, "María is not telling all the story. The reason was we still were trying to get used to being U.S. citizens, learn English and get used to hamburgers instead of tacos (he laughed saying "No hay hamburguesas esta noche!"). A lot happened, mostly good, from the late 30s to the 60s now. The railroads got us all green cards and most everyone evolved to become citizens. We are very proud of that! Most all of us in my generation served in the U.S. military and certainly our kids do. They all go to public schools from grade school, junior high, high school on up. And hey, you've got two of us at the Juco. But you'll notice most of the kids really don't know much Spanish, just snippets. If you were going to blend in, even just some, in Abilene, you had better know English and not speak with an accent. That is the case for sure with our kids. But most of us in our generation are still speaking with a bit of a Mexican flavor. You know, some still call us pretty bad names – wetback or spic – but on the whole it's better. Miss Stromberg up at the High School has educated a lot of white folks into Spanish and Mexico, and Nara Baldini the new teacher is terrific, taking students to Mexico every summer. It all helps."

"Ernie, Maria, David, I'm one of those products from Miss Stromberg's classes!" There's one more thing I'm curious about, and I hope it isn't a sore point. You are all or at least were Catholics; I've seen some of your family's grave stones out at the cemetery. But other than my baseball buddy Ronny and your daughter Mariela I've don't recall seeing you much at church. Maybe we went to a different mass."

Ernie laughed, "Miguelito, that is a long story and a bit touchy. I would rather have another beer and then do some more music, but I'll just finish and try to answer your question as well as I can. It goes way back to Mexico. You know with your history studies and language study in Mexico that there is a real anti-Catholic undercurrent since 1910. In fact, the Revolution was deeply socialist and anti-religion. But there's a reason for that. The church in the whole history of Mexico and especially in recent centuries has been tied to the upper class. The rest of us were "peons" and really invisible to the church. Big donations came from the landholders and lately the industrialists. But since the Revolution, priests and nuns were prohibited to wear their cassocks, roman collars and robes in public. And that still holds in a lot of places today. And the churches were often ransacked in the battles during the Revolution and even used as barracks. They were full of real gold painted altars, gold chalices and such, and even gold-thread lined vestments. That gold came from the mines where Indians and the rest of us poor Mexicans worked. To put it bluntly – we were second class citizens.

"So you can't ignore what your fathers and grandfathers experienced and told you about the 'old days.' Mike, at least for us here, there is still some of that going on; I mean the nasty names, the suspicion we are living off the government, but yet while we're doing most of the manual labor here in town. The kids say that mostly in school everything is going all right. And we are really grateful for old Miss Stromberg and young Miss Nara up at the high school, and especially what you are trying to do at the Juco. That's why we taught our kids at least until a couple of years ago to not speak "Mexican." They understand a lot at home (their grandparents still speak Spanish at home, us not so much, but won't use it away from home). As for religion, we are still Catholics, but believe a lot more in Nuestra Señora de Guadalupe than the parish priests.

"Hey, enough of that, I just remember teaching you some Mexican swear words and talking some down at the Ice Plant. 'Muchacho,' you have come a long way! Sorry you don't like our 'mole poblano.'" Ernie laughed until he was almost in tears. The rest of the night I sang, they sang, we all danced and María kept trying to get Mariah to eat more goodies. She ate a bit (told me later she'd have to get to the gym), but danced a lot. All the locals were extremely curious to know about her (they knew plenty about me and the O'Briens) and were complementary of her great Spanish (the accent of an educated Mexican and not a "gachupín" from Spain, her ancestors lived in Andalucía and did not have that Spanish "theta" or "lisp" as some detractors called it). María drew me aside as we left, gave me a big hug and said, "Andale muchacho. Esta vale oro!" ["Get going young guy, this one is worth her weight in gold!"]

Not only did we have a great time but a few blanks were filled in on Abilene history, I daresay, "blanks" not provided by the usual Anglo sources.

16

VANDALISM AND AN
OVERDUE EXPLANATION

All was going well, back to classes, Spring moving on until one morning in April when I went out to the car with all my stuff in a briefcase ready for school. All four tires were flat as a pancake, slit on the sides. What to do? I went back in and made two phone calls, one to Mariah to please tell folks at the Juco I would be coming in late, an unavoidable delay, and would be walking to school. She immediately offered to come by and pick me up, but I wiggled out of that. The second call was to Sheriff Wiley. I explained the situation, he was quiet, a good listener, and said to sit tight, he would be right up in the regular county car. He said to not touch anything on my car or make any more footprints around it.

I waited until I saw his car outside the window, walked down the back stairway and said hello. Still chilly weather, we both had jackets on but Sheriff Wiley had on his usual felt cowboy hat and cowboy boots along with official attire, the blue uniform, the weapon in its strapped holster on his waist, and a walkie-talkie on a shoulder strap. He bent down and then got down on his knees to inspect each tire and then said,

"Probably a switch blade, the usual, I've seen it before. Mick, I've got to report this to the police, and they will report to the paper. For now, I'll suggest vandalism by local rowdies, but I'm going to dust the area around the car for tire markings and footprints and finger prints. Chief Earl really has jurisdiction on things like this, being in town, but I've got joint jurisdiction, being in the county. Luckily, we generally see eye to eye. Since your car is new, I suggest you call the Chevy dealership, explain what happened, tires slit during the night and have them send out a pickup with four new tires, but wait until around noon to call them. I'll need the time to check everything out. Do you need a ride to school? Wait, on second thought, might be better if you walk and we keep this under our hats for a few hours. No sense them seeing the patrol car."

I said, "The landlord lives on the first floor and I'm sure she will have seen your car. And she will be on the phone to all her lady friends with this. I think you should talk to her and maybe suggest in your best sheriff's tone that would she please not say anything until noon, 'just regular procedure ma'am' or whatever you say. For that matter no telling how many people will have seen your car pull up."

"No problem Mick. Standard procedure and investigation of vandalism. Give me a call this afternoon, or better, come by the office. I think I'll know something by then, or maybe nothing. We'll see. Sorry about this. You and I both know it may not be a random tire slashing by punks in town. I don't mean to alarm you, but until we see if there are other cars and slashed tires, it's still my thought. Almost all these cases involve multiple cars."

I called the Chevy dealership, told them my problem but that I had Sheriff Wiley's instructions to not do anything until after noon. Could they bring out the new tires then, put them on and I'd drive by later this afternoon to settle up. I was assuming my insurance would handle it. I walked the twenty minutes on up to the Juco and was actually only one-half hour late to my first class. Dean Halderson had cancelled it but the second, American History, was still on as well as the SPA 201 class after lunch. Just a couple of colleagues knew I was in late and asked what happened, was I okay, or maybe sick. I assured them all was in order, just a delay getting out of the house this morning. I could not get by with that at lunch break, Mariah joining me in the cafeteria. And not wanting to alarm her I just said that my tires were slit but that every so often we had that in Abilene, just punks or "hoods" as we called them out for a joyride and making trouble. And I said after the p.m. class and office hours I'd be walking home and getting the car and going down to the Chevy dealership. She seemed to accept that saying, "If we were in Kansas City, they would have keyed the finish too, or would have forgotten the tires and just disappeared the whole car. Hey, call me at home after you get settled with it all. Sorry, what a bummer after our great fiesta at the Gomezes."

After school, all was according to hoyle, the car with new tires on it and a bill taped to the windshield. I drove down to the dealership, wrote a check and they said they would corroborate anything with the insurance company when they called. They would "naturally" reimburse me. I tried to be as casual as possible and asked if there were any other cases like mine today, and they said not at the Chevy place, but there were three more dealerships in town and two tire service places. I thanked them and drove over to the Sheriff's office. Sheriff Wiley was there, on the phone but motioned for me to sit down saying it would be just a minute or two. I grabbed a cup of his well-known strong but not particularly good tasting coffee from the reception area and twiddled my thumbs for what seemed like an eternity until he motioned for me to come into his office.

"Hi Mick, it's been pretty busy around here. Lucky in Abilene there's never too much going on that the same time, at least not normally. First thing I did was check all the dealerships and tire stores to see if they had calls for slit tires; no such luck, looks like it's just your car. So the wheels started turning upstairs in my overworked brain wondering about you know what. There were shoe prints around the car, we dusted them and took pictures, but nothing matches the prints from the fire and those gasoline cans at your folks' house back in '59. There were no finger prints or foot prints down at St. Andrew's. And your parking space outside the boarding house is off 10th street, so whoever did it did not drive into the alleyway but stayed on the pavement, so once again no possible evidence.

And Chief Earl tells me there were no calls or reports of suspicious activity and his night shift had no such case either. Damn! I'm still not ruling out local jerks, we have about half a dozen kids who hang out at the south pool hall and have been in trouble, but why would they pick one car, and yours at that? I'm sorry Mick, but that's all I've got. I know it isn't easy, but try to stick to your regular routine. I'll get Chief Earl to have his night shift be sure and do a drive-by at your place a couple of times a night. Okay? He patted me on the shoulder, shook my hand and saw me to the door.

The "Reflector Chronicle" had just a blurb on the tire slashing in the local "police watch" column but noted the address, up on 10th and Buckeye. So no "red" flags on that except that lots of people know I am renting at that general address, including Mom and Dad and Caitlin and Ron. And the drinking buddies down at Frank's and a few folks at the Juco. All I could say was that it looked like vandalism by local punks. That was until a frightened and angry Mariah called me and said we had to talk right away, "You've been holding out on me." Uh oh.

17

MICK TELLS ALL AND MARIAH REACTS

We talked and decided to meet up at the A & W on north Buckeye. You can tell when this lady is on the warpath, and she was. As soon as we got a corner booth in the back with no one around us, sat down and I got one of those great root beer floats, she didn't order a thing, just water, and glared at me. "What in the hell is going on Mick? Since you weren't at home, I called your Mom and Dad's house and talked to your Mom. They had just got the afternoon paper delivery and had seen the blurb on the tire slitting at 10th and Buckeye, put two and two together and were as worried as me. That was all I knew but your Mom inadvertently blurted out, 'There's been so much going on lately since the fire.' I said, 'What fire?' You could tell she knew she had said too much, but just said, 'I think you better talk to Mick about that. He knows more about it than we do.'" Not wanting to make more waves than I already did, I just said 'Thank you Mrs. O'Brien. I'll get hold of him. But tell him I called." She said, "And thank you Mariah was being so good to Mick. I hope there's no problem with you two." I laughed and said, "Not at all, peaches and cream as far as I know. Thanks. I'm sure you'll hear from him or us soon."

Peaches and cream indeed. I wolfed down the float and said we better have some place more private than this to talk. "It's a long story and not for anybody else's big ears." We drove out to the Catholic Cemetery; folks around town knew I was always out there taking pictures of tombstones, a safe place to talk. It's just a ten-minute drive from the A & W, but she was quiet the whole way.

"Okay, Miss Hot Temper, I'm going to tell you the whole thing. Mariah, you've got to know why I never said anything before. At first, not much had happened and I don't think it warranted any panic scene, but later because I did not want you to be frightened. Mariah, I care too much for you and did not want to scare you off." I put my hand in hers when I said that, and she flinched but did not remove it. "Okay Mick, I'm listening."

I proceeded to tell the whole story, from the Enterprise Bank Robbery and the attempted kidnapping back sophomore summer in 1957, the tussle with the redneck up at the high school, and then the fire out home and almost dying with Mom and Dad and me barely getting out of the burning house. Mariah held my hand tighter in hers and gasped, "I had no idea. My god, what else?"

No way I could gloss over what came next, so I told her about Jeremiah, his Mom and Dad and their church the same night as the fire. Then how Sheriff Wiley and the police found the gas cans and gate post painted with KKK, and the same at Jeremiah's church. They traced the gas cans to a purchase at the local RHV store where the dummies were remembered by the clerk. They were found out west of town near Solomon, arrested and hauled into jail. The law had the goods on them, and they ended up at Lansing for twenty years. And then I told Mariah about the whole KKK crowd being discovered southwest of Solomon and that they had a mass move from there on up to Idaho. Mariah interrupted, "God, that's horrible, but surely that was the end of it." So I had to tell her the rest. "Mariah, the three robbers got out of Lansing in 1962 on 'good behavior' and haven't been seen since, although they have to report to parole officers and Sheriff Wiley gets a call each week. But there's been a lot of buying of land from forced sales to farmers who can't pay their mortgages up in the north part of the county, all connected to a KKK front company up in

Idaho. Finally, we had rocks thrown through the sheriff's office window in 1962, the windows broken at St. Andrew's just a couple of months ago, and now my tires. I can't deny it, something is going on."

Mariah was silent for a few minutes, either in shock or else just thinking. She turned to me, put her arms around me, hugged me and kissed me and said, "What a burden you've been carrying. Too much for just one innocent person. Mick, and I'll tell you more later, and so will my Dad, we've had our moments too. I'm not afraid of those bastards. We've learned if you ignore trouble it comes right back at you. So you've got a friend; we're in this together."

"Mariah, no one has tried to attack me or rough me up. And whoever it is knows the local law people are aware of possibilities. There is one thing – Sheriff Wiley got me a pistol, and it's a powerful one, and has been teaching me how to use it. I'm a lover not a fighter and I'm just minding my business here doing what I love – teaching – and have had the good fortune to meet you. I think it's got to be business as usual for now. Teaching, working on the research for the history book, living life. But I'll understand if you want to cool it with me for a while."

Mariah said, "This is all pretty much of a shock to me right now, but I'm not one to run from trouble – I'll tell you more about that very soon. Let's just go on like normal, or maybe "**as** normal" like the English teacher would say. It's just about a month and a half until school is out, and we can see then what all we're thinking and what is brewing. I had some ideas for summer coming up, just wasn't the time to talk of them, but maybe the time's soon. I think both of us out of town for the summer won't do any harm. That's what teachers do – summer school and all. I've got some ideas. Right now, let's go back to town, both of us have to teach all week. Trust me Mick, I'll get through this and so will you. You Kansas country hicks have your hillbilly music which kind of nauseates me but that gal is all over the radio, 'Stand by Your Man.' Hey, that's me! That sappy music may have more to it than I thought." She kissed me again, I said thanks and we drove back to town.

18

GOOD NEWS FOR THE
NEXT SCHOOL YEAR

That's mostly what happened for the next seven weeks. A couple of good things happened, one for the research and one for teaching. I had applied for what they called a "guest researcher" library card down at the Eisenhower Library; they not only had everything about Ike and Mamie, but about Abilene all those years after the Eisenhower family moved from Denison, Texas, really all of Ike's growing up years. Up until now, and more to come, I've been looking into the "old" stories from Abilene, but the Eisenhowers would be important for about forty years in the 20th century. I would start basically in September when fall term began at the Juco. That was the other good news – Dean Halderson was happy with my work and wanted me for another year, provided I start on that promised Master's Degree, and even with a $500 raise. Better yet, they offered Mariah another year and raise as well, me finding out about this on a date up to Salina and the supper club. I, myself, was not so sure she would be interested in another year out in the "sticks" of Kansas, but she said yes and explained her decision to me.

"Mike, I've had a really good year teaching and it has opened my eyes to young people that are often very bright but with limited economic possibilities and still with a drive to do better than their families in the past.

Almost all are first time for any kind of post-high school education. And I think I've made a difference. Particularly with the young girls. They see me as "big city" but a model for what they could do – juco, college and maybe a career teaching. That's for openers. Then, there's Abilene. I can't separate the town and its history from you and all the places you have taken me to and all the tidbits of local lore you seem to know. And I think there's a lot more to come. It is so different, the whole experience, small town living, small town entertainment, farming and cattle raising. But even more all the beautiful old places, the mansions, the Victorians, and the Eisenhower complex. And local history. It would all be tourism without you.

"You have been wonderful to me, totally open to my background and family, maybe even a bit of a zealot when it comes to learning about Judaism. I would not mind if you tempered that a bit; I've learned to see it all with some perspective as well since being away from Kansas City and the family. In my way of thinking, Judaism is no different from Catholicism or any other major faith; good and bad, some things outrageous, others mindful. The difference is we 'lost,' by that I mean Judea and Jerusalem's history, the diaspora and the pogroms. But it has made our entire people stronger, more resilient. And in some cases, more fanatical, but you've got a bit of that going on in the Bible Belt. And Rome! I do declare! Anyway, it's a badge (wrong word and connotation there) we wear. Enough already as we say.

"More important is what I've grown to know about you, the Irish-American background, the humble farm background, the Catholicism you grew up with, your family, your school buddies, but also all your accomplishments, and openness to other cultures (that's obvious, a Spanish teacher!). We have some of that in common. What is worrisome is what I've just learned – the whole KKK story up to just a few days ago. I don't know where all that's headed, but like I told you, I'm not afraid of a fight, and you aren't either. I'd like to keep us going."

"Me too, Mariah. Agreed. It's a done deal. So what now?"

"The idea I had a few days ago, really since K.U. and Kansas City, is why not both of us enroll in first summer session down at K.U.; we can get six or even nine hours toward the Master's degree, I of course in English, you I guess in Spanish and History. Sorry, some prejudice – both areas are much better in Lawrence than Manhattan. Here's the kicker: we can share an apartment off campus. I know that will raise some hackles with the O'Briens and the Palafoxes! But I think you would be surprised. Both think we are a good match. Six weeks in Lawrence might go a way to see if that's really accurate. But the rest of the "brilliant idea" comes after summer school. I am sure I can arrange free lodging and more at the Palafox connection in Mexico City. No strings attached! They are Reform as well, not Orthodox, and being in Mexico you act like "conversos" anyway. We would have about four weeks to really get around to see the sights and work on your Spanish (pardon me, "Lo siento," it's not perfect yet.) I figure it might cost us each about $2000 and it's a tax write-off at least for you anyway. Think about it."

"I don't have to think about it; there's nothing I would object to or change. I had thought of a possible arrangement in Lawrence but was a little afraid to mention it. As for Mexico, I'm all in. And it's not really a bad idea to be away from Abilene for the summer. My landlady Mrs. Stevens will save my spot until September. I don't think wagging tongues would allow us to have one apartment for the two of us, not in these times. Maybe we can figure that out later. I just want to thank you for everything. You indeed have become my best friend and also an object of my amorous intentions!"

We laughed, toasted each other, had a nice meal and danced a bit before driving back to Abilene. There were still some loose ends to tie down before finals. One was to take Mariah down to the new (pardon me) "old" Abilene town south of the Santa Fe tracks.

19

OLD ABILENE, ST. ANDREW'S CATHOLIC CHURCH – COMING TO GRIPS WITH REALITY

I never figured out whose brainstorm it was, one of the local businessmen or Rotarians maybe, but they came up with a "surefire" tourist attraction for the town – the re - creation of an entire street of old Abilene built on vacant land southwest of the Eisenhower Center. Problem was there wasn't much left of the real old Abilene, but they did find three or four old original buildings that they moved lock, stock and barrel down to the new location. When Mariah and I visited it was pretty forlorn, before the summer schedule. Some locals formed "Old Abilene, Inc." and created the supposed business street with the Alamo Saloon, Merchants Hotel, General Store and Great Western Cattle Company. To me it seemed like tourist glitch or maybe kitsch is the right word. In spring and summer they have a can-can show in the saloon and a gunfight out in the street. I think Dodge City does the same thing but on a bigger basis. Local high school cuties form the can-can brigade and wannabe sheriffs and bad men do the gunfight. I had seen the whole thing a year or two before in summer. The idea was to corral (pardon that old Abilene word) overflow from the Eisenhower Center. I won't go so far as to call it a tourist trap because they won't get too much of your money, but it's more like a western B film. My opinion is subject to someone convincing me otherwise. It's hokey after you've seen some real history, I mean the Eisenhower Center. Mariah was not overly impressed with the phony store fronts in old Abilene either ("Like 'Shane'") but what she did love was the Eisenhower Center. The original museum and the freshly opened library were wonderful. It all was very dignified, well done especially with the murals of WW II history in the foyer of the museum, and all the historic photos, gifts to Eisenhower when he was president, and World War II memorabilia including the brown colored staff car and jeep. Mariah was comparing it to Kansas City's (Missouri side) own Truman Library, but said honestly Harry's place couldn't hold a candle to Ike's.

I told her about my or rather my students' encounter with Harry Truman the summer before I started teaching at the Juco. The reader might recall I taught a short course in English to foreign students at the Jesuit College on the Missouri side the summer after graduating from college, needing to make some badly needed shekels. We did some cultural outings in the city, down to old Union Station with the feds' and gangster bullet holes in the side, to the glitzy Plaza Shopping Area, to the Kansas City Art Museum and the Thomas Hart Benton Collection, really well done, but the most memorable out to Harry's library. After touring the library there was always a short appearance by Harry himself in the small auditorium to answer visitors' questions. One of my students came up with a lulu, all unexpected. He was from Japan and raised his hand and asked Harry why the U.S. still had troops in Okinawa. Harry, known for that quick temper, basically lost it! He looked directly at my student and said, "You Japanese #$^&$! We saved your @%^$%^ country and are there to keep the Communists from North Korea and Communist China from taking Japan." He probably said more, but that's what I remember. Quite a memory. And to go along with when I met Ike and Mamie (more later on that) and saw JFK and Jaqueline when I was in Mexico City.

We did not get to see too much of the spanking new library, most still open only to card-carrying researchers (I would get my photo I.D. the next fall), but the marble walled entry way and foyer were magnificent. I took a side trip just across the street west and showed Mariah the interior of our old St. Andrew's Catholic Church including the stained-glass windows, three now in repair status after the incident a few months earlier. The old traditional marble altar was gone, replaced by a really beautiful dark wood modern altar. The communion rail was gone as well, a relic of pre-Vatican II just a year ago. Our tour was by the current young assistant pastor, not old Monsignor Fahey from growing up days. When I told him who I was, Mom and Dad's long membership in the parish, my altar boy days and summer school over at Lincoln Grade School (recently demolished for Eisenhower Center stuff), and Catechism days with Monsignor Fahey, he was more than glad to do the tour. And he said he was familiar with my parents who bragged a bit about their son's job up at the Juco. He mentioned in passing that they still did not know who perpetrated the vandalism at the church, a real shame.

I sat with Mariah that afternoon, the sun streaming through the high round stained glass windows and the remaining ones lower on either side of the central aisle and pews, and thinking of years past and told her some stories. By the way, all of this was in "Rural Odyssey" started in 1959 after the fire and me off to college, culminating in a senior writing project for Honors before graduation in 1963. Mariah was moved and thanked me, "Another part of the O'Brien puzzle I guess. The altar in some ways is like our synagogues with that dark, beautiful wood, but with all the added images and of course the crucifix. And I'm still worried about the vandalism and all that's happened since." I said, "There's been a lot of water under the bridge since then in regard to my faith and religion, but we can talk about all that later." She said, "Yes I would definitely like to hear about all that. We'll swap stories. I'm not the Jewish American Princess you gentiles hear about. Ha. Do you know what a JAP makes for dinner? Reservations! (She laughs again.) Mick, maybe you've never heard all the Jewish jokes. All kidding aside, there never was a chance of me being anything like the stereotype – not enough money, not living in New

York, and parents far enough distanced from that whole New York scene to even begin living it. But everybody of Jewish descendance knows about it. I'm thinking; no way you would know any of this coming from Abilene and the farm, or for that matter, from that Catholic semi-ghetto college. Whoops, didn't mean to say that. But am I right?"

"You're right as rain. I knew nothing and I mean nothing about Jews or Judaism other than a general idea of what happened with Hitler and World War II. It all seemed so distant, another place and another time. We saw all the TV shows, the comedians and movies and had no idea most of the good stuff came from your people. And although I never would have admitted it at the time, you're right, college was if not exactly that old Catholic Ghetto mentality, a strong reflection of it. Most of the guys were cradle Catholics, graduates of Jesuit prep schools in St. Louis or Kansas City or Catholic High Schools in Kansas City and other towns, whereas the rest of us were just from Catholic families. I and a just a few buddies were different – public education in farm towns in Kansas. There in fact was some discrimination from the city boys, but I never but never regretted being a part of all that in rural Kansas. It saved the day for me as far as I'm concerned. Mexico and Guatemala enforced the Catholicism but also the anti-clericalism we never experienced at home. Gives you some perspective. Oh, and one more thing; I was in an old – fashioned dance band at college, and the band leader was Jewish and from Chicago. We all remembered him, well, as a bit 'pushy.'"

Mariah repeated an oft-used phrase, "Enough already. I'm hungry. What's the plan?"

"How about a hamburger up at the Inn N' Out and later out to Lena's again? You seemed to like it last time, the food's good and we can take a bottle of wine. I'll get you home by nine!"

"Fine with me, but come Sunday afternoon you have a command performance – to my house for dinner that I myself prepare, lock stock and barrel as you cowboys say, está bien chico?"

20

MRS. O'BRIEN'S CONCERNS

Sunday afternoon rolled around. I met Mom and Dad at 10:00 mass and went out to the house for Mom's bacon and eggs and a visit. They wanted to know what I had been up to, rather, what Mariah **and** I had been up to. I talked about the cemetery, drives around town, the Mexican dinner, Old Abilene, the Eisenhower complex, St. Andrews and, oh yeah, the trips to the supper club in Salina, and finally, the K.U. Relays and meeting her folks in Kansas City. What else? School, and the good news about a contract for next year. Mom asked, "What about Mariah? Did they renew her?"

"Yes, Mom. And speaking of that, we are becoming pretty close friends, but still just friends, no engagement ring or anything like that. She has been very supportive of all the stuff going on here, I mean the tire slashing and all. And I had to fill her in on all that stuff on the farm, the Enterprise thing, and most important the fire, the KKK and the criminals sent to Lansing. She was pretty shocked to hear it all, and that would have been a good time for her to bail out on me. But she didn't. Actually, we are working now on summer plans. You know we both have to get hours toward the Master's, just like Caitlin did for years, and we think K.U. is a good choice. I'll get an apartment down there; we'll both do the courses in first summer session and then take a vacation. Mariah has distant relatives in Mexico City, but they have connections to set us up with some travel all around Mexico. Good for my Spanish and a great traveling companion!"

Dad as usual said little, but you could tell he approved of my girlfriend, remembering her help out at the farm garden. Oh, I told him we could come out late May before Lawrence and help weed or pick whatever was ready. He perked up about that, said, "I've got a couple of extra hoes, and the early vegetables will be ready – lettuce, onions and maybe a few tomatoes. Corn won't be ready yet, but maybe we can go out again when your summer school is out and before you go to Mexico." I said that would work. Mom was pensive, you could tell something was on her mind. I said, "Mom, out with it! What's bothering you?" She hesitated and then basically told me everything.

"Mick, you haven't said anything about Mariah's religion, and you haven't had her down to mass or anything. And I'm still wondering about her name, Palafox. Your Dad or I have never heard of it, and I asked Caitlin and Ron and they haven't either. It sounds English. Is it? And I'm wondering if you both are in school at K.U. and you have an apartment, where's she to be? And I'm wondering about the travel arrangements in Mexico. Maybe it's none of my business but I am your Mom and we Moms think about these things. I'm sorry."

That was more than Mom asked me in eighteen years growing up in Abilene, and she wasn't worried during college days, after all I supposedly was in the care of her "beloved" Jesuits. "Mom, that is indeed a bunch of questions. I'm going to answer some of them but not all because I don't know some of the answers yet myself. Mariah does not go to any particular church, (no dishonesty there, she doesn't), but I have never met a better person. You don't need a front row pew at St. Andrew's for that. Her family, way back, comes from Spain, and her good looks by the way. The Palafox name goes back at least to the early 19th century and there was a famous Spanish general with the same name. You know her Dad is an M.D. with a very decent practice in Overland Park; her Mom is like you basically a housewife, but with a lot different life than you, more citified.

Mariah has two brothers both out of college, one a lawyer in Kansas City, Missouri and one an engineer for Monsanto in St. Louis. Now most Spaniards are Catholic, but she does not talk about that. Spain was split apart on religion with the Civil War in the 1930s and Franco's dictatorship ever since. Many Spaniards left Spain to save their lives because he was directly connected to Hitler and Mussolini. Unfortunately, the Catholic church was a big ally of his, but it was brother against brother. I don't know her parents well enough to ask about all that. You know stuff can happen, look at Dad's brothers and how many took their families out of the Church. I don't know much about the relatives in Mexico except that they are wealthy, linked to pharmaceutical manufacturing and medical supplies. I guess I'm lucky she didn't go into Medicine or I would never have met her. That's all I can tell you for now except that we really get along well, have a lot of common interests, and not only does she really care for me but loves you and Dad! Hey, I'm done. Do you feel better?"

"Thank you Mick, I do feel better, not all together better, but better. But you know that things turn out better when both parties are religious and the same religion. Maybe you can find out more as you get to know her. After all, it's still been less than a year." "Right on, Mom. I'll do that. And you'll be happy to know she is whipping up a big dinner for me later today, won't tell me the menu but said I'll find out what a good cook she is. How about that? Hey, I've got to run. We'll talk soon."

I think I weaseled out of that without telling any lies (a no-no burned into my young Catholic psyche at an all together young age), and yet satisfying Mom, and probably Dad as well. I don't know. Time to move on.

21

MORE HISTORIC HAUNTS IN ABILENE - MAINLY CREEPY

There were still places to check out for the Abilene History, mainly the old downtown buildings, and there were a lot of them, but many remodeled and losing that old pioneer charm. One residential place still stood out, just down the street from my apartment – the Seelye Mansion and some Abilene History. When I grew up two ancient surviving daughters still lived in the place, and it was run down and in need of a paint job. Little kids thought it was haunted and were afraid to go to the door even for trick or treating. There was a gazebo in the huge yard, a fish pool and the lawn often needed mowing. Even now in 1963 you could just drive by, but it was the "queen" of such places in Abilene. A.B. Seelye was an inventor of patent medicines, purportedly some 85 in all, and had a network of salesmen in horses and buggies to peddle them all over the country. Disparaging remarks were heard – a "snake oil" salesman! The house, so they say, has 25 rooms including a ball room, an old-fashioned bowling alley, original Edison light fixtures, a music room with a huge Steinway, and a Tiffany decorated fireplace. We tried to use history as an excuse and get a tour, but no such luck. At least I got a picture from the outside, this after they finally let go of some patent medicine dollars to get it painted.

There were probably at least a dozen buildings downtown linked to the old days, the best source for them a reprint of an old, small book touting Kansas, Abilene and its golden future (to get people to come to Kansas and specifically to Abilene, 1887), courtesy of our old First National Bank of Abilene. Just a few were still the originals like the Citizens Bank, the Lebold Mansion already seen, the old Court House, the St. Joseph's Orphanage up north on Highway 15, the First National Bank Building, the Presbyterian Church, the old Shockey and Landis building, the old United Real Estate Building, and many of the old Victorians scattered around town. The Sunflower Hotel where Ike gave his first campaign speech was a bit later, 1905, catty cornered from the United Building on 3rd street. I told Mariah I was on a 4-H float myself, depicting a "young Eisenhower," in front of the Hotel in a parade honoring Ike that same day as the campaign opened in 1952. She said, "Hmm, you are already beginning to lose some hair up there, just like Ike" and heehawed. We drove by most all of the places mentioned and I took slides on a Kodak of the old ones and some remodeled, not knowing if they might be of value for the potential book, but maybe. One place full of memories was where I went to Jr. High in the very early 1950s; it used to be the high school and there is a famous picture of Ike Eisenhower and his buddies in their baseball uniforms posing for a photo in front of the building.

I have vague memories of the 1940s, probably when I was eight or nine years old - the old Toothpick Building with a barber shop we frequented; it had a tin roof, ancient ceiling fans and spittoons; the original J.C. Penney's store with the old cable cash-change boxes sent upstairs on a maze of cables to clerks who would make the change, write a receipt and send it back down to the sales counter. I remember often going in the old Post Office and even the old courthouse and just once up to that wood paneled court room. Lucky I never had to end up there because of any shenanigans. I told Mariah the night just five years ago when we all went out to paint the water tower on the west side of town. I was scared to death to make the climb but some buddies did. The cops came and we were all admonished and told to "git" - "go on home." But no fines, no arrests. Those were the days, a traffic ticket for running a stop sign or speeding in town was $5.00. I didn't brag, but told her she could find out a lot more of the O'Brien family and my growing up days in that college project turned book in "A Rural Odyssey – Living Can Be Dangerous." She wanted a copy and said she devoured it in bedtime reading; she did not comment on the literary quality of the book, ha, but said it surely filled in a lot of blanks and reinforced her idea that the O'Briens and I were okay people.

There was one kind of creepy place to check out and we did it after yet another foray to the Catholic Cemetery. Just at the east corner before Highway 15 was what we all called the "orphanage." The official name was the St. Joseph's Home and Orphanage, dating way back to the early 20th century when it was actually founded as a girls' school by the same St. Joseph Catholic nuns out of Concordia Kansas (I told Mariah of bus rides for about two hours to Concordia, Kansas to play junior high football, singing "99 Bottles of Beer on the Wall" until we were all sick of it.) If you see old pictures, and I grew up with the original four story, brick building, it looks like something from Mel Brooks' "Young Frankenstein." It was however eventually turned over to the St. Joseph nuns of Wichita who operated the place until 1912. The order in Concordia took over again, housed the elderly in Concordia and the Abilene place became an orphanage with as many as 80 kids there. In my day in the 1950s for a short while they took in local Catholic kids as day students for grade school, and a good buddy spent a year up there. I also knew a couple of orphans from the school that I had as buddies all the way through high school.

A nun actually started the prize-winning Holstein herd and dairy across the road, to give jobs to the boys from the orphanage; its main owner in my time, a former orphan there. The same high school buddy worked there, and my Dad in the old days of the 1920s and 1930s would buy Holstein calves and bulls each year for the old homestead up in the Buckeye district north of Abilene. That was how it was even in my high school days. Mariah was fairly subdued in her comments on the place. "If it were a motel, I'd say it would be Norman Bates' place in 'Psycho' by Alfred Hitchcock. Every girl I know remembers Janet Leigh in that shower and what happened to her. It still gives me the creeps." With that in mind, we finished classes, exams and were getting ready for Lawrence. There were no more wanderings during that first year at the Juco. Oh, I haven't said much about farm history in Abilene, and that's a big part of the story, but it's all in "A Rural Odyssey."

No more strange incidents took place, but neither was there any news about the ones that did – the rock through the jail house window, the broken windows at St. Andrew's and my slit tires. I would still check in with Sheriff Wiley now and again but he said there was nothing new, just be aware and be careful. That's pretty much how we left things late that May, finals done, work up at the Juco tabled until September. My landlady, Mrs. Stevens, said she didn't think anyone would want to rent on just a short summer's three months basis, and since I was such a good "renter" (who might bring in other new juco personnel), she would keep the same place for me in the fall, with one proviso – a $100 deposit "to pay the electric and garbage bills." We could keep the phone connected to me, so no cost to stop or start again, but a "summer vacation hold" bill. The phone company, old Ma Bell, a descendant of Brown's old Power and Light and Abilene Phone Company had you where they wanted you. Mariah got a similar deal.

22

SUMMER SCHOOL AT K.U.

After saying goodbye to everyone in town, including Mom and Dad, we drove down to Lawrence the last of May, found a furnished, clean but simple apartment just four blocks from campus and went on and enrolled for first summer session at K.U., me with two Spanish Literature Courses, one Modern U.S. History Course, and Mariah in three advanced graduate courses in English language and American literature. We would be up to our necks with that schedule and huge amounts of compressed homework, but worth it we thought so we could get five weeks off afterwards to go to Mexico and then visit her folks and mine before Fall Term. What can I say, no one will believe me. We actually had separate bedrooms, each with a desk and "study area." I asked Mariah if she was sure about that and heard a resounding "You bet." Then she came over, gave me a big hug and warm kiss and said, "Está temprano, mi amigo! Don Quixote said all comes to he who is patient (when Sancho complained about not getting his island)." And she laughed. I guess I was not going to get in the real estate business quite yet.

Just as well, the work load was even more than we both imagined, maybe underestimating it or else our capacity to study. The classes however were not a bit disappointing. My 20th Century Mexican Literature class was great preparation for more travel to that country, the main emphasis on my favorite writer Carlos Fuentes. He was a tough nut to crack, big time lexicon including about thirty per cent vocabulary I had to look up in my Cassell's Spanish Dictionary. I shall never forget one word: "chingar," - the "f" word in Mexico. Fuentes did an entire page of some fifty lines with a hilarious account of all the grammatical ways it could be used: noun, verb, adjective, adverb, and especially exclamation point! But he was really important for describing, albeit in fiction, the 1950s in modern Mexico City ("The Region Where the Air Is Clear") and all of twentieth century Mexico with its heritage of the 1910 Revolution in "The Death of Artemio Cruz." (There would be a big surprise about him in Mexico when we got there.) He was a leftist in politics and an avid anti-clerical, but hey that is the essence of much of Mexico all the way to the 1960s. And like in much of Latin America, you can be a political leftist and be an upper class capitalist. I liked him because I learned a huge amount of Mexican culture and history I had not learned when in summer school at the UNAM. "That was an irony," said Mariah, "You studied literature from Spain! And in Mexico! I guess one could study English Literature at Harvard or Yale though, huh?"

The Modern U.S. History was a good refresher from college and more. The Civil War revisited was much needed, the Western Expansion, the Boom Days of the 1920s, the Dust Bowl and Depression days (which my parents lived) and especially World War II and Korea – a link to Ike and Abilene. Mariah's English courses were "okay" with an Advanced English Grammar but a great 20th century novel course with a recent addition to the core – Flannery O'Connor's stories and novels from the South. Mariah said, and I agreed, "Those folks remind me a lot of Kansas. I mean the leaded Bible Belt Religion and the country hayseeds (her term), but really her genius in creative writing. We women have a lot to teach you men! Too bad she died so young, who knows what else we might have. I swear I have even heard some of the language in Abilene." I said, "I'm not expert on southern speech but every time I read her, I'm reminded of people and customs I think I could recognize. Maybe a coincidence."

23

SUMMER FORAYS – THE O'BRIEN'S AND THE PALAFOXES

We made two forays on busy weekends, a long one on the 4th of July out to Abilene where we saw Mom and Dad, helped pick vegetables in the big farm garden and one afternoon I regretted – volunteering to help Ron bale hay with his brother down on their parents' river bottom land. The truth - I "played out," a nice way to put it, the culprit being the ambitious German farmers with their 80-pound bales (as opposed to maybe 40 to a max 50 on Dad's farm growing up). I could stack Ron's bales two high on the hayrack and that's all. He laughed but didn't kid me, and Mariah got to ride the tractor in front of the baler for a couple of rounds – and got filthy dirty from her efforts. I haven't mentioned, she had a place to stay with one of the girls from the Juco and I stayed out at Mom and Dad's. When I told Mom we had separate rooms in the Lawrence apartment, I could see a bit of relief on her face, and then she laughed, "Mick you are a good Catholic boy. We brought you up right!" "Right, Mom." Dad just smiled. A good extra, Caitlin fixed one of those farm hay balers' meals – mounds of fried chicken, potatoes and chicken gravy, fresh peas, green beans and especially from Dad's garden, and strawberry short cake for dessert, the berries from the old patch on the east side of the farm house. (Ron kept that when he and Stan were building the new house after the fire.)

The second foray was the one that was different and taxed me a bit — once again meeting Mariah's Mom and Dad but this time at their house in Overland Park. It was an easy drive, and it turned out the house was huge by Abilene standards with five guest rooms, one for me. We drove down in Mariah's car and she prepped me and may I say even coached me and encouraged me — "Still just friends, good friends to be sure," and checking in before Mexico but also maybe satisfying Mom Ariel's curiosity and Dad Benjamin's (Ben's) promise to show me all the Sephardic stuff. Confession time — I had gone back to my college Spanish textbook and checked out the 11th century Spanish lyric poetry related to Arabic and Hebrew poetry. I lugged that old textbook along with me to Overland Park. Kind of homework I guess, and in a sense, it paid off.

We went down on a Saturday morning (Mariah's idea, not quite ready or appropriate to rush into the house on Sabbath Preparation Friday evening), okay because they don't celebrate the Sabbath itself except if it falls on Jewish holy days. Ben suggested lunch down on the Plaza which would give him a chance to be a Rotarian and explain all the pseudo-Spanish architecture and fountains (some of which were legit — copies of places in old Sevilla in Spain). We did go to a Jewish Deli "one of the best in the city" and got those great Pastrami sandwiches and cheesecake for dessert (and a "goy" St. Louis Budweiser beer to wash it down). Somewhere in the conversation I mentioned I had played guitar and sung at an Italian Restaurant up on 50th street the summer after college days; Ben knew it, said he knew some insurance people, and it was famous for having burned down three times, and all legit and covered. He winked when he said that.

I really enjoyed the Plaza tour, I had always related it in some distant way to my studies just up the street on 68th street and the Jesuit College. Ben suggested we go on out to the house, Mariah and her Mom could catch up and I could finally see his library (uh oh O'Brien, get ready). That happened. Aside from History, Literature and Science, Benjamin had all the usual medical books, but also some ancient bound replicas of both Averroes' and Maimonides' treatises, from Caliphate days in Córdoba in Spain.

I don't expect any reader to be very interested in the next paragraph much less understand it. Go ahead and skip it.

I showed him my Spanish Literature Anthology and the three (!) pages on the Arabic and Hebrew lyric songs - "muwassahas" and old Spanish "jarchas." The text quoted some "cancioncillas" [little songs] from before 1040; they were the oldest known songs of European lyricism in romance language. The songs really were "jarchas" - poems in old Spanish (romance) at the end of each Hebrew "muwassaha." (Get it?) The latter were found in manuscripts in an old synagogue in Cairo, Egypt! Later, Spanish "jarchas" coming from Hebrew and Arabic "muwassahas" were written in Hebrew and Arabic characters, but the language is old Spanish Mozárabic (language of the Iberians living under the Arab rule) dialect. Benjamin was awed with this explanation (which I was pretty sure I didn't really understand). He patted me on the back and said, "Mick, for an Irishman from Kansas your interests are far from the wheat and corn fields. Thank you. All this corroborates what I believed about the role of Hebrew in old Spain."

I think I was just informally put on Benjamin's "okay list" for his only daughter. Things were far from that serious yet, but good times were ahead – the trip to Mexico. We were all in the living room having drinks before dinner when there was another surprise. Mariah's brother Josh came over, the lawyer, met me, and said, "We've heard nothing but good things about you Mick! Wow! A trip to Mexico and seeing the long-lost relatives. You're in for a good time, I think. Better take a coat and tie Mick, and sis, your best dress! Those folks live in high social circles. No overalls Mick or those farm boots with the manure on them ("just kidding"), but don't worry about a yarmulke [Jewish prayer cap for men]. They are all "conversos" [Jews converted to Catholicism to avoid the Inquisition] anyway, at least to the Mexicans.

I looked over at Mariah and said, "What's this? Down what paths are you taking me? All I wanted to do was to get back to Mexico, speak some Spanish and have some fun." Josh spoke up again, "Don't worry about that; I have an idea you'll have all you can handle."

24

ANOTHER WORLD – UPPER CLASS MEXICO

We flew out a few days later on Mexicana to Mexico City, were met at the airport by no less than Mr. and Mrs. Palafox, quite an honor their coming in person. They didn't just send the chauffer to pick us up, but he **was** driving the black Mercedes limo. They were all smiles, gave Mariah a big hug ("It's been so long, you were just a little girl last time, you have bloomed nicely"), she turned a bit red and said I want you to meet my colleague at the Junior College where we teach, my best friend, and in fact my boyfriend Michael O'Brien. "Habla bien el castellano, ya estudió en la UNAM, y se interesa muchísimo en México, especialmente la cultura pre-colombina y la cultura y arte de la Revolución." Señor Palafox smiled again and said (all subsequent conversation was in Spanish), "Welcome Michael. It will be our pleasure to show you some wonderful sights in Mexico and perhaps introduce you to some of our most renowned cultural figures!" Señora Palafox hugged Mariah, took her arm and said, "Let's be off, straight home to a fine dinner and time to get reacquainted again."

The Palafox home was a "déjà vu" moment for me, I mean the outside entry; as a student three years before I had walked along the Paseo de la Reforma in Mexico City and seen the huge walls with iron gates hiding who knows what behind them. The "casa" was behind such a wall just down from the "Angel de la Independencia" monument. Once inside one was greeted by a beautiful garden with all manner of tropical plants and even orchids (how these survived at 7000 feet I did not know), and of course fountains. The house itself was large, three stories, stone on the outside. Inside was a polished wood entry way, a large wooden staircase leading up to the first floor (our bottom living floor in the U.S.), with the living and dining rooms that were light and cheery with comfy yet modern furniture. My room on the second floor (I was instructed to settle in and meet everyone else later down stairs), one among many guest rooms, was comfortable with a desk and I noticed a good reading lamp, a TV in one corner, a window with a view of the Paseo, two easy chairs and of course a private bath. I was told to just let the maid "Concha" know of any of my needs, including laundry, a "cafecito" or "merienda" at any time. A butler, for lack of a better term, took my large suitcase and backpack with my camera up to the room.

We met in the living room, like I say, comfy furniture with easy chairs, divans and many handy coffee tables everywhere. And a large fireplace which indeed would be used on cool Mexico City nights. I was still in a bit of shock and would only appreciate the décor and the paintings later. That was when Señora Palafox showed me a small oil by Diego Rivera depicting rural school teachers, and another by Frida Kahlo with a monkey on her shoulder. Only Rivera's meant something to me because it reminded of pictures I had seen of the staircase murals in the National Palace. I knew little of Frida. Sara said they were constantly in the news the last few years, particularly when Frida died. She remembered the pictures in the newspapers.

I'm not going to say I was totally comfortable with the huge house and its décor, and in fact, nor was Mariah, both of us used to the small apartment in Lawrence and the same in Abilene. Although her home in Overland Park was a bit genteel, it was nothing like this. Sr. Palafox, saying call me "David," offered us drinks, imported scotch or national beer, wine for the ladies. We would meet Mariah's cousins later that day, all working and busy but curious I guess to meet us, all together at dinner. Mrs. Palafox, "Llame-me Sara," ["Call me Sara"] wanted to know all about the family in Overland Park, how Benjamin and Ariel were doing, and (she could not remember exactly) Mariah's brothers. Mariah filled them in, all in that beautiful fluent Spanish. Oh, by the way although I am writing in English, almost all the conversation in Mexico was in Spanish. In my case when talking to the Palafoxes, it would still be "Señor y Señora Palafox," at least for the first few days or so.

They were most gracious to me, for the moment not asking too much about my family, but really curious about the original travel and trip to D.F. and my experience at the UNAM. I told them of my farm background, a small wheat farm in Kansas, Ike Eisenhower's home town, then college in Kansas City with the Jesuits, the business degree with a Spanish minor and the trip to Mexico in 1962. "I probably stood close to this house watching John and Jacqueline Kennedy come down the Paseo de la Reforma in an open-air Mercedes limousine with President Adolfo López Mateos and his wife!" David said, "I remember it well, a wonderful moment for both our countries, those were good days. I add our personal condolences to you as a U.S. citizen for his untimely death. We all felt it and mourned for the family. Oh, by the way, your Spanish is excelente! Not perfect mind you, but we can't quite tell you are a gringo! Ha."

I said Mexico had a lot to do with it, Guatemala a little, but mainly Spanish at college and my efforts to speak as much as possible with students from Latin America at school (I told them the joke from Anglo friends, my prize for "most outstanding foreign student" senior year). I was not yet ready to talk about the O'Brien modest economic background, that I had taken a bus fifty hours from Kansas City to Mexico City, but had wonderful good fortune to be with a Mexican family who hosted me for those few months, living on Calle Londres, just a few blocks from the Palafox residence. Over the course of two drinks and the evening dinner I told them the rest – the wonderful classes on Spanish Literature at the UNAM, but limited local sightseeing highlighted mainly by a trip to Acapulco (interest piqued by Carlos Fuentes' novels) but the once again adventurous trip to Guatemala by bus and the experience there. I mentioned the wonderful host family – The Meiers - and the job offer at Industria Farmacéutica, and how that had turned out. Sr. Palafox was immediately interested, saying he knew the company well and even had met its owners. So we had a bit of something in common, just slightly.

They wanted to know all about Mariah's life as well, and she told them of college at K.U., the degree in English and American Literature, and the juco job in Abilene, and of course meeting me. She pulled no punches either, saying she needed to get away from home after a bit of a sheltered upbringing and saw Kansas as a big adventure. She noted she could have gone to Yale or Harvard for the advanced degree, but was not quite ready for that. The Palafoxes did take note of the latter. They had certainly heard of Eisenhower but were just vaguely familiar with Abilene and Kansas, the "wild west," "cowboys" and John Wayne to them.

The door bell rang and two handsome, well-dressed young fellows in business suits came in. Among much laughing, carrying on, hugging their father and mother, they came over. Jaime, the most outgoing, looked at Mariah and said, "Ay, too bad we are relatives. Ooo la la! I could go for this one!" He laughed, gave Mariah a respectful hug, and then saw me. (I was in a long sleeve dress shirt, a sweater – vest and slacks.) And it's Michael the Spanish teacher and historian! Our aunt and uncle in Kansas have spoken of you. If you're unlucky, you will inherit that dusty and musty library of Uncle Ben's. Un chiste mi amigo! [A joke my friend!] Welcome to Mexico, I hope I can be of service!"

The second brother, Lucas, was a bit quieter and just hugged Mariah and shook my hand saying, "Igualmente! Jaime can handle the clubs. I'll see you get to the museums!" We all sat down to a sumptuous dinner with the main subject being what did we want to see in Mexico and what they could do to help us. I explained that even though I had been at the UNAM for several months three years ago, it had been mainly study, some local tourist sites but travel limited by both time and budget. I added that

I had indeed studied a lot about Mexico, knew more than the average "gringo" of its history, a little geography but was open to suggestions – the Pre-Colombian sites and important colonial cities high on the list. Mr. Palafox said "That indeed is a big order for just five weeks, but we've got some friends in the travel business (it turned out they had friends in many businesses including airlines, buses and hotels as well as travel agencies themselves). I'm owed a favor or two from medical conventions when I brought some high – roller M.D.s to town, so we can call in a marker or two." Mariah objected, "Gracias Tío David, maybe just some hints and pointers." "Veremos mi amiga!" ["We shall see, young lady!"]

25

TOURISM – MEXICO D.F. THEN PRE- COLOMBIAN MEXICO

What ensued was a whirlwind five weeks leaving us exhausted but incredibly happy and satisfied, experiencing a veritable cram-course in Mexico. Lucas escorted us in Mexico City, driving a family car to the Zócalo, the National Palace and the Diego Rivera fresco "History of Mexico," an essential for understanding 20th century Mexico and all that went before it. Even though Rivera was an avowed Marxist, there is no one in Mexico that came close to his mural painting depicting: Pre-Colombian Aztec Tenochtitlán, Spaniard Hernán Cortés and the conquest, the colonial period and the oppression of the Indians and the poor by the rich, ruling class in agriculture and mining, Independence from Spain in 1810, then the Liberal-Conservative battles of the 19th century, and finally the 20th century and the Mexican Revolution and "workers' state" (whew!). All this appears in a huge stairway in the old presidential palace, all in mural style (paint on wet plaster, a technique Rivera got from Italy but also from the Mayas in Bonampak). His choice was to employ an almost comic book style, "black and white" because of his Marxist Dialectic – you were either a hero or a villain. Whew again! Rivera left no doubt as to his sentiments, and I for one certainly did not agree with him, but the art was overwhelming.

We stopped in the Cathedral, the largest in the Americas, and mainly tried to stay out of the way of the workers on scaffolds; the whole place needed shoring up. I remembered it from Sunday mass on quieter days in 1962, with the lousy p.a. system, empty pews and men smoking during the sermon. Lucas knows the entire church history vis a vis the Revolution of 1910 and how priests and nuns still have to "lie low" with the prohibition of clerical garb in public. U.S. citizens cannot imagine such a thing, but live and learn.

Nearby was the "Sinagoga Sefardi" in the old historic center. Lucas said, "Tit for tat or whatever you say in Kansas City, something for the Catholic, something for the Sephardic Jew! This is our oldest and is still frequented by those who work downtown." We made a very short visit, but Mariah seemed happy to see it. "After that monstrosity of a Cathedral and now this, I begin to understand the 'pecking order' in Mexico. Así sea. [So be it.]"

Lucas was proudest of the "Museo Nacional de Historia y Antropología" in Chapultepec Park. We spent the entire day going from one room and salon and one culture to the next. Lucas proclaimed it was the best introduction to Pre-Colombian Civilization in Mexico. I thought the whole place was amazing but also overwhelming. From Teotihuacán to the Toltecs in Tula, the Toltec move to the Valle de Mexico and the huge Lake Texcoco, the late arrival of the Aztecs and the making of Tenochtitlán, the Zapotec culture around Oaxaca, but especially the Maya in the jungle south – Palenque the crown jewel - and finally the Maya-Tolteca Civilization in Chichén-Itzá and Uxmal in the Yucatan.

After that long day at the museum, Sr. Palafox set us up with a family friend, owner of a major travel agency, and they in turn helped us with local day tours to Teotihuacán and Tula, close to Mexico City, Then we set off on a flight to Oaxaca and the day trips to nearby Monte Albán and Mitla, another fight to Tuxtla Gutierrez and our favorite modern Mexican small city, San Cristóbal de las Casas with a side trip to San Juan Chamula, then by car to Agua Azul and to Palenque. Finally a bus to Vera Cruz, nearby Las Ventas and finally the Yucatán. It took two full weeks but would provide the basis for me for a huge injection of Mexican native culture into my history courses at the Juco and for "culture days" in Spanish classes. As I write this, I have to remind myself and the reader that this is not a classroom at the Juco, and is just part of the tale of that phenomenal summer, I am just scratching the surface of what Mariah and I saw and experienced.

Mariah did not have any previous study or for that matter intense interest in the Pre-Colombian era, but she was a fast learner and could scoot up those tall pyramids ahead of me. And there were at least a half dozen each higher and more impressive than the last. It helps to not have a fear of heights; I recalled maybe at age twelve, sitting on the barn roof on the farm, trapped like a cat, and taking an hour to get up my nerve to get down on the rickety ladder. Must have been eight feet. The pyramids were hundreds of feet high, but fortunately many had a chain in the middle of the stairway you could hang on to. Sitting with my back to the outside wall on top level of the "Castillo" at Chichén Itzá says it all. All too much to say here, but one major impression aside from the main pyramid at Chichén was the small temple nearby with the skull racks of the sacrificed warriors – just like we saw in Teotihuacán – proof the Toltecs brought human sacrifice with them from central Mexico to the Yucatan and the late-classic Maya. Mariah was very intent about it all, and a good listener. She often would understand the Spanish of the diverse tour guides better than I and fill me in. "Aren't you supposed to know Spanish big boy? I expect a nice gratuity or something else special for this."

Aside from my fragile stomach and the disturbances you can imagine, it was a great trip. We did share rooms by the way, but they all had the small, narrow single beds, so no harm done most of the time. Mariah and I were very used to each other by now, and can I say, more intimate. More than anything else we were great friends, laughing and serious as the times dictated. After those two weeks we flew back to Mexico City, had a reunion with the Palafoxes, rested three or four days, well, almost, and then did what I like to call "Part II."

26

<hr />

A RETURN TO D.F. - FUN AND GOOD TIMES

Back in Mexico City, socially I had only one request, a throwback to three years ago: a visit to the nightclub where they played and danced "flamenco" - "Gitanerías" - and featured as well the great Mexican classical guitarist David Moreno. The one tv program I remembered from my student days, that program solely dedicated to the guitar in Mexico, featured him, but was a thing of the past. The whole family went to the restaurant, maybe because of the Spanish connection, and we ordered a huge "paella" for all. My comment to Mariah, "Not as good as yours." She laughed and asked me if I knew the meaning of the word "facsimile!" Ha.! The food was terrific, the flamenco dancing the usual (much foot stomping), but I paid attention to the guitarists, "Fenomenal!" Sr. Palafox ordered wine from "La Rioja" and a good time was had by all.

After we got home there was a chance for me to talk about the guitar playing we had just heard, my interest in the classic guitar, all the hours of practice, but learning on my own since sophomore year in high school. Jaime, the livewire, piped up, "We're going to check you out on that Miguel. I just happen to own one of the finest classic guitar models in Mexico, trouble is, I never really learned to play it. I was going to serenade one of the señoritas living in Chapultepec, and I did, but wisely left the guitar at home and just hired some really fine mariachis." He ordered the maid to bring out the drinks, went to his old room and fetched the guitar from under a bed. When he took it out of the case and handed it to me, I think I broke out in a bit of a sweat, but no time for excuses. It indeed was beautiful once you opened the dusty case (his apologies and jokes and excuses), and it needed a new set of strings, but it was quite playable and was still with amazing sound. After a couple of rounds of drinks, the strings and I both limbered up; I managed to play for about 30 minutes (the Palafoxes urging me on), basic Classic including a bit of Fernando Sor, and of course the obligatory "Malagueña." I could also do some "ersatz" flamenco based on an old LP of Carlos Montoya. Mariah knew I played. She was all smiles, but said in English, "Hey you weren't kidding me about that huh? I know you can sing too. Why don't you do some of those songs we did at the Gomezes in Abilene?" That was a bit more difficult; all I knew were the corny old Mexican classics like "Adelita" and "Cielito Lindo" and the Cuban "Guantanamera" from college days. I do believe, just as in Guatemala with the Meier family three years ago, I made some "brownie points." Something for everyone, Sr. Palafox liked the Spanish flamenco and classical, Doña Palafox the Mexican ditties and the boys pretty much everything. Jaime said, "I've got a new girlfriend up in Lomas, this time you can join me and the mariachis. I'm serious. I'll let you know. And Miguel, while you are here, feel free anytime to ask Concha (the maid) to get the guitar for you. Felicitaciones muchacho!" Quite an evening!

Later Sr. Palafox wanted to know more about our trip to the archeological sites and our impressions. That took a while, Mariah maybe having more to say than I. It grew late, but all decided that tomorrow, a Sunday, we could have dinner and plan Part II.

I went to mass at the Cathedral in the Zócalo on Sunday morning, met Lucas and Mariah afterwards and we walked to the nearby construction where they were digging and finding amazing remains of the old "Plaza Mayor" from the time of the Aztecs and then Cortes's palace. The most amazing was a few blocks away - a construction worker had slammed his pick and shovel into what turned out to be a beautiful carved round stone - depicting a woman but she cut into pieces. It was proof they said of the legend of the Aztec sun god Huitzilopochtli's revenge on Coyolxauhqui his sister, the moon god, who had joined her allies the evening stars to murder their mother Coatlicue. Lucas was sure it was the case and waxed enthusiastic over it all. Jaime said it was a fake. Where is truth? I'm with Lucas, and so are the experts.

Later with conversation of drinks before the big afternoon meal, when asked by Don David (a nice Mexican way of addressing him) of the plan for Part II of our travels, I said that to complete or at least move along my knowledge of Mexico for Spanish classes (and maybe tourism for the students) there was a big gap with me: the well-known colonial cities with all that history of the boom years of gold and silver. Mariah was open to it all and voiced her approval. Lucas, piped up at that: "There is now a complete 'gira' or tour and I think it would be perfect for you. Do you want the list? I've done it and it's spectacular. You start near us here with Querétaro and San Miguel de Allende, then Zacatecas, Guanajuato, and Guadalajara. You will see the highlights of the mining years but also much of the story of Mexican Independence from Spain and the highlights of really what is the Colonial Period. Personally, and I study such things, you and Mariah by the end of this will have it all – Pre-Colombian, Colonial with the 'gira' trip, and Diego Rivera's mural –"Historia de México" - here in the National Palace."

Mariah joined in, "Just one more thing, there are some great beaches and ocean in Mexico, and I'm not going home without a tan." Sr. Palafox spoke up, "There is something you might be familiar with – Acapulco. It was the favorite place of the stars of Hollywood in the 1950s, including our acquaintance Liz Taylor. Guess what, we have a Sephardi connection with her, and we can get you a beachside condo on what may still be the prettiest beach in Mexico. The government is making noise about developing all the Gulf of Mexico beaches on the east coast, but that's still in the planning stage. I personally think you'll find all you want at

Acapulco." I interjected, "Terrific! I know a little bit about it from Carlos Fuentes' novel 'La Región Más Transparente del Aire.' And I first saw the ocean (a Kansas farm boy) at Acapulco three years ago." Sr. Palafox seemed surprised, "Oh? We need to talk about that book later." Lucas said, you can get a short flight over from Guadalajara, tie it all together and we'll have a reunion back here to celebrate your trip. I'll be tour agent for all this, with some help from Dad, just a few phone calls. I'd love to go with you, but think maybe you and Mariah might appreciate the adventure together, Verdad?" Mariah protested, but only slightly, and in three days' time we were off.!

27

MORE THAN WE NEEDED TO KNOW ABOUT COLONIAL MEXICO

The "gira" or tour was done by one of the agencies the Palafoxes knew, so they assured us the tour people were not only honest but would take good care of us. It was four-star accommodations, most meals and local tour guides, but with plenty of time on our own. We were all packed and me with a run to the "farmacia" for Pepto Bismol, my "health insurance policy" for Mexico. What we did not expect was that Sr. Palafox had arranged a private van just for us, the driver on call the whole time, and an expert on the whole itinerary. So "ándale muchacho" and off we went. I'll just hit the high points – remember! I'm teaching History at the Juco!

First was the short drive to Querétaro (I vaguely recall driving through it on the bus three years ago, no memories whatsoever. I think it was early in the morning at the end of that fifty-hour bus ride from Kansas City). The main sight was the huge aqueduct done from 1726 to 1728, supposedly at the request of the Santa Clara Convent (some nuns must have had good blood and money connections to the Spanish crown, hence the governor or Viceroy, not unheard of; unmarried daughters indeed "went to the nunnery"). The city seemed very large and frankly industrialized to me. They said most of the Baroque churches and art were plundered in the

War of Independence in 1810. Its claim to fame was that French Emperor Maximilian, put on the throne in Mexico by no less than Napoleon III in what was called "The Second Empire," was executed in the main plaza in 1867, thus ending the usurper's power grab in Mexico in the 19th century. One folkloric anecdote remained: supposedly, jealous wife Carlota wanted to keep track of Maximilian after work in the Zócalo in Mexico City and ordered him to build the broad and beautiful Paseo de la Reforma all the way from the Zócalo to Chapultepec Castle where they lived. The idea was to see him leave from work and come straight home! Did he? I doubt it.!

Next was San Miguel de Allende on the very east end of the State of Guanajuato, a real delight and pleasure! Originally the territory was that of the Chichimecas, a bit before the Aztecs. San Miguel was at its height in the mid – 18th century, the time of the silver boom in neighboring Zacatecas State. It was on the main road carrying the silver to Mexico City. Today it is a major art center in Mexico and the largest U.S. Ex-Pat colony. David Siqueiros, along with Rivera and Orozco, the big three of post - revolutionary art in Mexico, taught there. There were many churches, some plundered, but "La Parroquia" was perhaps the best to see. The priest Miguel Hidalgo "Father of Independence in Mexico" in 1810 served here. The most ornate architectural colonial style of the "churrigueresco" was here in the "Iglesia de San Francisco." And another major tourist attraction was the "Casa de la Inquisición." Mariah said we could skip that. We were both overwhelmed by all the art galleries.

Then on to Zacatecas, the real "king" of silver mining in Mexico all through the colonial period up to present days. Also, little known, it was the beginning of the "Camino Real" of Spanish exploration and discovery up into what is modern day New Mexico and the founding of Santa Fe as its capital. A minor personal note was that my high school Spanish text book was indeed titled "El Camino Real," now a "relic" of instruction in the 1950s. So what did one see – dozens of tiny shops selling all manner of objects of silver, the most common a silver-dollar sized "coin" with the "Aztec Calendar" on one side and the snake and the cactus and the

Mexican flag on the other. Tourist kitsch, but still pure silver! Zacatecas was at an altitude of 6000 feet, the mines in nearby mountains. They claim that in the 18ᵗʰ century one fifth of the world's silver came from here. Father Hidalgo's army twice roared through the town, and in the major battles of the Mexican Revolution against President Porfirio Diaz and his main general Victoriano Huerta, "la Toma de Zacatecas" [The Taking of Zacatecas] by no less than Pancho Villa remains a high point in modern Mexican history.

Then to Guanajuato, our driver steady on the itinerary, always full of information, jokes, Mexican songs, and also discreet about any amorous hugging and kissing of his passengers. This place, also part of the silver boom, came to be known and symbolize a perhaps touchy part of Mexican history – the place of the largest "haciendas" of the rural upper class, the scene of almost total serfdom of the rural workers, and the rule of the owners of the ranches ["hacendados"] and powerful Catholic clergy. All the above were major causes of hate before and retribution after the Revolution. My studies of the Mexican "Novel of the Revolution" dealt with it all, mainly the national iconic work – "Los de Abajo" ["The Underdogs"]. My favorite writer Carlos Fuentes would retell a similar story but in Avant Garde literary style in "La Muerte de Artemio Cruz" ["The Death of Artemio Cruz"]. Padre Hidalgo, like Kilroy (pardon the "gringocismo") was here for battles of Independence, and it was the scene of the Catholic "Cristero" battles in post-revolutionary Mexico, in opposition to the oppression of clergy and Catholics in the late 1920s. Incidentally Diego Rivera was from here and the most famous of all folk artists in Mexico, José Guadalupe Posada of woodcut fame on the Mexican ballads ("corridos") and especially the skeletons (las calaveras) got his start here, so it was an important place for me as a college Spanish teacher.

Mariah and I were really getting tired by now, thinking we bit off more than we could chew, but just one more big colonial stop – the huge city of Guadalajara. I confess we really did not do it justice, we were just "touristed out." Mariah said, "If I see one more Catholic church I'll barf." Pretty much the sentiments of her Irish-Catholic traveling buddy as well. Much of Guadalajara was like a smaller Mexico City, the churches, the museums, the government buildings (don't tell this to either DF people or Guadalajara people!). We did make it a point of getting to the famous "mariachi" plaza for the State of Jalisco's most famous item, and the mariachis all decked out in the "charro" Mexican cowboy outfits. My take on the latter: The Plaza Garibaldi in Mexico City was no less fun (dating back to too much tequila and women of the night in the Tenampa Bar when I was a student). I told Mariah about the latter but added that way too much tequila plus buddies taking care of me saved my virginity that night! This raised an eyebrow or two but she said, "We can talk about the 'Macho Kid'- later."

So it was a warm goodbye to "chofer" Guillermo at the Guadalajara airport where we boarded Mexicana to the last destination, glorious Acapulco! The flight was short, two hours, and we rode via taxi into that dazzling beach and ocean city in the late a.m., and were taken to the promised condo in an old, but great location near Caleta and Caletilla beaches. We were traveled out, but had a quick lunch at a nearby café, donned swim suits and were off to Caleta Beach. Speaking of dazzling, Mariah was that and more in a green "maiô" or one-piece bathing suit that suggested if it did not reveal all of her attributes, including a nice view from below her dark hair, green eyes and smooth shoulders. I comment because now in 1964 bikinis were coming in to vogue, but the "maiô" was in my mind, well, more sexy. I had on a boxer style gringo suit and with skin asking for a major sun burn. (I had the mother of all sun burns on the previous visit just one year ago.) Mariah applied plenty of sunscreen, a pleasurable moment, and I had a big Mexican straw cowboy hat I had bought in Guanajuato, so no major damage done. She had me do the same for her, a pleasure, but already had a naturally darker skin than I, so she would get that tan she wanted in just a day or two.

There was time to tell her of my first visit to Acapulco, up to that time a major event in the farm boy's life. When the Greyhound "Special" Cinco Estrellas Bus from Mexico City came out of the forest and over the last hill, and the Pacific Ocean was before us, I thought I had arrived in paradise, the first view of the ocean, any ocean, for the landlubber from Kansas! I stayed in a moth – eaten, cockroach infested "hotel" the first night but then moved Caleta Beach, proceeded to roast myself for three days on beaches and manage to not drown in the waves of the bay. I got up to the "Quebrada" for the view and the cliff divers, walked all along Playa Hornos and took a scary motor boat ride to Puerto Marqués before leaving Acapulco in the rain and back to Mexico City. I told Mariah that the whole thing was inspired by Carlos Fuentes' description of the Acapulco of the Mexican upper class and foreign tourists in the 1950s, from, once again, "La Región Más Transparente del Aire."

She listened but said, "We are going to make our own story and adventures! We've got three days, so are you with me?" It was enjoying the beach, the water and waves, meals at the plethora of restaurants in the area, the long beach walk all along Playa Hornos and dancing in the clubs in late evening. We decided we were a good fit in most every way. I dragged Mariah back up to "La Quebrada," and it was no less impressive now than before. All the "hocus-pocus" of the sea divers' ritual (which I suspected was for tourists, but maybe not): one has to wait for the waves to come in between the sharp rocks of the cliff, all very closely timed by the divers, then the ritual of kneeling, making the sign of the cross and "pum!" the dive into the waves. Almost, or perhaps more fascinating, was the divers' climbing back up the cliff before the next dive. Those rocks looked rough and I wondered about bare feet. The bonus was the great sunset that followed, then more dining and dancing. It was like a honeymoon, wait! Not quite, but there were intimate moments. But no talk of any lasting bonds, at least not spoken. We were both still very young, really just out of school and fortunately in that almost make-believe time of rookie teachers. But neither of us could deny strong emotions, feelings and total agreement that this, indeed, was life to be lived!

A downer – I left the rolls of slide film in the hotel in Acapulco, so no trip photos. Oh well. We had plenty from the first weeks.

28

LAST NIGHT IN MEXICO, SOME "CONFESSIONS" AND SAD GOODBYES

And so be it, we caught that same "First Class - Superior - 5 Estrellas" bus back to Mexico City and a taxi to the Palafoxes on the Paseo de la Reforma. It was a very happy reunion but Sr. Palafox suggested we rest up that night and save most of our stories for the next day - there was only one way to end our stay in Mexico: as his guests at the posh restaurant – night club on the top floor of the "Torre Latino Americana" Mexico City's tallest skyscraper and symbol of Mexico and its future. And so it happened. We made the reservations for Mexicana back to Kansas City for two days later and got our baggage, tourist stuff and memories together before that last night.

Sr. and Señora Palafox, Jaime and Lucas, me and Mariah, all at the elegant and "modern" "Restauran del Cielo" ["Restaurant in the Heavens"] the next night. The chauffer drove this time, all of us getting out in front of the glassed-in lobby, then whisked to the 39th floor (the top was observation and full of antennae). Taken to a large table near one of the corners, all was glass around us and we could still see a bit of Popocatepetl Volcano (or is it Ixtaccihuatl?) through the evening Mexico City haze. I was in the only suit I brought for the trip, Mariah in her favorite color – green – cocktail dress. Wow! What a looker! Everyone else in Mexico City finery.

We started with champagne at Sr. David's suggestion, "Nacional pero está buenísimo." Appetizers were large shrimp in red sauce, taquitos or mini-chimis, ("an American invention we all enjoy now") all delicious. We all ordered different items, me once again the shrimp favorite – "gambas a la parilla con arroz" – and others assorted Mexican favorites. There was much laughter, perhaps because of never empty champagne glasses, jokes about Jaime's latest "squeeze" in Lomas. Oh, he apologized saying he really was serious about that "serenata" with me on the guitar; we agreed for next time. Lucas said we would all be ready for easy chairs by the time Jaime ever got around to proposing – too many "Lilies of the Field." Sr. David wanted to know how we have survived the intensive four weeks (including Moctezuma's revenge) and what do we think about Mexico after all the travel, and that gave me an opening to thank him, Jaime, Lucas and Señora Sara for their suggestions and help. The tour agencies had been great. I neglected to say to the reader, but did say then to Sr. David that we never got a bill, just always the response, "Está en la cuenta del señor Dr. Palafox." Mariah and I had budgeted for all this, maybe not as high end as it turned out, but budgeted just the same. Dr. David repeated that he had markers from the tour agencies, "Many, many accounts have been credited to them for our medical conventions here in Mexico City. This is just a fraction of what I've done for them. You can be tranquil ('tranquilo'), it's all 'hecho y pecho' [a done deal]. Oh, tell Benjamin and Ariel in Kansas we took good care of you." He laughed.

Mariah said she had something to say before I got long winded about the trip. She toasted the Palafoxes, thanked them profusely for the hospitality, and said how happy she was that we took the big step of contacting them and planning the trip, a bit "forward" on our account since the connection with the Mexican relatives had been gathering some dust. This was received with protests and assurances that it indeed was a very good thing to keep up such relations. Perhaps one day Ben and

Ariel, David and Sara would meet and renew acquaintances. Jaime popped up saying "Mariah, surely there are some beautiful 'gringas' even out in Kansas that would enjoy meeting a real Mexican gentleman!" More laughter and "Cuando quieras, primo!" ["Just give me the word, cousin!"]

The rest of the chit-chat around dinner was a rehashing of the trip, a lot from me, but equally important, from Mariah. On my account I assured all that the experiences and mainly all the slides I took (that is, the ones I got home) would be center stage on "culture days" in the coming year's Spanish classes, plus really adding to my growing knowledge and appreciation of things Mexican, perhaps to good advantage in future graduate studies. Mariah seconded it all but said, "Most important of all this to me is the renewing and strengthening of family bonds. You have been amazingly wonderful in that. And you are indeed what Mom and Dad call "Buena gente." She got up as she said it and went around the table with hugs for all. Sara who was on the quiet but perceptive side said, "Mariah, you are the daughter we never had, and the apple of my eye. (Mariah blushing). And this 'jovencito' is perhaps the most enchanting [a Mexican word: "encantador"] North American David and I have ever met." She lifted a champagne glass in a toast and I think might have been tempted to say more about us, but David nudged her a bit with a wink. "My sentiments also."

There was one more cultural note, this time initiated by Dr. David. "Miguel, you mentioned Carlos Fuentes on more than one occasion, and I had an immediate reaction but withheld it. I want to tell you why before you leave. I think you know about Enrique Krause, one of our major historians and also man of letters, but not a novelist. He and Carlos used to be the best of friends in the early days, but no more. Politically they are on opposite divides, Carlos an avowed leftist, recently supporting Daniel Ortega in Nicaragua, Enrique a free market capitalist and conservative. Enrique just recently wrote a scathing article about Fuentes, saying he is an 'intellectual dandy' who plays to a United States' audience and spends most of his time there as a guest lecturer on Latin American Literature and affairs. Fuentes took it personally, responding in one interview, 'I eat these critics for breakfast!' In short, Miguel, I and some of our family friends are good friends of the Krause family; they are also Jewish and we have much in common. I have read all of Fuentes' novels and believe his place in Mexican and in fact Latin American Letters is justified, but I was not and am not in any position to arrange any type of approach to him or a meeting for you. Besides, like Enrique says, I think he is currently in the U.S. at Harvard. Is there some intellectual jealousy on Enrique's part? Perhaps, but certainly religion. I believe Fuentes is at least agnostic if not atheist and certainly anti-clerical. He follows much of the old socialist PRI line from the Revolution yet lives the life of the upper crust and is quite wealthy. Seems a contradiction in terms."

"Thank you Dr. David. I had indeed heard of this spat and read of both in the papers even when I was a student at UNAM three years ago. I think Mexico has room for both."

The evening ended in front of the fireplace in the home on "Reforma" with all reminiscing of the past five weeks. There was lots of talk of the Pre-Colombian heritage, of the Spanish colonial period and of post-Revolutionary Mexico. As expected, the Palafoxes could in no way excuse the history of Spain, its Inquisition, but were generous in their remarks of recent Mexico and the fact that the Jewish Colony was allowed its freedom and how it has contributed greatly to Mexico. Dr. David said, "Ethnically of course we are Jewish, but we are also Mexican. Our people have survived by adopting the 'converso' experience in Spain." The night and all of us tired, to bed, a final breakfast and then the chauffer took Mariah and me to the flight at the airport. Almost on time, it was a "directo" to Kansas City and our first of two family reunions at home. We both were ready for that, but we had three and one-half hours on the airplane to let it all soak in and talk a bit of the future.

Over drinks and a lunch on Mexicana I thanked Mariah, for it was her connection that allowed for the terrific trip and experience in Mexico. She in turn thanked me for the enthusiasm and knowledge and interest which had spurred her own. Most of the flight was spent musing about the coming year at the Juco and in Abilene. I had plenty on my plate with teaching, local family, plus the new research at the Eisenhower Library related to Abilene history. She had the English classes at the Juco, and, well, me. The subject of the Klan did come up and my reaction that we would just have to see if there were any developments over the summer.

Mariah said she was committed for the next academic year but perhaps not beyond that, depending, a long pause, on how it went, and us. She admitted the Juco had fulfilled her objective of a change of scene, getting away from the city and family for a while, but was not sure Kansas offered that much for her interests and future. I guess this was the first time we even had to think of anything beyond the present. It was a sobering thought, but we both made a "pact" to make the best of Abilene and the Juco for this one year. We did not quite use the word "love," the most important in the English language, but did say how much we cared for each other, how great life had been the past few months. It was not only Mariah's reticence; I was not sure that being a junior college teacher was the final step in my future either. Abilene seemed kind of small.

29

KANSAS CITY AND HOME TO ABILENE AND SETTLING IN ONCE MORE

The reunion at Ben and Ariel's was fun and pleasant. It was mainly Mariah who filled her parents in on the Mexico trip. They were first of all interested in the relatives, the Mexican connection as it were. Mariah told them in great detail about David, Sara, Jaime and Lucas, how well we were treated and lastly what Sara had said about her being "the daughter we never had." That was a moving moment for all. I seconded Mariah's comments about the Mexican Palifoxes and added that all our objectives were more than met – getting around Mexico and speaking a lot of Spanish. Over dinner we talked of all the places we saw and how good Mexico had been for us. And I rambled a bit about the great Pre-Columbian sites and colonial cities we got to see. Mariah said we did get to the Sephardi Synagogue, but only briefly, and that in her opinion the Palafoxes were very low key on religion, maybe a result of most Jews surviving in Mexico as "conversos" [Jews who 'converted' to Catholicism rather than being thrown out of Spain and Portugal, but who contributed in great ways to the Crown both in Spain and the New World, but also were main targets of the Inquisition which came later]. There was no big Jewish Reform movement in Mexico, and Orthodox ways were not that of the family. Ben nodded his head, said, "Sometimes it's a matter of survival. It surely appears he has done better with Medicine than I." Everybody protested that, Mariah saying it was just different and in fact we hardly discussed Medicine or the family business in Mexico.

We briefly talked of heading back to Abilene and work, sharing some of the plans for my classes, the Eisenhower Library and Mariah's plan for English classes. There was one decision – Ben and Ariel at some point in the next few months would come to Abilene for a visit. Mariah looked at me, smiled and said, "Dad and Mom, I think about two days would do it. After that it's all cows, tractors, wheat and corn and small-town gossip. Mick and I will cook up an itinerary for you, hmm. Two days, shouldn't be too difficult." Ben said, "Perhaps a Friday, Saturday and Sunday would do it; I won't even have to make any contingency plans at the practice. Mick, I **am** interested in Abilene's history (another world for us), and Sara wants to see those Victorian houses you have been raving about. The Eisenhower Museum and Library are a must, and hey, Mick, it will be fun to get to know a little of your world. Farming and all that. You know we aren't known for farming in Kansas, although you might of heard about the experiment at Beersheba. You haven't said anything about your Mom and Dad but it would be our great pleasure to meet your parents. Okay?"

I quickly said, "Sure and I would like that. I guess I am a bit nervous; Mom and Dad are farm people, and Dad had only an 8th grade education, but Mom had two years of college and is really a part of western history – a schoolmarm in a one-room school house in Eastern Colorado teaching eight grades and more. Dad had to quit school to help run the farm, but he and his brothers were really good at it. I'm proud of what he did. I think you will see they are no 'hayseeds,' but also that Catholicism was and is their life. And Mom succeeded in getting all her boys to Jesuit colleges, with a lot of scholarship help. I guess I'm a little defensive. We have not told them Mariah is Jewish. That lack of information to my family is my choice and embarrassing for me. I personally will correct that gap before you come. The big city, medicine, and being Jewish are another world to them."

Ben said, "Mick, none of what you said offends us, and believe me, we have dealt with similar situations all our life. I mean folks who really don't know too much about us and our traditions. The way you are, the way you have treated our daughter, the values we have seen in you, did not come from nothing. I believe your parents will please us greatly; I hope the vice-versa is true. Don't worry, how do you kids say it, 'We'll be cool.'"

30

BACK TO ABILENE – STRANGE!

We still had our own cars in Overland Park, so we drove separately to Abilene, meeting at Mariah's apartment. There was one word for it – "strange!" We had been inseparable for the past three months, and now back to separate apartments! It was a bit depressing to think about. For both of us. We agreed however, that for the present, taking into account small town gossip and not creating any embarrassment for anybody up at the Juco (remember we were barely out of the 1950s), living separate was the plan. Mariah laughed, "The neighbors all know your car when it's out front, and that goes for me too at your place. So no shenanigans O'Brien!" We would see each other for lunch Monday up at the college.

Meanwhile I checked in at Mom and Dad's, once again for mass on Sunday at St. Andrew's and then Sunday dinner. Mom wondered why I didn't bring Mariah but I said she was tired from the trip and had a large amount of work to get ready for school on Monday. Summer in Abilene had been uneventful since our short visit before Mexico, the Rodeo Parade and Rodeo, the County Fair in the park near to them, and the usual out at the farm. Dad had pretty well picked the produce from the garden; the only thing left the potatoes coming in the Fall. He said the only unusual event was a big barn fire out south of town, everybody saying it was hay baled too green, put in the barn and spontaneous combustion started it. We knew the farmers, Germans in church at St. Andrew's. Dad said most farmers had insurance for their buildings but not the hay crop so it was a big loss. I had witnessed only one of those fires, maybe ten years ago; we had all driven out south of town and seen the flames. Dad always thought the Germans were too much in a hurry, what's a nice way to put it? Maybe too greedy to get a crop in and start irrigating for the next. We never had even a bit of trouble along that line, and Dad had always had the patience to wait until the hay was dry for cutting, stacking or baling. But Dad said it could happen to anybody, and he had at least 50 years of experience to say that.

I gave them a brief version of the trip, raving a bit about how much we saw of Mexico and the great hospitality of Mariah's relatives, promising I would bring her out the next week for a full-blown report. Mom just said, "Are you two still serious?" I laughed and said, "No more than last May, and depends what you mean by serious." Dad just laughed and said they would be looking forward to the visit.

I called Caitlin and Ron, just checking in and gave a shortened version of what I had given Mom and Dad. Caitlin I could tell was pretty anxious to hear about us and wondering what news there was about that. I told her pretty much the same as I told Mom and Dad. She said, "That young lady is a terrific match for you, not many like that around, but I guess you know that." Ron got on the phone for a minute, said he missed me for the rest of the hay baling (laughing) but was glad to hear all went well. I mentioned Dad had talked about the barn fire, and he hesitated a bit, saying there might be more to it than the spontaneous combustion theory, but didn't really have anything more to say about it. I promised to see them soon, if not before, at church on Sunday.

Mrs. Stevens was glad to see me, assured me I would find things just like I left them in May and was glad I was back. I said it was mutual and moved in. I had my head in the books the rest of the weekend until planning days up at school on Monday. I probably had 400 slides to go through, organize and cull out the bad ones, and get them all ready for the Kodak Carousel for Spanish classes that fall. Monday rolled around too quickly but it was back to routine. Something must have gone well because enrollment jumped a few for both Spanish classes and the U.S. history was a full room at 30. My boss, Dr. Halderson said he was happy to have me back and was looking forward to a good year. For my part I said I wanted to do more liaison with Miss Stromberg and Nara Baldini at the High School and would be starting on that soon, the idea to let them know what a good thing we were offering at the Juco.

Mariah was doing two classes of English 101, meaning the basics of writing, grammar and with a lot of papers to grade. She was happy to get some relief with an American Literature class and some very bright students. So, no surprises on her part. Her big project was to arrange a field trip to all three "big" schools, Emporia State, K-State and K-U. and let a few students see what might be in store for them if they could go to the next level. A good plan, it gave them lots of incentive to really hit the books. She actually would be able to do it on a long day each, but up at the crack of dawn to the school to visit classes, lunch, more classes and home late. It would total just three days, but all on Fridays during the fall. We met for lunch and set up dinner, take out from the In' n Out, malt, fries and burger, for that night. She said she missed me and would be especially glad to see me at home. That happened that night.

As promised, I did visit the high school and was graciously welcomed by both my old teacher Miss Stromberg, still teaching Latin, and former high school friend from my senior class Nara Baldini who was teaching Spanish and was in line to fill Miss Stromberg's place, due for retirement the end of the year. I set up the Kodak Carousel and showed highlights of the Mexico trip, accepted with some enthusiasm especially in Nara's classes. She was doing a terrific job and in fact had started taking promising students each summer to either Spain or Mexico. As much as I liked teaching and was good at it, chaperoning a dozen or so 17-year old kids away from home perhaps for the first time was not this fellow's cup of tea. But my "spiel" of what we were doing at the Juco meshed well with Nara's work; she did in private mention she was interested in getting her top kids into the big universities but that there would always be a dozen or so that would be good fits for the Juco. Miss Stromberg on the other hand was just happy to have a former student, sometimes not always on his good behavior, especially in the Latin classes, but much better in Spanish, come and show that her work could reap good benefits. We three had lunch in the student cafeteria afterwards; both invited me to the Spanish Banquet (provided I would bring the guitar and do the Flamenco and then Mexican songs). There was no need to do the visit too often, you had the same students, but twice a year we figured was a good idea.

The Abilene history project was still in the works and the plan from last year was to come to fruition and take up yet some of the time, the reading at the Eisenhower Library. It turned out not be as much as I figured, but it's worth telling.

31

FILLING IN THE BLANKS ON IKE AND ABILENE

I was greeted at the Library by and put under the wing of another AHS and K.U. graduate, Don Winston, a full-time employee at the library who knew the collection inside and out. He later would be the one to write a major book dealing with Ike's journey and importance as soldier, politician and president of the nation. He asked me my interest and I said it was a lot more limited in scope than his work – the "saga" of the Eisenhower family in Abilene and their experience after coming back from Texas, a short sojourn from Abilene, and then Abilene through Ike's leaving for college and the military. Strangely enough, what I found was accurate but sketchy. Just as valuable it turned out were the memories of my occasional drinking buddy at the tavern on main street, the local photographer. His father had gone to school with Eisenhower and later followed his career; both took pictures whenever Ike returned to Abilene. He had a good memory of recent times, like the 1952 Presidential opening campaign speech, but a lot more told by his own Dad. In 1963 not much was available except snippets from newspaper articles and a few old pictures.

One can read it all in the archives, which I did, but really found just a few basic facts for my very limited interests. A group of families, the Eisenhowers among them, originally moved from Pennsylvania to Abilene in the late 1860s; they settled just east of town in an area called Belle Springs. It was the location of the last of the Drover's Cottages from cowboy days and later became a creamery where both Ike and his Dad worked. And the creamery eventually became an ice plant where both worked, and I worked as a teenager for two summers in the late 1950s. Then it did not take in cream any more but did store ice cream for the big dairies that would later distribute it to the grocery stores in town.

The original settlers were what they called River Brethren and were farm folks, thus the link to selling their products at the creamery which River Brethren people established. The original house had three acres and a huge garden was planted to provide for the needs of the family, Ida and David, Ike's parents and his six brothers! Lincoln Grade School was to the west of the house. Ike was big into sports by high school playing both football and baseball, the latter his favorite. He had aspirations like a lot of farm and small-town boys of that time to become a professional baseball player. But being accepted into West Point (also an economic decision because it was free if you got in) changed all that and to some extent the history of the nation.

I ended up going to the library just a few times because there was no need for more with my limited objective. To summarize it, the family was really of modest economic means, the area by Lincoln considered a "less prosperous part of town," and the end of it all - it developed into an amazing but real American story of what hard work, education, ambition and a few breaks can do. All six boys did well, some more than others, but Ike's story in the military, the War, at Columbia University and later the White House brought Abilene's focus on him, the Museum and Library. If you added the old history of the cowboys, Chisholm Trail, Tom Smith, and Wild Bill Hickok, it made for a small gem for tourism and put Abilene on the map. And of course one could add some of the amazing entrepreneurs like McCoy, A. Brown, and the others I've already mentioned and their beautiful Victorian houses. But even then, there's just so much to see in a town of 7000, and my memories were of Mom and Dad and us kids on the farm, the church, the school and the buddies, and now a job, the Juco and Mariah. That's the story that needs to be told, what happened the next school year.

32

"DÉJÀ VU ALL OVER AGAIN"

On a visit out to Ron and Caitlin's with Mariah keeping me company we had a chance to catch up on our doings of the last summer and how things were shaping up for Fall. Caitlin was still part-time at the high school, subbing for the Home Economics and English classes. "I guess I'll never get it out of my blood. Must have inherited it from Mom" ("Me too," I added). Caitlin now with three children and a new house to decorate plus being a farm wife had her hands full. Ron always with a bit of a mischievous smile, told Mariah they would look forward to seeing more of her, betting she could learn to drive the new big dually John Deere in a flash. She laughed and said, "As long as you have one of those air-conditioned cabs with a radio, I'm good for that."

One thing led to another - I had something still on my mind from our earlier phone call. I asked Ron what exactly did he mean about that barn fire out south of town during the summer. He grew serious and said, "Mick, it might not have been spontaneous combustion like the paper reported. Ben Schmidt is a relative of mine, swears that he did not bale that crop too green, and there were some tire tracks around the barn and a hint of kerosene by the burned frame of the foundation. And he said he never kept kerosene near the hay barn but just up by the storage shed for the farm equipment. Sheriff Wiley looked into it and said he smelled kerosene as well. And he's trying to trace the tire marks. But for now, he asked Ben to keep it under his hat. By the way, (looking at her,) how much does Mariah know about all this, including the church windows at St. Andrew's?"

"She knows the whole story, including the whole thing with the Enterprise bank robbery, the attempted kidnapping and my close call, and really all the rest, including the fire here with Mom and Dad in 1959. And by the way, just between all of us, there was a tire slitting on my car by the apartment last spring. I haven't told Mom and Dad my suspicions about that. It's all getting a bit weird isn't it?"

"Since we are telling 'secrets,' here's another one for you. Stan and I are missing two heifers from the herd, and there are two cases up north of town, both on farms incidentally owned by Catholics in the parish, with maybe half a dozen or more missing. This has all been reported to the sheriff. Hell, Stan and I are the most anal farmers in the county and we know **exactly** how many cows and calves we have. There are some farmers, believe it or not, who may not have an exact count. Everyone is supposed to do "branding," but what we do today are ear tags rather than that old-time hot iron to the back; but I'm not sure everyone does it. The only way you can get those ear tags off is to cut them off with wire clippers, and of course cows with no tags would be a pretty good sign of foul play wouldn't it? Between cattle out on grass in the pastures and cattle in feed yards it can get complicated, but you know a grown heifer can be worth $800 and a cow and a calf each year a lot more."

Mariah spoke up, "I thought this stuff was from the cowboy movies!" Ron said, "You'd be surprised; there are statistics that over the entire area west of the Missouri up to five thousand cattle "disappear" for one reason or another each year. The sheriff said he would let us know if anything breaks on the cattle 'rustling,' meanwhile we are keeping an extra watch on the feed lot, have set up perimeter motion detectors with cameras; that's about all we can do. But Mick, sooner or later someone will make a mistake, and we'll get them. I don't think any of us, I mean Catholics in the area, are in danger, but I know down at the Knights of Columbus meeting at church people have been apprised. Your tire incident was not discussed, just so you know."

"Thanks, Ron, I'm due for a talk with the Sheriff anyway; last time was in late May. Okay, we'll be on our way, both of us have extra duties at the Juco, but you'll see us around. Like the cowboys used to say, "Keep your powder dry.""

That next week before I could get a chance to get down to the courthouse there was another headline in the Abilene Reflector Chronicle:

CATTLE THIEVES APPREHENDED NORTH OF TOWN

Two young men living on a farm on the Dickinson – Clay County line were arrested by Sheriff Wiley yesterday for what he called "cattle rustling" and related felonies. Wiley said that modern "branding" of ear tags revealed that about one dozen cows and heifers belonging to three different Abilene area farmers were found in a lot on one of the farms. The two persons responsible are currently awaiting trial in the Dickinson County Jail. Wiley added that there may be a connection to the Schmidt barn fire of last August as well. Judge Raleigh has ruled no bond in the case and first appearance will be this Friday. Pending developments, there may or may not be a trial until next month. The sheriff added that he and his men arrived just in the nick of time; there was a large cattle truck parked in the barnyard ostensibly to haul the stolen cattle away. And they had wire cutters to cut off the ear tags.

The "Chronicle" awaits developments and will be on top of this story. It appears the old "Chisholm Trail Days and Cowboys and Rustlers" are not over, not by a long shot. This is one more case of the type of behavior our respectable, Christian town cannot tolerate."

The courthouse was full for the hearing, including yours truly. I overruled Mariah's wanting to be there with me, saying if these criminals were some of those still out for revenge on us from 1959, there would probably be friends in the courtroom, and I did not want them to see her with me. She said, "I'm going anyway; if it makes you feel better, I'll sit in the back of the courtroom with Jenny (a young teacher from the Juco who was a good friend of both Mariah and me)." Ron and I agreed too that it would be better if Dad were not there, and he did not argue with us. The same attorney that handled the conviction back in 1959, Mr. Reiman, a good friend of Dad's from down at the Elks Club, was present. The county District Attorney was doing the prosecution of the case. It didn't take long, Sheriff Wiley testifying with what he saw up on the farm, showing pictures taken of the rustled cattle (the ear tags with numbers clearly shown). Ron and Stan and the other two farmers from up north testified and gave evidence that those tags belonged to their cattle. The two criminals, both in their late 20s who incidentally did not resist arrest denied any wrongdoing, saying they had no idea how the cattle ended up in their corral, "Must have gotten mixed up with ours during the fall roundup (a likely story)". So Judge Raleigh said, "So be it. The trial date is set for two weeks from today, October 15 in this courtroom. Prisoners will be returned to their cells until that date. Court dismissed."

To make a long story short, again with a full court room, the trial was held as scheduled and completed in one day's time. The county defense attorney was on hand to defend the accused, but really had no new evidence to present. It was not a jury trial, the judge declaring that all evidence had been presented and taken into consideration. He sentenced the rustlers to five years in the state prison at Lansing, but offered a "carrot" to them, suggesting if they had any other defense or statement to add, he might reduce the sentence. He intimated that there was evidence of arson at the barn fire south of town and wanted to know if they had anything to add about that. Surprisingly one of the men blurted out, "Yeah. We did that too. Just more payback, Judge." "What do you mean by that?" said the Judge. "Nothing your honor." Judge Reiman got red in the face and said, "I'll not permit such blatant disrespect in my courtroom. And that burned barn and hay cost Mr. Schmidt the difference between a profit and loss this year to his livelihood. Five more years on the sentence. The prisoners will be transferred to Lansing tomorrow. Court dismissed."

You can imagine; that was the main talk around town, but things settled down in a few days, no further incidents, and most people thought that was the end of it. A few of us weren't so sure. Still too many loose ends to tie up. No one in town knew the two guilty parties, but it was becoming general knowledge that strange happenings were being associated with the north county, this from the "Reflector's" articles plus general gossip around town. I talked to Sheriff Wiley and he said not to worry, just be vigilant and business as usual. It was busy up at school, and I had already incorporated the Mexico trip into "culture day" in the Spanish classes and Nara Baldini had me back to talk to the advanced Spanish class at the high school. Mariah and I had reminisced more than once over drinks or dinner of what a great time that had been. There was not a whole lot she had not seen of Abilene, but I convinced her that we should take an entire Saturday for a walk all around downtown and I'd tell her the stories of the places and any connection to growing up days. It sounded like fun, so we did it.

33

THE WALK AROUND TOWN AND ALL THE MEMORIES

As Mariah and I walked south on Buckeye from my apartment and then Mariah's, the first big place was the Seelye Mansion already spoken of. It is a Historical Georgian Mansion with 25 rooms, 11 bedrooms, a one-lane bowling alley, a ball room, and Edson Light Fixtures. One source says it was built in 1905 for $55,000 and renovated in 1920 under the direction of no less than Frank Lloyd Wright. It all had to do with the founder of the A.B. Seelye Medical Company, 1890, selling 85 products sold via horse and buggy over 14 states. Two daughters lived in it when I grew up. Still overgrown now when we walked by; it needed a paint job, both on the house and the gazebo in the big side yard which needed mowing. I guess Mr. Seeley offered cures for man or beast. Snake oil?

We walked on down Buckeye and then west over to Cedar to Garfield School where all of us O'Brien kids attended grade school. It was built in 1942 and was one of three grade schools in town, all named after assassinated presidents! Lincoln on the south side the oldest, then Garfield on the "north side" and McKinley on the west side. A product of the Federal Works Project Administration, it broke with thirty years of architecture for schools in Kansas. They called it "Modern and 'Art Moderne' Architecture, "blond brick, concrete construction, horizontal lines and bands of windows, steeped bays and simple form." What do you know about that! We didn't. It had a great gym for basketball with a real wooden floor (converted into an auditorium for school plays) and was next to the old Jr. High (Ike Eisenhower's High School.)

Then we walked down Cedar to the Public Library that I grew up with, checking out as many as eight books at a time, the favorite science fiction in the early 1950s, anything with a trip to the moon or space. I had no idea then of its history: early funding from a William Jennings Bryan speech, from the Parker Carousel Company and no less than the Carnegie Foundation. The first building was in 1908 with many renovations since. The main book collection was from Dean Malott the Chancellor at the University of Kansas, then President of Cornell. So Ike and family would have used the library.

From the library as you walk two blocks more downtown, you cross Buckeye east to 2nd street, and there is this run-down but impressive old Victorian. It's known locally as the Kirby house. It seemed to me in my days Abilene had lots of such great places, but only some of them in nice shape. The others were basically boarding houses that needed paint and this was one of them. The Kirby Place was done in 1885 by a then successful banker in Abilene, but it turns out he bought it from no less than Joseph McCoy who brought the cattle trade to town in the 1860s by extending the Chisholm Trail from Wichita and then built the mansion with some of his dough. Pretty impressive. Mariah was getting used to me showing these less than perfect places. Her reaction: "There's a lot of money all over our country and interest by folks who love these places; the Abilene Chamber of Commerce needs to do some research. But wow! What a treasure for a small Kansas farm town!"

From the Kirby house just north of the big flour mill by the tracks, we walked back west, across Buckeye and back down to 2nd street and the Union Pacific Station (the old Kansas Pacific from 1867 and the cattle drives). This was a must! The "new" station was built in 1928 in Spanish style, and Dad for a few years after World War II had a cream station on the south side of the freight depot; I remember the old iron wheel baggage carts and huge steel cream cans. Dad said government changes to farm prices and commodities caused the business to gradually go downhill, not his doing, but that it was good income for a few years. After that endeavor, the main thing for Dad and Mom was the farm where I grew up.

A second train station was south of the Union Pacific Station, the tracks just north of the Catholic Church and the depot to the side north, the Atchison Topeka and Santa Fe. It was started in 1859 by Cyrus Holliday and by 1869 was the first south to north line in Kansas; from Abilene it went West to the cattle trails at Dodge City. Yet a third train was the Rock Island Line which arrived in Abilene the same time as the ATSF. That depot was smaller but still important. So for a town of just 7000 three major train lines were amazing. Incidentally, it was the Rock Island Line coming in from the North (a freight line only) that almost caught us in a jeep driving on the tracks over a trestle after fishing up north of town, cousin Elfred the driver and culprit ("It must be one of those freights, a bit early I reckon").

On a different occasion after visiting Mom and Dad, and just a couple of blocks from Mom and Dad's house in Abilene, on the edge of Eisenhower Park was the huge old locomotive (an amazing sight) I climbed on like a little kid when I returned to Abilene. It was the Atchison Topeka Santa Fe Steam Locomotive built by the Baldwin Train Works in 1919. The ATSF ran it for 34 years and then sold/donated it to Abilene in 1955. Although not the original locomotive from old Chisholm Trail Cattle days (one like that would have ended up at Promontory Point in Utah west of Salt Lake where it met the Central Pacific and they did the Golden Spike), it was a big part of Abilene History for most of the 20th century. I told Mariah I am sure I rode on it as a little boy to a Catholic Youth Convention in Hays Kansas about 1950.

Back to the Union Pacific Train Station; just two streets south was the street we always used to drive to the grain elevators for wheat harvest time. Another old wreck of a surprise was there – the old Elms Hotel. It was across the street from our main grocery store growing up, run by a Catholic family on the south side. The Hotel was three stories, made of red brick with a long porch it front, the original building from 1919. It was part of Abilene's old downtown area, of the 1870s cattle trade district. Originally called the "Forster Hotel # 2" it was built by Jacob Forster who did three hotels in the two blocks from the rail lines. I told Mariah in my day it was I guess a boarding house or apartment building, low income I suspect on the South Side. I don't think I ever ventured inside. It seemed creepy.

As we walked around town that day, I told Mariah of memories of downtown while growing up, saying all this while we were stopping in the old drug store and having a root beer float. It wasn't like the memories and places were historic - just memories.

There was the pool hall on third street where I and high school buddies mainly played snooker and drank draft beer when we were 18. You could get a Kansas stand-by – tomato beer – if you wanted. Mariah said, "Ugh!"

Next door was the old barber shop where we went all my growing up days. I recall the big glass window in the front of the shop – I think so you could see everything going on out on 3rd street and who passed by. And the hot lather machine, leather strap and straight razor the barbers used, and a never-ending series of talk and laughter.

Just down 3rd street was the old Abilene National Bank (in the original bank building) where Dad, then us, did all our banking. The owner was a member of St. Andrew's and also the man responsible for giving me the $500 loan to go to Mexico City in 1962 (signed with Dad), and me paying it off right away after the Juco checks started coming in.

There was the drug store (where Mariah and I were now) where we went after school and got root beer floats or all kinds of flavored cokes (lemon, even chocolate), this for years. On a more serious note, this was where we filled any Dr.'s prescriptions.

Duckwall's Five and Dime was across the street from the drugstore, recalling the huge grave stone in the cemetery and all its history, maybe my favorite store growing up. That was mainly because of the toy department where you could see the new **Red Ryder B-B** guns and other cowboy stuff and where I bought lots of bubble gum and packs of baseball cards. A treat was a lunch during the school year with brother Joe and sister Caitlin – a 35 cent lunch of a toasted cheese sandwich, mashed potatoes and gravy and a small coke!

And just down the street on the same side was the town's only photography shop with the owners I've already talked about, including the beer drinking friend and "history informant" of Abilene. They did all the sports teams for the schools, all the graduation photos, and most importantly, weddings and anniversaries. A special aside were the photos whenever Ike Eisenhower was in town.

Down the street across 3rd street was a really important place for the O'Briens and all the local kids. The Music Store which also sold all the school books, obligatory each Fall. For me more important yet was they sold music and it was there I bought my first guitar at age fourteen, a Stella with steel strings for $15! It's main virtue: it stayed in tune and the fretting was good for the price. That's what I learned on, even classical guitar, until about age seventeen when I bought a Kay Electric (with small amplifier), a shiny copper color like the customized cars in town. Oh yeah, Joe and Caitlin bought their trumpet and violin and band music there as well. The end of that story is important: I bought my first classic guitar (nylon strings) through the Sears-Roebuck Catalogue in 1959 for the grand sum of $50. Money earned from the ice plant.

On the next street west was the old Greyhound Bus Depot, used by us very little I could recall, with maybe just two or three arrivals each day, a hole in the wall place you could buy a bottle of Coca-Cola or RC Cola. Farm and town folks, maybe with the exception of the country club set, still rode the inter-city buses then, even if just sporadically. I could not remember who or when but told Mariah we did go down there to meet people, maybe even older brother Paul coming home from the military.

Across the street on the corner was the United Trust Building with all its commercial and business history of Abilene, going back to Brown the founder I've already written about. It was real estate, mortgages, insurance, and investments in my days. I don't think I ever set foot in the place growing up.

Across the street south was the favorite teen age hangout of my entire growing up years, including all the "big kids" from brother Joe and sister Caitlin's days. It had a soda fountain, booths where four or more kids could talk, laugh and carry on and flirt. For me the pinball machine in the back for a nickel was important, the juke box with a song for a nickel and five for a quarter dollar, that and the magazine rack in front facing the street where I could see the latest "Sport" or "Sport's Illustrated" magazines for 25 cents, buying one if Mickey Mantle was on the cover. (The other important purchases for me, for 25 cents, were the "Top Hits" song magazines, but we got those at a scurvy news shop across from the Post Office; the owner let his Chihuahua doggies poop on the magazines on the bottom row.) And you could sneak a look at the girlie magazines along the side, "Playboy Magazine" the new kid on the block. This place was probably important for at least ten years! In earlier days I would go and get a coke and get a ride home with brother Joe; later we even rode bikes or drove a car.

There was the J.C. Penney store just down the street south. That's where the O'Briens bought all their clothes; the price was right. Dickie jeans instead of Levis. And where Caitlin worked for a few years after school. I just remember the old cable system, the little box the clerk placed your money in, the staff upstairs on a balcony who made change and wrote out receipts and sent the box zipping back downstairs.

I told Mariah that huge memories were from the town movie theaters, the slick Plaza nearby and the modest, even poor Lyric near the pool hall on another street. B-Westerns, comedies, newsreels, great cartoons were the memories. And the price – a quarter dollar allowance and you had it made. 14 cents for admission, a nickel for a fountain coke from a new-fangled coke machine, a nickel for a sack of popcorn or a package of Milk Duds. And a penny left over for a bubble gum or root beer barrel after the movie. I could write pages of what all went on in that place, and told Mariah I had written more in "Rural Odyssey" the senior writing project of now two years ago.

There was the more refined, "fine clothing" store east of the movie house block, and one final place I forgot about: the "general store," over on Buckeye, really three stores in one run by the Baldini family. Shoes in one, groceries in another, and hardware and appliances in a third – with the added attraction for me of great leather baseball gloves that smelled like real leather, and real Louisville Slugger baseball bats, with the names of people like Ted Williams, Mickey Mantle, Willie Mays and Stan Musical burned into them. This same store had livestock feed and a small creamery my Dad "traded" with – literally! He brought fresh cream in, maybe eggs, and got "Baldini" money in return and bought goods in their stores. We never questioned all this; seemed fine to us, but I guess it had a "whiff" of the "company store."

I don't know if even all this was the end of it, but from the "age of memory or reason" as the Catholics called it, and leaving town for college, at least 15 years, this was all we knew and was reason to be downtown several times a week. There was probably more, but that filled that Saturday.

Mariah could not believe all the stories but said that indeed this had to be small-town life in America, and what a town! She said she never experienced anything quite like this living in the big city, but had her own memories of places, stores and restaurants, a story she would tell me sometime.

34

THE TURKEY SHOOT THEN A VISIT

That Fall moved on, both of us busy, me up at the Juco, studying to be ready for classes, Mariah the same plus those field days with her best students at the State Universities (these took up several of her Fridays). One really different day was the Turkey Shoot out at the Wassman's farm by the river, sponsored by the Knights of Columbus at church. As promised, Sheriff Wiley showed me how to hold, aim and fire the shotgun for the skeet shoot (and how to handle a handgun as well). I did better with the small gun than the shotgun, mainly having to learn how to handle the recoil of that powerful pistol. All this instruction took place the day before the actual shoot. ("Mick, this is just an insurance policy; that's a good way to think of it. You get what I mean, right?")

The main event was the next day on Saturday. Very cool Fall weather and warm jackets and hats in order. As per tradition, there were a few flasks passed around, but under control, not a good mix to drink too much and shoot. But a swallow of that stuff did warm your cockles. It was as they say, "a custom." Everyone was there, the men and young men from church, including Ron and Stan, Dad, and a few of the wives who were in charge of the coffee and hot chocolate table with the cakes and pies. I probably knew all of them or at least by the last name and where they sat at church. A real community affair. Mariah insisted on taking a few turns with the shotgun (no end of volunteers to help with that, mainly Sheriff Wiley himself, and then Ron and Dad) and did better than I but probably made more points charming Mom and her church ladies. There was gossip in town about Mariah and me, and of course in this crowd wondering why I didn't bring her to church.

That brings me to the culmination of it all – the Palafoxes' visit to Abilene. It took place on a weekend between Thanksgiving and Christmas. It was preceded by a visit to Mom and Dad's by me and Mariah, (we both took a deep breath) telling them about her parents and what pleasant people they were. And, it was time, telling about the Palafoxes being Jewish. Mom got very quiet and Dad just listened as well. Mariah explained that her family was not Orthodox or really Reform, but basically Jewish by ethnicity rather than religious practice. When Mom professed she really did not know much about any of that, but that the O'Brien knowledge was mainly based on the New Testament and the general knowledge that Jewish people were very involved in Business and Medicine and Law and lived mainly in the East. (She laughed saying this.) And Dad knew a lot of the history of 1947 and David Ben Gurion and the British paving the way for the Jewish State in Palestine. Mariah smiled, was patient and said the same thing was true with most Jews – they knew "official history" of the Catholics and Christians by the Vatican, the Protestant Reformation and the never – ending number of different Protestant religions in Kansas. (She did not mention the Spanish Inquisition, the Edict against the Moslems, Protestants and mainly Jews in Old Spain, or the Holocaust of World War II days). She just emphasized that most everyone seems to get along now when they get a chance. She said the big difference between our families was just being a farmer or a doctor, or living in a small town or the city. She explained that it was me teaching Spanish, a language she knew from growing up and her old family tradition, and just being a fine young man ("He's easy to like and be around."). Mom and Dad seemed a lot less nervous and said they looked forward to meeting Mariah's parents, saying they must be good folks judging by how they had raised their daughter. We offered the idea of the dinner at the Brookville Restaurant and I think they liked that. Mom would not have to cook.

By now there were a couple of nice motels up by the Interstate (built during the Eisenhower Administration in the late 50s and whacking off 40 acres on the north side of Dad's old farm, "imminent domain"), and Ben and Ariel stayed there. Friday night there was a dinner out at Lena's with just Mariah and me, getting caught up on all our news. And some "prepping" Ben and Ariel about Sean and Molly (I gave them a copy of the book "The Farm" I had written about growing up on the farm and with all the stories about Mom and Dad). I think David read the entire thing that night and talked to Ariel about the family at breakfast on Saturday morning). Saturday during the day there was a whirl of tourism, the Eisenhower Museum and then a long drive around town seeing all those Victorians and some of those places of Abilene history I've been talking about. The big event was Saturday night when both families met at the old Brookville Restaurant for the big chicken dinner. I introduced Mom and Dad to Ben and Ariel, or rather did with Mariah's help. And Ron and Caitlin were there also. Everyone was dressed up for Abilene, nice suits and dresses.

I don't know what all was discussed, but the Palafoxes spoke glowingly of what a fine town, and, (red face) what a fine boy Sean and Molly had raised. There were similar compliments about Mariah from Mom and Dad (red face). Most talk was of the amazing history, architecture of the Victorians and the Eisenhower Center. Something new for me – Mr. Palafox had served as a medic in Italy and then Normandy during the invasion and could rattle off the names of all the Allied commanders and generals. Both Dad and Ron had military service as young men, Dad in the Merchant Marine and Ron in the Air Force. There was lots of talk about farming, and Ron chipped in on milling technology and "modern" farming. It was then Ben admitted he had read "The Farm" and that I should be proud of Dad's role as really a "pioneer farmer" and Mom with the stories of her teaching in the one-room school house in Eastern Colorado. On the other side of the coin, Ben and Ariel explained how they had come to live in Overland Park, start his medical practice, all after medical school at the University of Chicago. Ariel's background was there as well, a degree in Liberal Arts at Grinnell College in Iowa. The evening passed quickly, everyone got their fill of that famous fried chicken, potatoes and gravy, and enjoyed the wine Dr. Palafox ordered from the menu. We talked around the table for about an hour before Mom began to get a bit weary saying "Early morning tomorrow for church." It could not have been more amicable and pleasant for all. Ben and Ariel returned to the motel with our promise for breakfast before they would head back to the city, and every one else home. That is, except a visit and long talk with Mariah at her apartment.

"Well, what do you think?" I asked her over a glass of wine, both of us sitting on the divan.

"What do **you** think?"

"I think it all went great. There remains a lot to say that was not said, old Catholic questions and requirements. But it went great. I know now I've got at least one reader. Ha."

"Mr. O'Brien, me too, happy with it all. What do you mean exactly by 'Catholic requirements'?"

"It's the cart before the horse, Mariah. It slipped out; I mean raising kids in marriage to be Catholic."

"Whoa Mr. Goy! Maybe something is on your mind you haven't told me about. Spit it out!"

"Mariah, it was just a passing thought, involuntary at that. Let's live life and see how things go. I do think you know, if there is such a phrase, that I'm not an "Orthodox Catholic" and am a lot more spiritual than religious. I sense that in you as well. We both know that religion with a capital R has caused enough problems in the world. I'm tired, enough for one day. Let's get some sleep and be ready for that breakfast up at the Motel tomorrow."

Mariah yawned at that response, literally, said it must be something in the air. We kissed and hugged and all that for a moment or two and perhaps reluctantly went our separate ways. "Damned small-town gossips!"

35

BREAKFAST WITH BEN AND ARIEL - A PROMISE TO VISIT

It wasn't actually that late when we got to bed, so we were both pretty alert when I picked up Mariah and we headed up to the motel. Ben and Ariel were waiting in the breakfast nook of the place, he stood, smiled and Mariah hugged and kissed them both. We got coffee and a sweet roll before the rest of the food. Conversation was about how pleasant the visit had been, the tourism and meeting the family last night. Ariel admitted the parents were different, "But they are all good people, and we try to be the same, and that's what counts." Ben basically seconded Ariel but added, "Mick, you are indeed a writer (I read all that book), it must carry over from the skills of teaching. I feel like we really know and appreciate your family. I do have one reservation." Uh oh!

"It's not what you think, nothing about religion or parents' education, income or the like. I'm just wondering about both of you children, or should I say, young man and woman, thinking of your background, talents and interests and I wonder how Abilene and a Juco college can satisfy you or be the big plan for the future."

I told Ben I agreed; it was an important topic and observation. Mariah and I had only talked about this briefly, really in passing conversation and both agreed we loved our jobs, thought we were doing well and doing good things for our students. We both had mentioned the possibility of Abilene being temporary and both of us back to graduate school and its unknowns, but it was just that, talk. What we had not addressed was any long-term relation with each other, both a bit afraid to, I think. In fact, we had not talked about the next year, just about the end of term and the coming Spring Term. If we were invited to continue at the Juco it would mean a repeat of last summer, most summer school probably at K.U. Conversation had not gone beyond that. We told the Palafoxes basically what I've just said. Ben smiled and just added, "You're both young, getting your feet on the ground. You know us and our tradition about education; I'll just say I can envision both of you with Ph.D.'s and teaching at a fine university. Time enough for that and time will tell. So far so good; both Ariel and I think you are doing well. I suppose you will let us know events as time goes by. Hopefully you can get down to Overland Park and visit soon."

We both agreed, finished that plastic food breakfast, and made our goodbyes, Ben saying he had a big week ahead of him, Ariel the same. Hugs and kisses.

So it was back to the busy routine of December. Final exams, the holidays. I spent Christmas once again with the family. Mom asked, "Why didn't you invite Mariah?" I said, "Not yet Mom." Between Christmas and New Year's I did a visit to the Palafoxes in Overland Park, staying in one of the guest rooms at the house. Nothing unusual to report about that; we talked of plans for spring term and perhaps summer school at K.U. again. Then Mariah and I did our first skiing trip to Colorado, out to Breckenridge, but did include a night in Abilene along the way (Mariah stayed at Jenny's and I bunked at home). It was much the same as with Mariah's family; we talked of plans for spring term and then a return to K.U. for summer school, nothing too out of the ordinary. But you could tell Mom was happy to see we were still an "item." We were back in Abilene, ensconced in our respective apartments and planning for spring term in January. That was when more stuff hit the fan in Abilene.

36

TROUBLE RIGHT HERE IN RIVER CITY

In a way it was a repeat of what people already knew – the St. Andrew's Church windows, the cattle rustling and barn burning – and what they didn't know, my slit tires. It seemed like more vandalism than anything else. The two guys who had confessed to the cattle rustling and barn burning were, as set by the judge, doing time down at Lansing, so it wasn't them. But it pissed off Abilene.

The first damage was at the cemeteries. It was a shock for everyone in town to see that someone, and they had to use sledge hammers and crow bars in the middle of the night, knocked down the Catholic Cross (a crucifix with the figure of Jesus on it) in the Catholic Cemetery. There was more. They knocked down the Brown grave stone in the Protestant Cemetery as well and a couple other old ones shaped like small obelisks for good measure. Brown as we wrote of earlier, for Abilene History is almost a religious figure, a "messiah" for all he brought to the town! It turns out there was a precedent for such damage and vandalism to cemeteries by the Klan in Kansas, way back in the 1920s. I say "Klan" because that's what it turned out to be.

The Abilene cemeteries had no night watchmen, no need for such a thing in presumed venerated places; at least that was the thinking. Old timers in town knew about the KKK history in the South, the cross burnings or "lightings" as members called it. It was nothing new and had been done by Scottish Clans in the mid-19th century as a method to "light the way" for battle but to defend their Christian heritage. In the Post – Civil - War Klan era however the custom and meaning changed: cross burning was used to intimidate the black communities who were all Christian. The Klan itself was originally Christian in its own way but with a couple of strange twists. They were Aryan as well and anti-negro, this in the post 1860s. Back in the early 1920s some citizens thought the whole cross burning thing was a bit of a hoax and was not an attribute of Klan activity at all until a couple of novels and "The Birth of a Nation" in 1915 depicted burnings.

Back to the Catholic cemetery in Abilene. Some religious extremists could possibly understand knocking over a **Catholic** cross because it had the concrete Jesus on it. Sorry, it just popped into my mind and maybe not so funny under the circumstances: the same years I'm describing had that country song of "I don't care if it rains or freezes 'cause I got my plastic Jesus on the dashboard of my car." The same extremists considered the Catholic cross an "abomination," daring to portray the image of Christ (images were "craven images" - a no-no and "anathema" in almost all Bible Belt Protestant churches). The Klan in the twentieth century had added immigrant Catholics and Jews to their hate list. Still, knocking down the concrete cross was an insult to Catholics and a crime on top of that. St. Andrews and the Knights of Columbus took it seriously and demanded the sheriff's office and local police find the perpetrators and quick!

But there was more damage – spray painting (once again in red) of the KKK initials on barns of some German Catholics south of Abilene and of Ron and Caitlin's barn out east of town. For good measure they did the same on Sean O'Brien's (Dad's) horse barn up at the northeast end of the farm.

And once again it wasn't just the Catholics. They spray painted the KKK on the front of Reverend Watson's Ebenezer First Gospel Church (the reader may recall, he is Black) north of the athletic field and football stadium. It must have been chilly work because it was a cold night in January.

All this was discovered early that next cold morning. Nothing else was talked about in town and there was a lot of muttering about the efficiency of law enforcement and the local law officers. There were even rumblings about Sheriff Wiley and his continuous re-election. There was an emergency meeting called by the Knights of Columbus (they were a Catholic fraternal organization, did charity work, gave out Christmas candy at the Santa Claus party at the church at Christmas, but way back were seen, in part, as defenders of the Catholic Church.) But before anything at all could take place, William Donaldson of the "Reflector" produced a "bombshell:" the entire front page was dedicated to the crimes, including a two-inch headline, photos of the overturned cross, the Brown tombstone, and the front of the Watson church below the headline:

INTOLERABLE VANDALISM IN ABILENE AND DICKINSON COUNTY ONCE AGAIN!

"The 'Abilene Reflector Chronicle' is putting the local police force and Chief Earl Sampson as well as Sheriff Wiley on notice: enough already! We are reporting the most recent event first: unthinkable vandalism took place at our local cemeteries last night. The Catholic Cross at the cemetery was toppled to the ground and the Brown tombstone was turned over in our Protestant Cemetery. In addition, vandalism claimed by the KKK was once again evidenced in our community: the symbol of the Klan, KKK, painted in red on barns of farmers south and east of town and once again, recalling a major 1959 event, the same painting on the Ebenezer First Gospel Church north of the athletic field in Abilene.

"We here at the 'Chronicle' are reluctant to open old wounds but under the circumstances it is necessary. It all harks back to the arson-burning of Sean and Molly O'Brien's farmhouse in 1959 and the ransacking of

Reverend Watson's church at the same time. Those culprits were found, arrested, convicted and served time at Lansing. We understand they are free 'on good behavior' and up in Idaho with other refugees of the KKK from west of Abilene. If you add to the 1959 events the letter threat to Abilene we published in 1962 after a rock with a message tied around it was thrown through a window at the sheriff's office, the vandalism at St. Andrew's just this past year, the cattle rustling and barn burning that followed, (the culprits confessed and are also currently serving time in Lansing), and now, last night's activity, something indeed is awry in Dickinson County."

The unthinkable happened the next day, reported in that afternoon's "Reflector Chronicle" edition:

Abilene Reflector Chronicle Paperboys Assaulted

"Two different RC paperboys on bicycles on their afternoon routes were cut off by a pickup truck yesterday and were told to hand over all their paper bags with all the papers in them. Two ruffians then pushed the boys and their bicycles over onto the curb beside the street. The thugs who perpetrated this unspeakable offence have not been apprehended. Both paper boys said the men wore kerchiefs on their faces, the license plates on the truck were smeared with mud, and besides they were too frightened to get up right away and get a good look. They do however think it was a black Chevy, maybe a late 1950s model. We implore the local law enforcement officers to get to the bottom of this and quickly!"

This was not a minor incident any longer. Mariah confessed to being frightened for me and even for my family. And of course, for other Catholics and the small black community in Abilene. We had only the grand total of seven black students in the Juco, but one was Reverend Watson and his wife Stella's daughter, my friend Jeremiah's sister. Mariah said, "My people have been through this, past and present, so I know evil when I see it."

Somehow things got out of hand. No one knows exactly how but the names of the people and location of the farms of the Idaho – related "migrants" up north were discovered, maybe by seeing the tax records, but no less than what you might call a "vigilante" group of six pickup trucks, twelve men in them, all armed to the teeth with shotguns and hunting rifles, drove to the farms, three in all. This was done in broad daylight. The "vigilantes" making no secret of their identity - no masks, nothing to hide the license plates - drove up to the three farmhouses, two trucks in each group. The message: we're giving you one month to clear out or suffer the consequences! At one of the places a man holding a high-powered rifle opened the door of the house and shot three warning shots above the vigilantes' pickups. They returned the fire breaking all the front windows in the house. The fellow yelled out, "To hell with you!" and slammed the door. The "vigilantes" decided their message was received loud and clear and returned to Abilene by separate routes. No one knows their exact identity, but there are suspicions. General community response (there was soon gossip all around town about it) was that whoever it was, at least someone was fighting back.

Sheriff Wiley's and Chief Earl's reaction was understandably different. They went so far as to contact Editor William at the paper and placed the following article that day:

CITIZENS OF ABILENE AND DICKINSON COUNTY

We in law enforcement, responsible for safety in the community, are well aware of current events. We are not standing around with our hands in our pockets. The KBI (Kansas Bureau of Investigation) has been notified and a plan is already in place to address this problem. We cannot however countenance knee-jerk 'vigilante' actions. Ladies and gentlemen, that solution which is not a solution went out the window one hundred years ago. Any further such activity is liable as a crime and will be prosecuted to the full extent of the law. The community is put on notice. As soon as there is more to report, you will hear from us. However, we ask all citizens to be watchful; notify either of our offices, the Sheriff's or Chief of Police, of any suspicious activity, cars or trucks driving by houses especially at night, and in particular we advise farmers in rural Abilene to be especially watchful for the same. The unlawful and cowardly acts of the KKK will shortly be put to a stop. That is a promise. Sincerely, Sheriff Wiley and Chief Earl Sampson.

Three arrests were made the following week, three men accused of the vandalism of just a few days earlier as well as the attack on the RC paperboys. Their arraignment took place that same day with charges of vandalism, and much more serious, of physical assault to the paperboys. This time Judge Raleigh called for a jury trial. The defense lawyer had a bit of a problem finding 12 neutral jurors, but it happened. The courtroom was once again jammed in two weeks' time when the trial began. Mr. Reiman once again was the prosecuting county attorney and the accused had no personal lawyers other than the county defense attorney. They claimed innocence, but it turns out Wiley and others had been diligent and efficient. They found sledge hammers and crow bars, still with concrete power dust on them, and amazingly enough, several spray paint cans underneath some gunnysacks in one of the barns, the latter with vestiges of red paint. (How stupid can you be? Likely disposal places like the county dump, road sides, ditches and culverts all over the county would have been searched, and stream and river beds as well. No stones left unturned.) It took the jury one hour to decide; the three were pronounced guilty as charged and sentenced to ten years in Lansing. There was the beginning of quite a community down there.

The next week black cars with KBI on the side arrived at the three farm homesteads, armed agents talked to the remaining residents, and signs were posted: "Temporary Foreclosure Pending Legal Action." Within two days neighbors took note of a mass exodus of pickup trucks, automobiles, and big truck-trailers and cattle trailers hauling farm machinery and a few head of livestock away. This was the second large "exodus" of troublemakers in the area, the first after the trial back in 1959, so just four years later. The KBI took names, license plate numbers, and noted all vehicles, all I suppose for future reference.

The reaction in town was relief. Closer to home, Dad said he was satisfied and didn't expect any more troubles. He bought paint and painted over the "KKK" on the horse barn. Ron did the same with his barn but had a little more vehement reaction, telling Mariah and me when we visited the farm, "I'm glad they got those bastards, but I'm not sure this is the end of it. You know there's a minority in the whole country out to make life difficult for all of us.

"I'm not just talking KKK, and I think with their history, even though the organization is still legal (1st and 2nd Amendments, Bill of Rights), they've got enough sense to lie low. But it sure as hell puts all of us on edge. I think we should organize a permanent committee, don't know what you would call it, maybe 'Citizens for Public Safety,' folks who would take it upon themselves to keep an eye on things. There will be no shortage of volunteers, that's for damned sure. (He didn't make any reference to the "vigilantes" of the past few days, but had a bit of a crooked smile on his face talking about his new idea.)

"Mick, I'm more worried about the general situation here out west. I don't know what you want to call it, but you've heard of all that trouble up in Idaho. There are some really mean, angry folks up there in the woods, and I've seen the reports about them, all armed to the teeth and looking for a fight with anyone "tainted" with government connections.

37

BACK TO NORMAL?

So now it's the end of January, still cold enough to freeze the balls off a brass monkey (pardon the Abilene slang). Time was spent teaching for both of Mariah and me, my writing up some notes on Abilene history and study, class preparation and grading. I took Mariah out to Sunday dinner at Mom and Dad's a time or two, more later on that, and once out to Ron and Caitlin's.

We continued "date night" over at the supper club in Salina and a movie once in a while. James Bond was the new thrill and the Salina theater got that feature in pretty quickly. I don't know if it was expected but we both went regularly to the AHS basketball games and even over to Chapman for the rivalry game. That game could get pretty intense, both teams vying for the Central Kansas League championship. Some scuffling took place on the court but it was always more interesting what happened outside. The "Chapman Irish" were known for some hard drinking and love of fisticuffs. I told Mariah my brother Joe somehow or other dated one of the pretty Catholic girls there, but I desisted with her younger sister (I never had occasion to tell her that) because of some rumbling by the locals that they didn't appreciate "squirrely Abilene guys" horning in on their home grown dates. I was a very skinny guy in school and no match for people who liked hitting you with their bare fists. On the other hand I saved some gas money.

There were plays at the high school and a great memory for me, we spent the entire day at the old downtown city auditorium gym for the county grade school basketball tournament. It was a real hoot and I loved it; I think Mariah just liked the change of pace. There were games from 8 a.m. to 8 p.m. from tiny country grade schools from places like Herington or maybe Rural Center, all the way up to the "big" schools of Garfield, Lincoln and McKinley in Abilene. The fare was popcorn, hot dogs and cokes and ice cream. I confessed to Mariah that I had committed the fateful foul of a McKinley star when we were in sixth grade, me a substitute at the very end of the game, just barely touching his fingers on his shooting hand with a last second desperation shot to win the game. He dropped in both foul shots and they beat us. That was a sad and traumatic moment of growing up. To make things worse he ended up dating my girl friend a few years later in high school. Mariah gave me a hug and a quick kiss, "Gracias a Dios. Quedaste para mí." Somehow that did make it all better.

And we spent another entertaining full day at the annual 4-H plays up at the high school auditorium. As just one activity for 4-H Day, most of the clubs in the county would put on one-act plays. Where they came from I don't know and never took the time to ask. But they were corny and always funny. My club the Abilene Aggies seemed to have a "corner" on first prize for years, maybe because it was the "city" club in comparison to all the others in rural districts outside of town. My brother Paul who had a lot of amateur acting experience plus a great baritone voice in high school and St. Andrew's choirs directed and he was good at it. Joe, Caitlin and I all took part, but my time later because of the age difference. I probably had the "lead" but can't remember a single play, just that then it was easy to memorize lines. So, the tradition continued and Mariah and I probably saw three or four of those local productions in one day. Being an English teacher with experience in plays and singing of her own, Mariah got a tremendous kick out of it all. The only thing missing was the popcorn and coke – the high school wouldn't allow it in the auditorium but you could get goodies in the lobby. We saw lots of folks in town that knew us from school, and me from those old 4-H days. This too was a small part of Abilene history, but recent history.

Mariah had finished her "field days" at the colleges with prospective students. She gushed with happiness, not for her, but for those kids that had never been exposed to a big school campus and the thrill of it all. On three separate occasions she rode "shotgun" in a college van with a driver and six or eight late teenage girls in the back seats. They went to Emporia, Manhattan and Lawrence, toured the respective campuses, ate at the student union and visited college English classes (all arranged by Mariah beforehand). The girls had lots of questions, most of them not about school. The fraternity and sorority system was indeed total "Greek to them" (and to me as well), but they had heard stories about the pledge week and the parties. Mariah told them the truth (what else?), both sides of the story. "I explained there was a lot of snobbishness that went on, and that social class and money of your family unfortunately were factors for some. However, there are sororities and fraternities that get away from all that and are really fine organizations to make lasting friendships and make college days a real 'sisterhood.' I had the good fortune to experience the latter. But you have other matters to consider – keeping up your studies, making good grades, and getting a chance for scholarships." Mariah added, "I don't know if I felt like a school marm or a big sister; I'll take the latter."

What I know is that at Abilene Juco (that's what most people called it) she was known as a teacher who would do everything possible for her students, and she really was a role model for all. Mariah added, "The girls are constantly asking about us and almost every Monday look at my hand to see if there is a ring on it. I tell them, 'Don't be in a rush, girls. I might not want it! Just kidding, not yet, not yet."

38

ROWING AGAINST THE CULTURAL CURRENT

There was one night we took a chance, but I figured it would be worth it – I took Mariah down to Frank's Friendly Tavern and we really lucked out – several of the friends from the old high school days were there, plus Wally Galatin. I justified it all, and it was true, that the place was part of Abilene history, at least for the last ten years or so. I had warned Mariah ahead of time of the fact that Wally knew everything going on in town, and we would soon be an "item," so be on your good behavior! But also, Wally was a living encyclopedia on town history and the Eisenhowers, so if we kept conversation on that, no harm done.

But old friend Jeremiah Watson was there. We probably spent an hour reminiscing and getting up to date. Mariah had read all about him in "A Rural Odyssey," and we also got a chance to catch up on his folks' reaction to the latest KKK stuff.

He said, "It looks like history repeating itself. Mick, we keep a pretty low profile here in the Black community, but there are three or four families whose kids do well in studies, sports and in music up at the High School. Jeeze, this latest is nothing as bad as your house on fire in 1959 and them ransacking our church. Just think what that could have been! This time Dad's flock was right over to the church with fresh paint (after the sheriff and police checked everything out and gave us the go-ahead), and you would never know anything had happened. We read the papers too and there is a network of Black folks all across Kansas that shares news and information. The word is to be vigilant. I guess now more than ever; those hoodlums weren't afraid to say they were KKK. It's kind of "business as usual." My Dad and others are still the janitors in town, the Howlands run the garbage trucks, and Mr. Waverly has a pretty good trucking business. But three or four of the girls including my sister have done well in college and have fine jobs, one of them a high school principal in a big school in Wichita. In other words, they've "made it." The guys go into the military, one of our good athletes of just four years ago (Caitlin's class) is a barber up in Chicago. And (he laughed sardonically) no one's been strung up!"

"Not so funny Jeremiah, but I get it. But how about you? I understood you had gone down to either K-State or Emporia State when I left for Kansas City. What happened with all that?"

"Mick, that's not so funny either. I didn't get a music scholarship in spite of all that work in band at AHS, but started at K-State. It's simple. The money ran out. I couldn't make enough in the summers to keep up with tuition and board and room in Manhattan and didn't have enough money for a decent car to commute. So I've been working over in the foundry at Deershon's in Enterprise. It's hot and nasty work, but it's steady work. I'm saving a little; maybe in a year or two I can get back to school. There is one idea I'm tossing around, you may remember Linda Gallagher in band, our buddy Spencer's sister. She got a music scholarship to Oklahoma. I might be eligible for that. The problem is you have to tack on out of state tuition. I don't know right now. I'm playing in a band (black guys of course) over in Junction City on Saturday nights, and we are doing some really cool music, so that's what keeps me going."

"Level with me Jeremiah, would a couple of white dudes like me and Mariah be safe to check that out?"

"Mick, maybe yes, maybe no. I don't think so. The club is full of soldiers from Fort Riley. They are off duty, looking for some relaxation and they drink a lot of beer. And it can get pretty rowdy. Some of them have dates, and the others wish they did. Yeah, I'm sure; let's skip that for now. On the other hand, when it gets warmer this spring maybe you can get out the guitar, I'll tune up my electric and we can get Loren Beasley and his bongo into town and do a night out at the old bandshell. That would be fun."

For old times' sake, we asked him if both Mariah and I could come to church on a Saturday evening when they had a big service. He was amenable to that and said he would talk to his Dad and let us know. That would happen the next week on a Saturday night.

Wally wanted to know all about Mariah, so she told him of growing up in Overland Park, her Dad an M.D. and her experience at K.U. Wally was a graduate of K.U. so they went on quite a while about that.

Wally was in the process of doing a pictorial history of the Eisenhowers, to be a small book, so we were regaled with some great "inside" comments. It would trace in photographs from his Dad's era and then his own the whole story with short comments on the photos, when they took place and the situation. Early photos of the Eisenhower family grouped at the original house on the South side, Ike's baseball team photos in front of the old high school, Ike's early military career at West Point, and then the glory days of World War II, Normandy and the rest. Wally's contribution would be post-war with Ike and Mamie's visits to Abilene, the beginning of the 1952 presidential campaign (and maybe I mentioned it, when I was on one of the floats passing by the Sunflower Hotel where Ike gave the first speech, my 4-H float and me, ha ha, depicting a young Eisenhower), the presidency and the last being the inauguration of the Eisenhower Library. Wally regaled us with comments about the short conversations between the photographers and Ike.

Oh. Mariah had two draft beers, no more, and I probably had a dollar's worth (a glass of beer at 25 cents). I told Wally, "If there are any wagging tongues, tonight is 'research'! You, Jeremiah and this place are a big part of Abilene." He laughed and laughed and incidentally agreed. It turned out to be a pleasant night for all and no repercussions later because "two juco teachers visited a local tavern."

39

SERVICES AT THE EBENEZER FIRST GOSPEL CHURCH

A couple of weeks later, it was bit a "déjà vu," being back at Jeremiah's church, but there was a lot of water under the bridge, and this time Mariah would be with me. We were prepped for the proper clothing, me in a white shirt, sport jacket, dress shoes, but no tie. Mariah in a "modest church outfit." Jeremiah only had his sister and our high school friends as models. Mariah wore a long skirt, a long-sleeved sweater but with a jacket on top. No hats for either of us.

It was like last time, Reverend Watson and his wife Stella and Jeremiah greeted us at the door. They were all smiles and happy to have me once again (and my guest who was known to them, Jeremiah had talked a lot about Mariah). The Reverend said, "Mick I've heard what good work both of you are doing up at the Juco. Ernie and María Gómez are friends of ours and have told us how happy Mariela is up there. I didn't really figure on you being around here, Mick, maybe up to greater things, but it's a pleasure. If you two don't have anything planned, we would like to have you over to the house for coffee or tea and some fine home baked chocolate chip cookies after the service. I'll try not to be so long winded as usual and get us out of here by nine. Jere says he and you are going to have two or three gospel hymns for us, so come on in, get set up. Services will begin in about thirty minutes; you will have time to rehearse a bit. By the way I see your Dad and, in fact, Ron and Caitlin occasionally down at the Elks Club where I'm still janitor. They are always friendly and respectful to me."

We set up and then took places in the third row on wooden chairs. Soon churchgoers arrived, all dressed "Sunday Best." I recognized many and we exchanged smiles. Then the small choir filed in in their dark blue robes and sat in the front row on the right. It was much like the last time four years ago. Reverend Watson came in, wife Stella to his side, she took her seat on the left in front of the pulpit, along with family friends. Reverend Watson in a long black robe began the service. He did an opening prayer and then announced, "Tonight we once again have special guests. I am sure you remember Mr. Michael O'Brien, our son Jeremiah's good friend in times past and present. He is joined by his friend Mariah Palafox, a colleague from Abilene Juco. Tonight Michael and Jeremiah will renew their music performances, but this time with three spirituals, and will be joined by the voices of the Ebenezer First Gospel Choir. But you have to hear the readings and my shorter than usual sermon first. (All laughed, and you heard a voice in the back say, "Amen to that!")

I don't recall the readings but the message was clear: in times of adversity remember the Lord, have courage, and pray for deliverance. Reverend Watson in his sermon recalled the problems in 1959, the O'Brien house fire, the Ebenezer Church vandalism and the great community support in re-doing the church. He then recalled all the events of this past year, noting once again the local vandalism, the threats, and the arrest and conviction of the latest attackers. His message, "We must all be vigilant and remember that the Lord delivered the Jewish people from slavery in Egypt; we were freed by President Abraham Lincoln in the aftermath of the Civil War, but the devil and evil still exist in the world. We must repent of our sins and ask the Lord to help us."

There was thunderous applause, many shouts of "Alleluia" and "Amen Brother" and "Thank you Lord." He then introduced Jeremiah and me, we walked to the front, tuned the guitars again and launched into the three planned hymns: "Wayfaring Stranger," "Just a Closer Walk with Thee," and "Amazing Grace." I don't think I have felt closer to God than that moment. The best part was the incredible addition to our voices of the harmony and great spirit of the local choir. People were standing, swaying with the music, and once again with spontaneous shouts of "Amen," "Thank You Lord," and "Praised be the Lord."

Then came the call for those who wished to be saved to come forward for a blessing and a laying on of hands. Many did so, adults and children. Toward the end Jeremiah nudged me and said, "Mick, the Lord is still waiting. He has not gone away. You can go up again. And Mariah as well." Taken by surprise but remembering the last time (I was indeed 'slain in the spirit') I did not hesitate to step into the aisle. Before that however I looked over at Mariah, she with a surprised look and "What do I do now O'Brien?" look. I nodded toward the front and she stood, took my hand and we walked forward. We both knelt down, Reverend Watson put his hands on our heads and seemed deep in prayer. I could tell it was starting to happen again; I felt faint and began to sway a bit. Two strong robed choir members appeared behind me and gently held me up. Mariah was in tears, but happy tears. In just a few moments we were escorted back to our seats. Suddenly the entre congregation was standing and quietly applauding amidst murmurings of "Thank you Jesus." I just sat, my arm around Mariah, and waited. She dabbed her eyes with a handkerchief, smiled and hugged me, saying "This is a first for a Palafox. I do believe the God of Israel is the same as whatever is going on in this church tonight. Thank you, Michael."

Reverend Watson stood in the front, saying "We once again have been blessed by the Lord. Thank You Lord. Please stand and raise your hands with me and the choir will lead us in our last hymn, "Swing Low Sweet Chariot." We all stood and swayed to the music. I was sorry when it was over. Everyone filed out, many staying to shake my hand, greet Jeremiah and thank him, and gently taking Mariah's hand saying thank you and that they would never forget this night.

Stella Watson then herded us over to their house next door, saying the Reverend would be along in a few minutes, had us sit down in the living room and said "I'll start the tea pot and we'll have a nice talk in a little bit." I had not had a chance to talk to Mariah, not knowing whether to apologize or try to explain that I didn't know what would happen tonight. When I opened my mouth she just said, "It's all right Mick. It's all right. We'll talk later."

Sure enough, Reverend Watson and Jeremiah came into the room a bit later. We all had hot tea and maybe the best chocolate chip cookies I had ever eaten and then a frank talk about recent events. The reader knows about all that. Then the topic changed, all of us agreeing to get to know each other a little bit better. Of course, the Watsons knew about my parents, the farm and my times with Jeremiah. They were curious about Mariah, how we had met and all. She explained the decision to teach after school at K.U., the chance job in Abilene, and meeting me. She gave the short version of growing up in Overland Park, a "big" city girl. It was then I asked Mr. Watson what I never had the chance to do before, how they ended in Abilene.

"Mick and Mariah, it's a long story, and it's getting a bit late. I'll just give you the short version. Maybe you know of the settlement and town of Nicodemus up in north and western Kansas. After the Civil War and in full blown Reconstruction times, and the Homestead act of the 1860s, a few former slaves, all tied to growing up on the land, managed to move from Kentucky to the newly formed town of Nicodemus. My great grandparents the Watsons and also three or four other families you know in town were amongst those settlers. But it was no where near the end of hard times. No one had really any money at all, no real farm equipment or livestock, and early charity and kindness just went so far. For a while people tried to farm the land, and in fact life improved. The town incorporated but could never get the support it needed to really make a go of it. The town fathers tried to get a railroad to come, that would have brought growth, but none of the three major lines would come. Time passed and then in the 1930s the Depression. That was when most of us came down to Abilene, some chance of doing labor on the railroad (that's how we met the Gomezes). And we soon found that there were town services no one else wanted to do, janitorial work and the garbage collection. That is pretty much our story. I met Stella in Nicodemus, married her in that town, and we came here together, with hardly a dollar in our pockets. It was after we got here, me with janitorial jobs, that I felt the "call" and started this church.

"Life is still pretty much the same for us as thirty years ago, just making it financially, but there are good things. The kids got schooling, our daughter Ellie has done really well, some of the kids of our neighbors as well. But back to earlier on tonight, the dangers have not passed. Some people will never get used to having black people around so the word is "Be vigilant.""

I thanked Reverend Watson adding, "It's not the same, but you know the Catholics are also on that hate list. Fortunately, this is a god-fearing community with good people and recent events have seen us all pull together. I'm hopeful for the future. Opposition to the Klan in the entire country has grown exponentially these last twenty years. I'm hopeful they are on their last legs. I know that folks here are on the alert and law officers are keeping an eye on things."

Mariah added, "Reverend and Mrs. Watson, Jeremiah, and Michael, this has been an unexpected experience for me tonight. I never would have guessed its effect on me. You are a whole new world to me and it's made me thankful for you and aware of our shared humanity, struggles and rewards. I shall always remember tonight. My faith background is from old Europe, dating back in Spain, but like I told Mike, the God of the Bible is the same and was present tonight. Thank you with all my heart."

We all embraced, shook hands and amidst wishes and hopes we would be back at the Juco for another year, said good night. Jeremiah said, "Mick, what can I say? Keep practicing that guitar and maybe we'll do it again. For sure when it warms up out at the bandshell. This night was good for me, my people and thanks again. You O'Briens need to know: there are folks in our group that know how to defend themselves and you as well. We are ready just in case."

Sunday, the next day I was back at Mass at St. Andrew's and Sunday dinner at Mom and Dad's with Mariah. We told my folks about Saturday night and services at Jeremiah's church. Dad was all ears, and so was Mom, but she was still bothered that a Catholic would take part in a Protestant service, and what would Monsignor Fahey say about it! I started to protest, but Mariah stopped me, saying, "Mick, I'll handle this. Mrs. and Mr. O'Brien, you might imagine what an ethnic Jew and my parents would think as well. The truth is that from way back, I'm talking the 11th century in Spain when people were more tolerant, we were constantly involved with both Catholics and Muslims in Córdoba in Andalucía. Our lives were separate yet inseparable. I think I can safely say that you would have loved being in that church last night. What is it the Catholics say, 'The Holy Spirit is with us' or something like that. It was certainly the case last night. We've all read and heard that the Catholic Church Council is wrapping up in Rome, and it's historic. And one of the key words is Ecumenism – being with and accepting people of other faiths (The Eastern Rites, Protestants and even Jews). The Ebenezer Church and your son are well ahead of the times. Last night I experienced religion as I never have before, and that includes my family tradition. I believe what you call the Holy Spirit was present and touched us all. It must be something like what the next life is like – feeling good, feeling safe and feeling loved."

After I got up off of the floor (figuratively), I looked at this young woman thinking, what a blessing she has brought to my life. I didn't say it, but I thought it. Mom was moved to tears and gave Mariah a big hug, saying, "Thank you. And thank you for loving our son." Whew. She and I had not dared to use that word yet, like I say, the most important and serious word in the English language. Dinner was ready, the table was set and the food was scrumptious as usual. We moved on to more mundane topics – Dad would soon be planting the big garden, the end of the term was in sight, and we were thinking of that and beyond.

40

THE K.U. RELAYS AGAIN AND ANOTHER VISIT HOME FOR MARIAH

Spring arrived after some really nasty weather in late February, snow and a Kansas blizzard, and horrible winds in March. Ron and Stan were afraid the wind would blow the young wheat sprouts right out of the ground, so they rushed to the fields with disks and harrows to mitigate the damage. April finally arrived, the weather warmed but with some good rains, and Mariah and I planned a return trip to Lawrence and the Kansas Relays, and a jog down to her see her parents in Overland Park.

There's not much new to report for the Lawrence visit. The relays were great again, lots of Olympic quality athletes, another night for me in a frat house, the reunion with Mariah's sorority sisters, less satisfying for her because fewer of her old friends were around ("Mick, this may be the last go-round on this"), a fun but also enlightening visit with some surprises to the Palafoxes Saturday night and Sunday through lunch and the drive back to Abilene.

We drove into Overland Park in the late p.m. on Saturday, went directly to the Palafox residence, were greeted with great enthusiasm by Ben and Ariel and then whisked off once again to the Stockyard's Restaurant, Ben's favorite. He drove and said along the way, "Mick you know there's got to be a big connection between the stockyards here and Abilene. I doubt if anybody who works there knows anything but let's ask. All those cattle shipped east on the Kansas Pacific to Kansas City and Chicago – a good many must have met their end here." Mariah spoke up, "Is that why my steak last time looked a little green?" Everyone laughed, but Ben insisted, "We'll see. We'll see."

Sure enough, no one in the restaurant including the manager could answer the question but Ben was persistent and saw from posters and old photos on the walls of the restaurant that the stockyard was built in 1871. I spoke up saying that by that time the cattle from Texas to Abilene via the Chisholm Trail had begun to wane, and most Texas Cattle were driven on west to Ellsworth and famously to Dodge City for another ten years. But hundreds of thousands of head of cattle indeed arrived to Kansas City and on up to the even bigger stockyard in Chicago over the next almost 100 years.

We drove on back to the house, happy and satisfied with the fine meal. Mr. Palafox asked me to join him in a Drambuie liqueur in the living room and for me and Mariah to fill him (and Ariel) in on the latest in Abilene. Both reiterated the good times in their visit, complementing my parents as well and marveling at the history and old homes in Abilene, not to speak of the Eisenhower museum.

Mariah and I had decided to tell them about the recent happenings, including the vandalism and the KKK, but not without some trepidation. She was sure her Mother would want her out of Abilene as soon as possible and was not sure of her Dad's reaction. It brought some surprises. After hearing of all the recent happenings, including vandalism at the cemeteries, the Ebenezer Church, the assault of the paper boys, the vigilante trucks, the arrest and conviction of the three perpetrators and finally the KBI foreclosures and mass move of people back to Idaho, Mr. Palafox sat deep in thought for a while but then spoke up.

"Mick and Mariah, this is all highly disturbing. Mick, I know you have not been hurt, but it has touched your family."

"Yes, and Mariah with me, it affects her too, and indirectly, it affects you Mr. Palafox and Mrs. Palafox as well. This brings us to an even more serious matter to discuss with you. I guess now is the time. There was never a time to really bring it up before. Mariah knows about everything I am about to tell you. Ben and Ariel, the story in the "Farm" took you up to my high school days and all that went on the farm, Mom and Dad's story, growing up days. But after that, in the senior thesis at college, I brought it all up to date in another book "A Rural Odyssey – Living Can be Dangerous." There are two major events you do not know about, the "real" story of the final days on the farm before the fall of 1959. I'm referring back to 1957 and that episode of "The Great Enterprise Bank Robbery." The bank robbers tried to kidnap me that day. I weaseled out of their grasp, they traded gunfire with the sheriff and the Highway Patrol, were subdued and arrested, and thrown in jail for the robbery.

"The second event was two years later, early in the summer after I had graduated from high school and was working on the farm before heading off to college in Kansas City, now in 1959. It's all in the new book, but the long and short of it was three men living out west of Abilene (they turned out to be cousins of the bank robbers of 1957) set fire to Dad and Mom's farmhouse, with them plus me in it. Whether a miracle or not, I smelled the smoke upstairs, yelled "fire' and ran downstairs, and we all got out the front door, but just in time. The whole house burned down. It was devastating for Mom and Dad, for all of us. The community however was great; we got clothes, a temporary apartment, and eventually with the insurance money Dad and Mom bought the house they live in now, the one you drove by in Abilene a month ago.

"Local law enforcement caught the scoundrels, arrested them, threw them in the clink and there was a very swift trial (all Abilene was involved, the prosecuting lawyers, the judge, the sheriff, everyone, many being friends of Dad and Mom's). The bastards got twenty years in Lansing. But in 1962 squeaky hinges were oiled and they got out on "good behavior" and moved up to Idaho. Later that year the small "troubles" started in

Abilene, a rock thrown through the jail house window with a message promising revenge on Abilene, and two years later the beginning of the vandalism, a couple of times before all this latest surge.

"That is what Mariah and I decided jointly to not tell you. It was not the time. Our motives were simple: to not have you and especially Ariel worry. Everything seemed to be under control. And I daresay, now after recent events it seems to be all under control and no immediate danger. I think this time the KKK went too far. Local law enforcement is on constant watch and the KBI has entered the scene. It's a whole different story."

Mariah spoke up, sitting beside me and holding my hand as I finished telling the story. "Dad and Mom, I am totally in agreement with Mick on all we have done and heard and told you. I joked once saying I was one 'to stand by your man' from a hokey hillbilly song in Kansas. It's more now. I'll stand by the man I love."

There was absolute silence in the room. Mr. Palafox took a big swallow of his Drambuie, looked over at Ariel and said, "Thank you for telling us the whole story. I'm not sure how I and Ariel would have reacted had we known of it before our visit to Abilene. I'm not sure from everything you have shared with us tonight, that recent events are **not** related to that. I don't think those bad guys have forgotten you. And when I say you, now I say you and Mariah. I'm all the more convinced you both should think seriously of moving on with your lives after this school term finishes. You for sure don't have to decide tonight or even tomorrow, but I would think soon. I think maybe Mariah has experienced enough of the 'wild, wild west.' We can't run your lives for you, but we would be remiss to remain silent."

"This does not mean I'm not concerned, Mick, about your parents, sister and brother-in-law, and for that matter, other "targets." I believe your entire community should be put on notice for possible danger. However, it appears the sheriff, police and the KBI are on this."

Ariel was silent but in constant "touch" with what Ben had been saying.

"Mr. and Mrs. Palafox, don't think Mariah and I have not thought about this, and we've talked with a lot of 'ifs.' No decisions yet, but soon I think. Now that you know the KKK is involved, and who knows what other "rugged individualists" are too. There's not much for us to add on the matter.

"I know it is changing the subject, and I'm not trying to avoid the main issue here, but I think it's relevant. In your own case, your family, friends, your people. What can you tell us about the KKK and Jewish people? I know Jews have been a target since the 1920s and immigration."

"Mick, I won't and can't even begin to go into the history of anti-Semitism in the western world and especially the U.S. in the 20th century. There are dozens of cases. We wouldn't be finished by morning. It came from all sides and from abroad, the Holocaust the main thing but far from the only thing. Suspicion of Jews, Jewish bankers, and all that came from Henry Ford in his diatribes as early as 1915 but again in the early 1920s and even a Catholic priest, Father Coughlin in the 1930s with a big radio show and newspaper, that's just for openers. The KKK had gone on record in the 1920s against all immigration to the United States that might "soil pure Americans." That included Irish, Italians and Jews as well. I know that in Kansas City in the 1920s there was a major KKK presence, parades with the men on horseback dressed in white robes and hoods. While it was not directed specifically toward Jews, we were part of the target. Funny, I guess we and the Catholics and the Blacks all have that in common. Mike, it's nothing new for us, thus we keep a low profile as well. Most Jews don't advertise they are Jews and certainly don't flaunt their religion or wealth for that matter, that is, if they have it. Of course, Orthodox Jews with their dress and beards, etc. are a different matter, but that is largely in New York and other eastern cities.

"We personally, the Palafox family, have not had any problems but we are not unaware of the dangers. Mariah can tell you, when she was overwhelmingly accepted in Pledge Week at K.U. and then they discovered she was Jewish …"

"Daddy, I haven't told Mick about that. Mick, I pledged another sorority before the Tri-Delts, and in effect I was 'blackballed'. They never gave the reason, certainly not in writing, and I was heartbroken, I really liked the initial party and girls, some of them from Kansas City. Gossip soon revealed that the Sorority had a history of being anti-Jewish, that plus a perusual of the last names of the pledges before decisions were made. But the Tri-Delts also liked me and wanted me, so that's what happened, and now that's all water under the bridge, but it hurt. Granted, it's not like being shot at or burning your house down, but just something to keep in mind."

Mr. Palafox continued, "So Mike there are a lot of things unsaid and perhaps better not brought up. You judge character when you meet people and get to know them. In this case, Ariel and I are positive Mariah is in good hands with you. Uh, I mean for the present."

"Daddy, enough said of that. We'll let you know but not yet. The "goy-mensch" indeed treats me right. Enough for now."

I added, "All you have said is serious, but thank you for elucidating on this whole matter. I truly did not mean to overlook anything, and we did bring you up to date with the latest in Abilene. But what I have just told you from 1957 to 1959 happened long before I met Mariah. When we go back to Abilene this afternoon we'll be talking about all this in the car. And very soon the Juco will be issuing contracts for next year, so there will be decisions to be made. I'll just say for now, once again, and you seem to concur, there is no immediate danger in Abilene. And I think, in fact, with the KBI now in on everything, there's really no danger at all. Mariah and I have talked, very tentatively, about this coming summer but better for her to tell you about that."

"Mom and Dad, we've been thinking, really regardless of next year at the Juco or not, of going back to summer school. Another nine credit hours for each of us toward the Master's would be a good thing. But then, we both think a trip to Spain is in order, once again to speak Spanish, but for both Mick and me to see the famous places he has studied, some of Spain's tourist sites, but especially Córdoba and the Alhambra and Sevilla, all with our Sephardi connections. And the synagogue in Toledo, that's on my list. That's our thinking."

Mr. Palafox said, "Spain sounds good, terrific Mariah for you to see your 'roots.' And Mick too. We won't keep you from your drive, but keep us posted, good news and bad." Lots of hugs, handshakes, embraces and we were off. A fairly quick drive home rehashing the last twenty-four hours. We were both really tired so we made it a quick evening with a promise for lunch up at the Juco on Monday.

41

DECISION TIME

Things came fast and furious the next week. The Juco not only offered to renew our contracts but offered "substantial" raises of $1000 each. We would be teaching our "regular" schedules as usual, but this time both of us agreed to "field days" taking students to the big three, K-State, K.U. and Emporia State, to expose them to big campus life and prospective programs in English in Mariah's case, in Spanish in my case. Mariah took the lead, having already done it, telling me how to plan. With all that in line, we ended the term, said temporary goodbyes to Mom and Dad, Ron and Caitlin and friend and buddies in town.

It was full speed ahead for K.U. and then four weeks in Spain, a great plan we surmised.

42

THE RETURN TO K.U. SUMMER OF 1965 AND ON TO SPAIN

We put in our time at K.U., actually able to rent the same apartment as last year. There was little time for social life and the course work was strenuous. I did two more courses in Spanish, this time on Peninsular Literature to get ready for Spain; one on the classic "Don Quixote," another on 20th Century Spanish Poetry (including Federico García Lorca). I was pleased to see a graduate history course on Kansas History, perfect for the Abilene research. Mariah did one Spanish Course, Civilization of Spain (including Andalucía) and two American Literature courses, one on Faulkner, the other on female novelists of the 20th century. We got together for coffee occasionally in the student union, the evening meal, and pizza, beer and a movie on Friday or Saturday. That was it!

Classes ended after July 4th, we packed up intending to leave our cars, books and paraphernalia at the Palafox house in Overland Park, had a fun weekend with Ben and Ariel, getting tips from Ben on what to see in Spain, and got on the TWA to Madrid. The original plan of four weeks in Spain was cut to three, plenty to accomplish our objectives, two in the South and one in Madrid and day trips from there. We figured we could use the extra time later at home to visit relatives and rest up before Fall term.

A note: this was the first time for either of us in Spain and I'm not sure who was more excited, each of us for different reasons. Spain is the "Holy Grail" for Spanish teachers, and all my undergraduate courses were pointing the way for this encounter. Mariah had read and knew more about Spanish tourism than I, and was guardedly curious to discover part of her roots ("guardedly" is accurate keeping in mind the family tradition plus the Catholic Kings' Alhambra Edict of 1494 that added greatly to the Jewish diaspora). We were already exhausted from jet lag when the overnight flight landed in Madrid early in the morning, but held on for the regional flight to Sevilla. For our interests, Andalucía was older in Spanish history than Madrid or even earlier in the Catholic Kings' era of Toledo and Segovia, so it came first. We would take the bus to Córdoba, then Granada and back to Sevilla, staying in 3-star hotels along the way. After the night flight and then customs and the wait for the next plane, I was a walking zombie by the time we got to Sevilla and Mariah much the same. We went to a travel agency and bought bus tickets to Córdoba and made a hotel reservation. It was dinner that night in a "tapas" restaurant, a glass or two of wine and early to bed. All we managed to do was walk to the main plaza and look wide-eyed at the Cathedral and the Giralda Minaret. Amazing! Good things to see later. The bus would leave early the next day for Córdoba.

We had no trouble speaking Spanish, but it was interesting that here in the South of Spain, natives did not use the "theta" for the "c's" or "z's" as in Castile. So I couldn't use my "theta" joke my college prof had taught me, "Voy a Zaragoza a comer cigalas en la plaza de Zaragoza" (Six "thetas"!). In vulgar terms this means the "lisp" in central Spain. Caramba! The Spanish professor is coming out of O'Brien. Because a good many of the soldiers of fortune in Mexico and the New World came from Andalucía in southern Spain and the southwest province of Extremadura, Latin American Spanish does not use the "theta" as well! There are a lot of jokes about the Spanish and their speech. From statements from friends from Latin America, specifically Colombia which claims to have the "best Spanish" in America, there also is no "theta." End of lecture.

43

CÓRDOBA

The next morning after a quick breakfast of "café con leche" and "churros" (and a snack of fruit and rolls on the bus) off we went to Córdoba. It was a trip of two hours and the farm boy did not miss a thing: this was the basis of agriculture in most of Andalucía - huge orchards of olive trees, equally huge fields of Spanish sunflowers (the very large ones), vineyards of grapes, fields of wheat, and citrus groves, the "breadbasket of Spain." We would learn it was the Arabs in the 10th and 11th centuries that had established the irrigation for all this, notwithstanding the surprising Sierra Nevada Mountain range outside of Granada with snow year-round.

The first thing you see when you roll into Córdoba is the Guadalquivir River and the old Roman Bridge over it and to the left the famous Muslim Mosque of Córdoba. The place "drips" with history, no need to get into all that deep doodoo now, suffice to say the Romans were there first, from the second century B.C. and Córdoba became the capital of Roman Spain. The Romans ruled in Spain until the 5th century A.C., then the Muslim Invasion came in 711. The Umayyads founded a caliphate originally in Córdoba and all went well until the end around 1080. At that time a new wave of Muslims, this time fanatic Berbers (the Almoravids) were invited in to help Córdoba defend itself against the oncoming tide of Christians from the north in Castile (the era of the Cid and the Reconquest). The Berbers rebelled against their hosts and the end of a great era began. The

Almoravids (Berbers) ruled until being defeated in 1212 at the Battle of Las Navas de Tolosa by the Spaniards. That ushered in the rule of the Nasrides, the last major Muslim dynasty in Spain, the ones associated with the Alhambra, its glory from the 1200s to 1492 and final Spanish conquest.

Our "musts" for study and tourism in Córdoba were the original Mosque ("La Mesquita de Córdoba") with the amazing Spanish Renaissance Chapel in its interior, the Jewish Quarter, the statues of the Arab intellectual Averroes and the Jewish philosopher Maimonides marking that great age of learning. (A while later on the last leg of our trip we will talk of Madrid and Toledo and a related phenomenon the "School of Translators" of Toledo).

Through a series of accidents, the most beautiful and extensive mosque in Córdoba (to rival Bagdad, Jerusalem and Damascus), started at the end of the 8th century and modified the next two hundred years, was preserved, only because the Spanish Catholics much later built a Renaissance chapel in the middle of it. But science, mathematics, medicine, philosophy, history and agriculture thrived in a golden age of Moslem rule when the three cultures got along for more than two hundred years. The Mesquita (with 856 marble columns, red and white brick capitals at the top, and many other sights such as the Mihrab) was an amazing sight. The Spanish Chapel all done in dark, gorgeous wood choir stalls with a renaissance pulpit with a white marble bull in front of it and the Hapsburg Double Eagle to the side was equally impressive. An accident of history.

After the Mosque we went to the quarter where we saw the statue of Averroes, Córdoba's greatest Muslim intellectual. The biography blew me away: he wrote of philosophy, theology, medicine, astronomy, physics, psychology, and mathematics. What am I leaving out? Of greatest fame was his study, admiration, translation and commentary of the works of the Greek Philosopher Aristotle, for this receiving the title of "Commentator" by the Christians. This is what they mean when they say the Arabs were responsible for the recovery and development of Greek Philosophy in the West (much abandoned in Christian Europe after the fall of the Roman Empire). Thank you, Averroes.

And of equal importance was the move on to the old Jewish quarter and the statue of Maimonides. He was a contemporary of Averroes in the 12th century in Córdoba. Intellectual, philosopher, writer, he became best known for his commentary on Jewish Scripture, and an expert on the Torah and wrote his own "13 Principals of the Faith," the required beliefs of Judaism. What we saw in Córdoba was proof of that great age of relative tolerance by Muslim rulers, and an intellectual "renaissance" of the three faiths, Moslem, Jewish and Christian (meaning the Christians living under the Moors, called "Mozárabes," long before the Spanish crown would defeat the Moors in Al-Andalus at the end in 1492).

There was one remaining synagogue in Córdoba. It was beautiful with ornate stucco in the Arabic "mudéjar" style. Done in 1315, it may have been a private synagogue by a businessman or a trade guild's religious place. They don't know for sure. But something is better than nothing. We both were moved to see it. Our final and most important one would be later in Toledo.

Even though we did not **see** anything, a house or a statue, I can't leave Córdoba without mentioning the Golden Age Spanish poet Luís de Góngora. He was probably the best-known Spanish Baroque poet of the 16th and 17th century, known for his convoluted style and with the nickname "Príncipe de las Tinieblas" or "Prince of Darkness.' He was incredibly difficult to decipher in the undergraduate poetry class, but we did it. He was born in Córdoba and then moved on to the royal court in Madrid. He had famous predecessors in the city, the two Sénecas during Roman rule!

After sharing a bottle of white wine seated on the Roman bridge, we happily called the visit a success and moved on to equally amazing things in Granada, catching a bus the next morning, passing through rural Andalucía once again with the same farm scene. Next was the gorgeous city of Granada backed by the snowcapped Sierra Nevada. And the Alhambra!

44

GRANADA

This city is associated with the rule of the Nasrides, the last major Muslim dynasty in Spain, the one associated with the Alhambra Palace and its glory from the 1200s to 1492 and final Spanish conquest. Culture and people had moved from Córdoba to Granada where there was a true renaissance of Arabic Moslem Culture for about another 250 years before the Spanish "Conquistadores" and Catholic Kings saw and knew better (sarcasm intended).

You would think it would be difficult to match Córdoba for tourism, and more importantly, for my interests in teaching and Mariah's interest in searching out her Sephardic roots, but we were just getting started. Totally different, my non-expert comparison, maybe like Gothic to Baroque (nah) was the "jewel" of all Moslem Spain, the Alhambra Palace in Granada. From the massive yet beautiful Mosque in Córdoba, you entered an almost ethereal dreamlike palace in Granada, from marble columns and brick arches of the Mesquita to the filigreed, dainty, maze of "mocárabe" stuccoes (miniature stuccoes like "stalactites" and "stalagmites") of the Alhambra and channeled pools of flowing water everywhere. And there were the Arabic decorative tiles, "azulejos," on its walls, tiles used throughout Spain and Portugal and their colonies in the New World to come. And the gardens ["jardines"] of Granada. The gardens make me think of Washington Irving and his "Tales of Granada." And for the amateur guitarist there is nothing like "Recuerdos del Alhambra" transcribed by Francisco Tárrega from the classic Isaac Albéníz piece for piano. It is one of the more beautiful and most difficult of all classic guitar pieces, played entirely in "tremolo" or triplets! Arguments will never cease which is more important or beautiful. Ancient Greece or Rome? Córdoba or Granada?

We fought the usual tourist crowds but were in no hurry – this was a "lifetime" experience. We lingered in the maze of halls, rooms, and corridors of the main palace. There were dozens of rooms of columns, walls and ceilings decorated with a maze of "mocárabes" – the filigreed stuccoes (as mentioned before, like small jeweled "stalagmites" or "stalactites"). And many interior rooms covered with the Arabic colored tiles. A curious note – there were no representations of humans or animals, strictly forbidden by the Quran, but flowers, plants, and geometric figures abound. One room, my favorite, "The Hall of Two Sisters" had it all. I don't think you can do justice to the place without photos, paintings or such. The "Patio de los Leones" and the exquisite (Mick seldom uses this word!) fountains, channels for flowing water with the musical sound (maybe the Baroque poet Luis de Góngora did get to me) were not to be forgotten. I took rolls and rolls of slides just in this place.

The "Tenerife" or gardens outside were impressive, the flowers and fountains beautiful, but it was the interior that I would remember. Mariah and I did sit on a bench in the gardens. They say many wedding proposals happen here. No wonder. It may have crossed our minds, but it did not

We finished that whirlwind day with a visit to another of the famous sites – the "Caves of Granada" in the Sacromonte Hill facing the Alhambra. This is where one can see "legitimate" gypsy flamenco. We sat with glasses of wine while watching and listening to the stomping of feet and swirling of dresses by the ladies, the voices of the "cantaores" and for me, the fantastic performance of flamenco guitar. For a tip during an interval, the main guitarist regaled us with "Recuerdos del Alhambra."

While I'm talking of music and dancing, how about a little poetry? One of Spain's most famous poets of the 20th century, Federico García Lorca, author of the famous (for Spanish majors) "Romance Sonámbulo" ["Verde, te quiero verde …"] was born in Fuente Vaqueros, a small town just a few miles from Granada; he wrote plays and poetry flavored with Gypsy culture and was killed by the Franco forces at the beginning of the Civil War (a fact disputed yet). We had just studied him at K.U. before traveling to Spain.

Enough! I could now leave Granada. Which is what we did the following morning, a final bus ride back to the largest city of Andalucía, Sevilla, unique in combining the three cultures, but with a definite Spanish flavor.

45

SEVILLA

As they say, there was no time to lose. We had programed two days of intense tourism in this place, not nearly enough to see it all, but a good introduction, especially since we had done our homework and knew exactly what we wanted to see. First things first. The original natives of Spain were known as Iberians, then Rome came, and then the Islamic Conquest in 712. As already briefly mentioned (and it's never enough) Sevilla first was under the rule of the Caliphate of Córdoba, than became an independent "Taifa" ruled by the Almoravids until Spain conquered it in 1248. It became the main port for Spain to the Americas after 1492, by virtue of being on the banks of the Guadalquivir River which would flow into the sea, and Spain controlled all ships, men and supplies to the New World and the riches (gold, silver, etc.) coming back through the "Casa de Contratación." It only diminished in importance when the Guadalquivir river silted up and commerce had to move to Cádiz closer to the coast.

What other tidbits can I mention? Miguel de Cervantes lived there for several years working first as a purchaser of goods for the Spanish Armada. He deposited crown funds in a bank in Sevilla and the bank failed. He ended in jail for the first time as a result. It is thought his great "Don Quixote" was engendered in that time in prison. He worked later as a tax collector for the crown. He may have fudged some on the accounts for he was thrown into jail again in 1597. One of the great ironies of Spanish

173

history came a bit later when he applied for a post in the Indies, but was turned down. Had he gone, no "Quixote!" One of his most delightful "small" novels **Rinconete y Cortadillo** takes place in Sevilla, the two young characters part of "el hampa" or criminal underworld. There is no doubt Cervantes based it on his own experience and the diverse "characters" he met in those years in Sevilla.

The "Archivo de Indias" [Archives of the Indies] is still the main library anywhere in the world for anything related to Spain and its discoveries in America. Many book - worn and thread – bare scholars (I mean the elbows and elbow patches on their woolen coats) hang out there.

The Cathedral had to be first on the list. It is said to be the largest cathedral (church with a bishop) in the world but is third in size behind St. Peter's in Rome and the Immaculate Conception in Washington, D.C. (technically not cathedrals). I don't remember the details, but it is huge, cavernous, 413 feet long, 138 feet high. Built in the 16th century, it is Gothic in style with one of those amazing carved stone Gothic entrances with dozens of carved figures, (One figures Christ, the Apostles, all the saints and angels, but not necessarily). I do not know. Mariah and I just sat on a bench in the interior and took it all in. Filled with gold gilt, the central altar (the "reredo") is a dizzying mass of niches with saints, all done in gold. The largest altar in Christendom! Folklore in Spain has the saying (I paraphrase) "We shall build a Cathedral so large they will say we are mad." Say no more!

One thing more in the cathedral impressed me: the larger than life size statues of the Kings of the four main provinces of Spain (Castilla, León, Navarra, Aragón) carrying the tomb of Christopher Columbus. I read he wanted to be buried in America, in the Dominican Republic, and was, but the bones were moved to Sevilla the end of 18th century. Several places claim him. Mariah said, "And this isn't even the main attraction!"

Related to the Cathedral is the impressive tall tower connected to it, the most famous of vestiges of the Moorish era, "La Giralda" (the name comes from a revolving weather vane on top, a bit prosaic I think). It dates back to the 12th century and Moslem times; it originally was a minaret, then of course was "redone" by the Spaniards in Arabic "Mudéjar" style. Supposedly, the nobility went to the top on horseback up the many inclined circles of the inside ramp, and they say Queen Isabella did as well! I guess for the view. Tourists however can make the rather steep, long walk. We did.

The third "must" place in Sevilla was in effect a huge complex of buildings called the "Alcázar." It is a series of makeovers – from the Romans to the Moslems to the Spanish Christians. One sees mainly the Arabic "Mudéjar" and Renaissance styles of the Spanish Golden Age. Palace built upon palace, it was the residence of the Arab rulers, then Pedro I (El Cruel) when Spain took control, later modified for the Catholic Kings (Fernando and Isabella), and then again for the Hapsburgs Carlos V and Felipe II, the great kings of Spain's Golden Age. It is easy to see how the Spaniards copied the "Mudéjar" style of Granada in all the halls, corridors, interior rooms, arches and patios. "Mocárabe" imitation - the use of stucco, and especially all the tile work is dazzling. And overwhelming. After viewing the final part of Carlos V, we called it quits. I did note that the modern monarchs of Spain (the Bourbon dynasty) still have a residence on its top floor.

At the end of that second day, we honestly needed a break; we were exhausted from the previous days of intense tourism. The temporary respite came the next morning in a modern express train from Sevilla to Madrid, saying goodbye to Andalucía, and bracing ourselves for the huge, modern, congested capital of Spain. Madrid. Luckily, Ben Palafox had a tip on a nice hotel near the Prado Art Museum and made a reservation for us. (It was the Ritz but with a discount Ben arranged, another medical connection.) It is 1965 and Spain is in the process of modernizing its transportation because of the huge influx of tourists. The train was pleasant and comfortable; we had a private compartment to ourselves where we dozed, watched the countryside go by, enjoyed a fine full "almuerzo" in the dining car and had conversation over our impressions so far in Spain. And then while working on a bottle of El Toro wine we summed up the South. Mariah went first.

Mariah confessed that she was basically overwhelmed with the immensity of what we had seen and tried to absorb the last few days. We talked a lot comparing Spain and our experience in Mexico the year before and both agreed on some basics. In one sense Mexico's churches and colonial edifices are the "poor cousin" of Spain (in spite of their gold gilt and statuary from European artists), although modeled on the great churches and in some cases using the same architects. Nothing unusual about that; after all, Mexico was a colony of Spain's. But the Pre-Columbian grandeur of Mexico, Guatemala and Honduras is without parallel. It is an amazing heritage of Mexico and they are right to be proud of it and base art and even politics on it.

However, the Arabic -Moslem contribution to Spain it seemed to us is equally important. We both agreed that Spain is fortunate today to have saved some major places and based much of its later Spanish heritage on it. Of course, that pretty much ended in the 17th century and on. We were looking forward to the next few days and a new chapter in "exploration." I did mention, in an unguarded moment, the incredibly romantic places we had visited and how wonderful it was to share them with her. Mariah said, "No matter what comes, we will always have those memories." That brought on some spooning in the private compartment!

46

ARRIVAL IN MADRID, THE PRADO AND ON TO TOLEDO

We arrived at the huge railway station in Madrid, the Atocha, and grabbed a taxi to the Ritz, just a few blocks away. What a great location, near the Plaza Mayor, the beautiful Plaza de Cibeles and the Correos Building, and most important the Prado Art Museum. The very next day in Madrid, after arriving late evening the night before, we marched ourselves to the most important place for the entire study of Spain, the Prado Art Museum. I said we could easily spend a week inside those long halls, huge salons and the annex with one painting – Picasso's "Guernica." One is overwhelmed and can be easily tired, and I can't begin to talk of it all here. Suffice to say, the Prado has a bit of everything – the Italian Renaissance, the masterpieces of Flanders (Rubens and others), this due to the fact Kings Carlos V and Felipe II were Hapsburgs and the crown was the successor of the Holy Roman Empire, thus including the Low Countries in addition to Spain.

For me the highlight had to be the "Golden Age" painters, El Greco, Ribera and Velázquez, then Goya of the 18th and 19 centuries, and of course Picasso in the 20th. The first were the ones closely linked to the literature I had studied in Spanish classes the last four years, the 16th and 17th centuries, and, no surprise, to the religious history of this "the most

Catholic country in the world" as someone said. El Greco's paintings of earth and heaven ("El Entierro del Conde Orgaz" – "Vista de Toledo"), Velazquez's down to earth realist paintings of commoners in Spain ("Los Borrachos"), of military battles and views of the Court ("Las Meninas"), Goya's caricatures of the nobility and then the dark days of Napoleon's conquest of Spain, and finally Picasso's "Guernica," the condemnation of evil and modern warfare in the bombing by the Axis of the town in northern Spain, but in a wild and almost incoherent modern style – all were before our soon to be weary eyes. The Spanish major and the young lady of Spanish roots were in "art heaven." And just an aside, the dark side of Spain, the Inquisition and the "Auto da Fé" or execution of those "unfaithful to the faith" was also there with Berruguete's "Auto da Fé." No photos were allowed but I purchased many slides for the classes back home.

I can't help it; I've got to tell my undergraduate Professor's joke about the modern Spaniards and religion. It seems an American protestant missionary knocks on the door of a traditional Spaniard and shows him her Bible and is he interested in being saved? The Spaniard, smoking a cigarette and with a glass of cognac in his hand says, "Lady, if I've got the True Religion and don't believe in it how in the hell do you expect me to believe in yours?"

And another anecdote of Spain character (the "True Religion," the "Most Catholic Country in the World"): Two Spaniards were arguing and could not agree on how a word was spelled. One says, "That's the way it's spelled in the Royal Academy of the Spanish Language Dictionary." The other Spaniard says, "Well, it's obvious. The dictionary is wrong." Ah, the Spirit of Spain!

Jokes like these are common in the Spanish speaking countries from Mexico south!

Late that day we went to a travel agency and arranged for the short bus trip and lodging for two full days in Toledo, no less important than anything already seen, a "jewel" of the total Spanish heritage. We were exhausted, to bed early and arising early for that bus to Toledo.

The intercity bus delivered us to the bus station on the outskirts of Toledo and we immediately took a taxi to the famous overlook where El Greco did his "View of Toledo." It looked much the same as the painting (there are many copies of the famous painting, one of which we saw among the dozens of El Greco's in the Prado), but without those looming storm clouds. We had a beautifully clear day. We probably spent one half hour at the view trying to identify landmarks in Toledo like the Military Alcázar bombed by Franco in the Spanish Civil War of 1936 – 1939 and of course the Cathedral the next stop.

We imagined real architecture "aficionados" could spend a couple of weeks in this place, the Cathedral. It is Gothic inspired, modeled in some ways on the Cathedral of Burgos in north central Spain, and compares to the huge church in Sevilla we already saw. I won't go on and on, but the reader can imagine a list of let's say, twenty different aspects that are famous. I'll just mention a few and give our impressions. First, the place is huge, not quite as large as Sevilla, but almost. It dates from 1085 shortly after King Alfonso VI took the city from the Moslems (he is contemporary to the stories of Spain's national hero El Cid). And of course, there is a long history: originally a Visigoth Cathedral in the 6th century was on the spot; it was converted into a major Mosque. King Alfonso had an agreement with the vanquished Moslems to maintain at least part of the mosque, but in his absence his wife and a Bishop obliterated the whole thing! Inside, the central altar ("Robledo") is very reminiscent of the one in Sevilla, a maze of statues, nooks, most in gold gilt, and with a huge "reja" or steel screen separating it from the rest of the church.

The stained glass is magnificent, second, they say, to the best in Spain at the Cathedral of León, on the "Way of Santiago." The carved wooden choir for the monks of late medieval times in itself tells much of the history of Spain, its battles, kings and clergy.

One final impressive object remains – the huge, gold and silver Monstrance called "The Monstrance of Arfe" (for its designer) was overwhelming and may I say outlandish! Some facts before I "vent."

The monstrance is traditionally used to house the Holy Eucharist during religious processions particularly during Holy Week, but mainly for the Benediction of the Blessed Sacrament (I told Mariah that I recalled many times as a teenage altar boy at St. Andrews in Abilene holding an incense boat or a candle alongside the priest in all his robes carrying a gold (I do not know if gold, gold plate or just gold colored metal) monstrance in the Benediction ceremonies generally on a Friday night in Lent.) This monstrance in Toledo (some say monstrosity) was commissioned by Cardinal Cisneros for the Cathedral from a famous German silversmith, Arfe. Wikipedia has it that he wanted something "better" than that of Queen Isabella. Arfe spent from 1517 to 1524 to complete it. It is designed to look like a Gothic Cathedral, is over 10 feet tall, made originally of pure silver and gilded with gold in 1595. Eighteen kilos of gold were used, 180 kilos of silver, at a cost of 15 million "maravedis" (the gold or silver coins of Spain at the time). It is under lock and key and bulletproof glass in the Cathedral and it taken out only for the Corpus Christi procession each year.

It is also said that it contains gold from the original Christopher Columbus trips to the New World. That's another matter. We do know that most of the gold and silver for two centuries or more was mined on the backs of Indians or black slaves and we do know that many churches are filled with gilded gold altars. None come up to Sevilla or Toledo!

Is there a rational defense for such things? I do not know, but there is an explanation. Traditional Catholic Thinking: if the tabernacle in a Roman Catholic Church houses Jesus in the communion host, and if the house of God on earth should be the most splendid possible, i.e. the church itself, does it not follow that when Jesus is carried in procession, that the monstrance be the same?, i.e. precious metal or the like. Whatever the belief, that is what we saw in Toledo, and we saw "lesser" versions in Sevilla, but not by much.

We both wondered what is the lesson we take home to the Spanish classes at the Juco? The riches of the world and the rich of the world are not and never have been limited to one country or people, but there is no doubt that the driving force for centuries in Spain was to expel the Moslems and build monuments to the True Faith, i.e. the splendor of the churches and cathedrals and the people at the top who ran them. The splendor of Moslem Spain was just as evident, but not in gold or silver; that only came with the massive discoveries and mines in the New World. The rich will decorate with riches.

We made a rather quick stop at the House-Museum of El Greco, mainly to see one famous painting, "El Entierro del Conde Orgaz" which the critics say capsulizes El Greco's view of this life and the one to come, earth and heaven. It was not disappointing, but we had to stand in line with others to see it.

One last tourist stop was a must! The "Sinagoga del Tránsito" Spain's most famous and most beautiful. The synagogue was founded by a particular Jewish gentleman who served the King and whose family had served the Spanish Kings for generations: Samuel ha - Levi Abulafia, this in 1356. It is surmised the Crown gave the Jews permission to build to make up for pogroms and past persecution. After the Jews were banished in 1492 it was converted, what else, into a Catholic church. More history: first given to the Spanish knights of Calatrava, then to the Benedictine Monks, it was even used for troops in the Napoleonic War. Today it is restored beautifully and is a museum. It is not complete but what you see makes you think you are back in the Alhambra! Nasrid stucco, arches and inscriptions in Hebrew praising the King and ha -Levi.

As we sat on a bench in the long, narrow and tall room I could tell Mariah was moved, the last of her heritage. She dabbed at her eyes with a kerchief, and just said, "Think what could have been!" I made sure to take several photos so we would have an accurate record of what we saw. I held her hand, saying nothing, and for a change, was patient until she stood up, lips moving in personal prayer, and then motioned for us to go.

It was late in the p.m. but we both were ready to say goodbye to Toledo, thinking that one day we would return to Spain and see many important places in the center and north like Ávila, Salamanca, Segovia, León and Santiago de Compostela. That would have to wait. We got the late afternoon bus back to Madrid and were in the hotel for evening drinks and a final dinner. We had reserved the TWA flight to New York the next morning and a late flight to Kansas City that night. We were exhausted emotionally and physically and both admitted rest at the Palafoxes for one or two nights and the quietness of Abilene were in order. Only later would we be able to sit back with our photos developed and realize what a huge chapter of Spain and Spanish was accomplished.

47

━━━◆━◆━◆━━━

TWA TO NEW YORK, AMERICAN TO KANSAS CITY TIME TO THINK AND PLAN

The Palafoxes and the O'Briens

On the long flight to New York before growing weary and getting just a little sleep I wrote more of the travel notes and we talked of what we had seen and the days to come. Mariah was sure her parents and brothers would want all the details from Spain, but that her parents would be more interested in our plans for the coming year, including the news from Abilene (meaning KKK news). We had been seeing each other and basically now were inseparable for two and one-half years. How long would that go on? Any announcements? And that included the curiosity from the O'Briens and relatives in Abilene. Mariah and I talked of this and asked ourselves the same questions on the flight. We had basically avoided the big question: if we were to "get serious," (ha!) what of the religious question?

It called for some good old-fashioned soul searching on both our parts. The good news is that both Mariah and I had evolved from the strict teachings of our respective faiths. In Mariah's case it was not so difficult simply because the Palafoxes had now hundreds of years to evolve to their ethnic and religious practices in the 20th century and had chosen the route

183

of less religion and more spirituality. Out of necessity. I learned one can be ethnically Jewish and not necessarily religiously Jewish. In my case, it was not so cut and dried. The fact of the matter is that education and seeing some of the world does indeed affect such things. Perspective it's called. Catholicism was so deep rooted in me, much of it customs and memory of growing up for fifteen years practicing it (not necessarily by own will). On the other hand, I had examined many of the notions of the faith, the church, its practices and seen that I could not accept some of them as outmoded, sometimes fairy-tale notions and some contrived by clergy and not by Jesus. I was sure about God, but not so sure about some other things. Did I think that background, religion and ethnicity would keep me and Mariah apart and from loving each other? Absolutely not. So there you have it.

Ben and Ariel met us at the airport in Kansas City, Missouri and drove us immediately to the house. We were exhausted but had part of the afternoon to fill them in on all we saw. Ben was exceptionally happy we saw the Andalucía highlights and the synagogues, and we raved about the Tránsito Synagogue of Toledo, the Alhambra, and the cathedrals in Sevilla and Toledo, and of course, the Prado. As a back home treat we returned to that terrific deli in the Plaza, had the huge pastrami sandwiches, pickle, an icy beer to wash it down, and of course cheesecake. It was to bed early that evening, still with jet lag, and a conversation at breakfast the following morning. Over more than one cup of coffee we basically told Ben and Ariel what we would be doing this next year, classes, otherwise, business as usual. Ben wondered if this would be our last year at the Juco and if we were doing any thinking about graduate school, finishing the M.A. and maybe more. Basically we said, "We'll let you know." We packed up, said goodbyes and drove back to Abilene.

After unloading the stuff we drove out to Mom and Dad's that p.m. for a wonderful reunion. Mom wanted to cook dinner but we asked for a raincheck – fried chicken on Sunday – and we spent two hours going over the trip once more, and then plans at the Juco, once more again. We were both anxious to know any news in Abilene, not mentioning specifically the past troubles, but expecting anything. Fortunately, things had been totally quiet along that line, a regular, busy Abilene farm summer. Dad at the vegetable garden, Ron and Stan in the farm feedlot or out in the fields. It had been a good year for wheat, no weather problems so a big harvest and decent prices, and three good crops of alfalfa. With more rain than usual, it looked like there might even be a corn crop in the dry-land farm acreage as well as the irrigated bottom land. Mom was feeling good, had an amazing flower garden out back and Caitlin was busy with the kids.

So promising the following Sunday visit (me at mass with Mom and Dad) and dinner later, we begged off and went home to catch up on work. We would report in to the Juco on Monday, see any developments or changes in plan and then full speed ahead for classes in September. Small town routine and no surprises was okay.

48

TIME MOVES ON

Monday morning up at the Juco brought routine and as hoped, no surprises. Good. I had the usual two Spanish classes, 101 and 201 and Western Civilization - History. Mariah was back to English 101, two sections (ugh, lots of papers and grading) and one Introduction to American Literature Course. Because it had worked out so well last year, Mariah began the process of setting up plans for the big school's visits, one-day jaunts with interested students from her classes in the Juco van to Manhattan, Lawrence and Emporia. She would show them the campuses, visit a class or two and generally try to raise enthusiasm to apply for college acceptance, scholarships, other financial help to continue their education. What was new is that Dean Halderson thought I could do the same thing for my Spanish and History students.

The more students who went on to four-year schools, the better for the Juco. We both had to work with the guidance counselors and registrar to check realistic possibilities, i.e. student grades, progress reports. But we knew from everyday work in the classroom who was a most likely candidate. No less than ten of Mariah's students from the previous year were now in the big schools, almost all on partial scholarship or financial aid, mainly thanks to her! We would not start the visitation trips until October, both of us actually going the same day, but in separate school vans. It means less disruption in the long run. Wednesdays turned out to be best, more people on the big campuses. It involved a passel of phone calls to set it up, but all worth it. The big schools were always "on the make" to increase their own enrollment, particularly the Spanish sections, and were generally glad to have us. We were the only Juco in the state to do this. Colleagues in Abilene I think were a bit envious and asked how we did it. I said, "It came to me as in a dream" (recalling a quote from a Mayan weaver when asked where her patterns came from!). We laughed, maybe not loudest, but last.

Meanwhile September and Fall were moving along in Abilene. That meant football for the high school where we were regulars at the Friday night games and saw lots of friends, a good corn harvest and trucks down to the grain elevators, regular visits to Mom and Dad and out to the farm. In another month or two it would be the Turkey Shoot out south of town. Mariah and I went over to Salina to the supper club about once a month, dined and danced and happily made our way home. We dared once again to go down to Frank's Friendly Tavern where sure enough Wally Galatin invited us for beers and wanted to know all about Spain (he had heard we did that trip). In turn I wanted to catch up on the progress of his Eisenhower – Abilene Photo Book. "Coming along, coming along," was about all we got out of him.

About the same on my Abilene history research. In truth it was winding down, having hit the high spots the last two years, all reported faithfully in these pages. You may be seeing a little restlessness moving in, both for me and Mariah. Abilene wasn't getting any bigger, so it really came down to a matter of routine. I can say we both were working very hard up at the Juco, preparing for classes, me digging harder for material for the lectures on the European History Class, Mariah teaching basic English and up to her ears in grading papers. We had another fun night at the Gomezes, more of that good Mexican food, Dos Equis beer and singing Mexican songs with me on the guitar. Timmy was now in one of my Spanish classes, getting over his shyness to speak Spanish and Mariela was a star of the more advanced class. Mariah reported both were challenged and working hard in her English classes.

Mariah admitted to spending time in the school library, looking at college catalogues, not only for her students but for herself. The University of Missouri in Colombia offered a great course in journalism, one of her special interests, but higher up on that ladder was Columbia in New York. And both Yale and Harvard English programs were tops! And she still thought of Law with her idealistic bent of getting involved in legal aid for minorities. And we both talked some of the Peace Corps.

The national government, after Sputnik back in 1957, admitted there was a knowledge race as well as a space race and instituted the National Defense Education Act to train qualified folks for the Ph.D. in "critical language areas," ostensibly to catch up with the Russians who were establishing "centers of interest" all over the globe. The program fit my interests perfectly, Spanish and Portuguese for Brazil, both languages on the "critical" list. All the top universities were participating and offering grants for full rides for their chosen candidates – Harvard, Yale, Columbia, Stanford, Berkeley, Texas and even a couple of Jesuit schools – Saint Louis and Georgetown. I was sure my undergraduate Spanish teacher would still write a glowing letter of recommendation, and the Juco work would be in my favor. I wasn't ready to get out the typewriter and make applications just yet, but it was a main topic of conversation for Mariah and me.

We figured that public relations work at the Kansas big schools would not do any harm either for impressing admittance and grant committees, although that was not at all on our minds when we first thought of it and planned it. Honestly, it was mainly to do some good for Spanish and English enrollment by small school kids to move up with more chances at the big schools.

That left that other topic of conversation – us! I think we were both afraid to tackle that one. It got tabled, like "motion tabled" in 4-H club model meetings. Not that we were not getting along well, we were. It just seemed different.

49

ALL BETS ARE OFF

Early that October I was down at the Eisenhower Library, still checking out sources on Ike playing baseball at Abilene High School and looking for that famous picture I had seen but now could not locate – the one where he is in uniform with all the team in front of the old high school (the Junior High when I was in school). I was running late, but was having a fine conversation with Don Winston the library research director about my research and the library's latest holdings. Everyone on staff had left, but he being a bigwig said to relax and he'd let me out the front door when we finished. (Even with a presidential library, Abilene is still a small town with small town ways.) He said he was staying behind to catch up on paper work.

I walked out of the library at about 6:00 o'clock; closing time was 5:00 p.m. I was walking to my car in the parking lot north of the library and west of the Eisenhower Museum when I noticed the entire lot was empty except for a large green van parked at the far east end close to the sidewalk going into the museum. Out of curiosity I walked over to it, wondering if it had a flat tire or something (ever the Good Samaritan; my Spanish teacher in college used to kid I would get stabbed with an umbrella by an old lady I was helping to cross the street!) There was a guy in the driver's seat dressed in farmer's blue bibbed overalls. He saw me, gave the okay sign with thumb and forefinger, so I turned around and was walking to my car when a pickup came down Buckeye and turned into the parking lot, a used but fairly new Chevy. It waited for me to pull out giving me the right of way which I did, but glanced back and saw the truck had mud smeared on the license plate. Something clicked or rang a bell I don't know what. Like an idiot I turned around and pulled up beside the driver's window and rolled down my window and asked "Sorry to bother you. Just wondered if anybody needed anything. I've got a jack and jumper cables in my trunk." He said, "Naw. I'm just meeting my friend here and we're deciding where to go for dinner. Thanks anyway." "Fine," I said, "good deal, just checking."

The sheriff's office was just three blocks north and something made me think I better tell somebody, maybe Sheriff Wiley, about what I'd seen. The minute I ran into his office he said, "Thanks Mick, I'd better check it out, maybe it would be a good idea if you rode along with me and could identify the vehicles. We don't see many vehicles parked after visiting hours at the Eisenhower Center. Do me a favor, grab that 357 out of your glove compartment just in case. But keep it on the floorboard out of sight. We'll take my patrol car, but I'll let the deputy know where we're going."

We drove down Buckeye, across the Santa Fe tracks and saw that the pickup and van were still there, with the motor running in the truck. As we pulled in Joe Weston the Museum night guard was walking down the sidewalk out of the Museum Entrance toward the lot, probably beginning his night rounds and checking the lot. Everything happened so quick at that point, it was a blur.

Joe walked up to the driver's side window of the pickup, and was leaning in saying something, probably asking the driver what was going on, and the guy from the van came from behind and knocked him on the head with the butt of a big pistol. Joe fell and the van driver jumped in the front seat of the pickup and it burned rubber, swerving around us on the way in. Wiley yelled "Damn!" and peeled out after them. We were about four blocks down Buckeye by the John Deere Implement Company toward the river, Wiley just getting on his radio to alert the office about Joe when we heard and felt the explosion. Wiley got on his radio, saying to me to his side in the front seat, "We got no time for the museum now;" he called an "Emergency - All Cars" to go to the museum. We found out later it was too little and too late.

He kept on the radio, saying "We're in pursuit of a 1963 Chevy pickup. Dark blue, no license plate numbers visible. Two men in front seat, probably armed. Put out an 'Emergency - All cars' to the Highway Patrol for Highway 15 south of the river, heading south." The patrol car was "hotter" than the pickup so although they were pushing 90 miles per hour, we were just tailing them, not too close. Wiley said, "I hope to hell no one is coming up over the hill." (I didn't get a chance to say before, Highway 15 is a narrow, hilly two lane with no shoulders.) He was one cool customer; I'd never seen him in such a situation. He said, "There will be a roadblock down the road pretty quick." There were no police in Rural Center eight miles south of town, but there were in Hillsboro about 15 miles down the road. And by this time state troopers from Salina and even Newton would have been notified and be heading our way. And police planes as well.

About four miles south of town on K-15, the Chevy suddenly hit the brakes, tires squealing and burning smoke and swerved onto a gravel country road heading west. Wiley slowed down, made the turn and kept them in sight. It was hilly country and the road was gravel, recently graded so in pretty good shape, a huge cloud of dust ahead of us. I don't know what they were thinking, but the car pulled off onto a section road two miles ahead and stopped. We pulled in behind at a distance. Sheriff Wiley had his speaker phone on and said, "Get out of the car, no weapons, hands up, and no one will get hurt." He was answered with bullets from a rifle, one breaking the front windshield, another whizzing over us. Wiley yelled to me, "Mick get down! I don't know why in hell I allowed you to come along, Damned well don't want you to get hurt." That was when I took the 357 out of the holster.

One of the men yelled, "There's more of that coming shitheads. Back up, let us by, and there'll be no more trouble." Wiley answered, "The

Highway Patrol, my deputies and the Abilene police will be here in a couple of minutes and they won't stop and talk like me. Go ahead and do as I say. Get out of the car, hands up, and no more crap! It looked like they had wised up and were going to follow orders. The two men got out of the car, dropped a rifle and with hands up, stood in front of the car. Sheriff Wiley got out, a shotgun in his left arm and hand pointed right at them and the holster strap loosened for his 357. He slowly walked forward, keeping an eye on both of them, saying, "Stay put and lie down on the ground." At that moment, one reached behind his back, pulled out a pistol and fired it at the sheriff, hitting the arm holding the shotgun. It was then I jumped out of the car with my pistol, shielded some by the car door, and fired as many shots as fast as I could pull the trigger, luckily hitting the man with the gun in the shoulder making him drop the gun, and me yelling to the other one, "Freeze, don't try to pick that f****** gun up." Wiley had recovered partially, a pistol in his good hand and said "Mick, walk up slowly and cover me." He kicked the pistol away from the wounded guy on the ground and when the other one made a motion to get up slammed him in the side of the head with his own pistol, knocking him to the ground.

So now the Sheriff was standing over the two fallen thugs, his left arm bleeding like crazy, but still with the big heavy duty 357 in his right. I had my pistol aimed at the heads of both on the ground. Soon there were sirens, and three Highway Patrol cars roared into the intersection, men jumped out, armed to the teeth, and Wiley just said, "Glad you're here, can you cuff these bastards?" It was then I started shaking all over and had to vomit. Wiley said, "Damn Mick, can't you take a little excitement? Just kidding son. I think maybe you saved our lives. Maybe that time out at the Turkey Shoot last year wasn't wasted after all." I said, "Sheriff it was blind luck, I didn't know what I was doing, Just adrenalin. I just aimed and kept pulling the trigger. Thank God I had it pointed in the right direction."

An Abilene Memorial Hospital ambulance roared in at that moment. Two guys jumped out, saw Wiley and said, "Damn, Sheriff, seems you can't stay out of trouble these days." They saw his bloody arm and said,

"Hold on. We'll get you to the hospital and fix you up right away." They put him into the ambulance and he said, "I'm not sure what shape Mick is in; better bring him along." The thugs weren't treated so kindly; both were already cuffed and were now frisked and pushed into the back of a patrol car with bars separating the back from front seat. A deputy climbed into the back with a shotgun trained on the two killers, one of them obviously in pain. The car wheeled around and headed back toward Abilene, I guess to the hospital.

Our ambulance got into town first and was heading up Buckeye, but not before we passed the Eisenhower parking lot and saw all the devastation. It looked like a war zone, ambulances from Salina and Junction City, police and highway patrol cars, and officers stretching yellow tape on all the perimeters of the Museum parking lot. Wiley told our guy to stop, an officer came up and said, "Sheriff it's all under control." Seeing Wiley's bloody, bandage wrapped arm, "You better take care of yourself first and then we'll see about all this." Wiley said, "Where's Joe? What's happened with him?" The officer got quiet for a moment and said, "Sheriff, he didn't have a chance. With the explosion we just found body parts. I'll come right up to the hospital and fill you in." Wiley wanted to stay but he was still bleeding profusely. One of the guys in the Hospital emergency team with a white uniform on jammed a needle into his arm saying, "Sheriff, you'll be glad for this later." Whatever the stuff in the needle was, Wiley had to sit down in the ambulance and nodded, "Okay, get us fixed up. And Mick here too."

They were waiting at the emergency entrance, two gurneys, guys in hospital green to the side, two nurses beside them. They took sheriff Wiley first, saying "Sheriff, just be quiet for a change; this isn't the jail and you aren't in charge! You're going right to emergency and we'll take care of that arm." I said I was fine, but they said, "Lie down." A nurse poked a needle in my arm and all of sudden I was woozy, just remembering I was being rolled into a room that was all white. They helped me out of my clothes, put me in one of those damned hospital gowns, said to lie down. I was semi-conscious but woozy; they were taking blood pressure and then ole Doc Bernard. came in with a stethoscope, smiled and said, "Mick we've done this before. Didn't plan on seeing you back so soon." He did all the usual, blood pressure, checked the heart, looked down my ears, nose, throat (like the good G.P. he had been for forty years) and said, after you get rested, you'll be as good as new in 24 hours."

Time must have passed. They had patched up Sheriff Wiley's arm, all wrapped and in a big bandage and in a sling. He came into my room, said, "Why don't us cripples drive on down to the Museum and get the low down? Doc Bernard says as long as you don't move too quickly and try to run around, you'll be okay." I smiled and said, "Now that we are partners in crime prevention, or sort of, that sounds good to me, but I have to make a couple of phone calls first, to Mom and Dad and to Mariah." I made both from the room, assured them I was all right (they had no news of what really happened, just gossip and all citizens were urged to remain at home the remainder of the day). I said I would be with Sheriff Wiley for about an hour and then come by. My car was parked at the sheriff's office, and I saw later with no damage but a layer of dust, powder, I'm not sure what all, on top.

We climbed into the patrol car, a deputy driving and drove straight down to the bomb scene. The law officers, deputies, police and highway patrol all gradually came up to Wiley, asked how he was, congratulated him on the quick thinking and good work with the whole episode. And everyone had heard the story. They all came up, shook my hand or patted me on the shoulder and said stuff like "Son, you ever need a job other than teaching, you've got one. No paperwork, we'll sign you up, fit you out in a uniform, pin a badge on and make that 357 legal (ha, ha, ha). But you start at the bottom, maybe "patrolman" but not sergeant! And we'll get you out to the gun range." One of the deputies came up, handed me my 357 and looking at Wiley and me said, "Mick, that gun was empty." Wiley looked at me and winked, "Best part of poker is bluffing." I had to go sit in the squad car until my knees stopped knocking.

The scene was worse than I had imagined. The west wall of the museum was crumbled, you could see part of that room where Ike's WWII jeep was parked, broken bricks all around (there was no glass on that wall). The entire north side of the old Eisenhower Home was in pieces, clap board everywhere, all of it scorched by the blast. The front of St. Andrew's across the street was intact mainly because it was of brick but the two entrance doors had been blown apart. The most unbelievable were the Santa Fe tracks directly north of the parking lot, the rails were actually bent from the heat of the blast. The Depot, a way west of the intersection, also of brick, had its windows blown out. And all the houses which fortunately were two blocks north of the tracks had windows blasted. To the south and southwest the damage was fortunately limited, the concussion of the blast going to the east and north mainly, and some to the west. The library could count its blessings being so far to the south of the museum.

Most amazing was no serious injuries were reported, just a few folks with cuts from blown glass, and incredibly no cars had been on Buckeye at the time of the immediate blast. The one truly sad fact was the death of Joe Weston the night watchman. In coming days he would be labeled a hero and the Eisenhower foundation guaranteed that part of his employment had been a sizable insurance policy (required of all employees) that would be available for his wife and family. Joe was near retirement and their two children were raised and living other towns. The Foundation added that its own insurance would supplement that policy. I'm saving more details from the special issue of the Reflector Chronicle that was rushed out the next day.

The call was out to state and even national law enforcement agencies (the Eisenhower Center was considered part of the national patrimony, thus under the federal umbrella as well). That meant forensics people from Topeka (the KBI) had already arrived on the scene and agents from the ATF would be in that night and early the next morning. There were people in the dark blue uniforms of the KBI scouring the entire area with all kinds of devices. One very odd thing, there was an acrid smell all through the area, from the explosion itself, the ensuing fire. Any farm boy could recognize it, the smell of farm fertilizer.

A little less shaky, I asked the sheriff to drive me back to the office where I made phone calls to Mom and Dad and Mariah, and arranged to pick up Mariah and drive out to the house on Rogers. When I picked her up at her apartment Mariah just hugged me for a long time, kissing my face and neck and saying, "Thank God you are all right. Rumors are flying all around; people are calling me. God, I was sick with worry. I knew you were down at the library, but there was no news, nothing, from anybody. I was so relieved when you called. Mick, I don't know how much more of this I can take, for me, but for sure, not for you." I said, "Mariah, I called as soon as I could and got here as soon too. Please bear with me and get in the car. We've got to go out to Mom and Dad's. I'll fill you in some, but we'll sit down out there and I can tell the whole thing all at once." She didn't argue, grabbed a jacket and said, "I just thought, have you had anything to eat? It must be at least since lunch and it's 9:00."

"I'll bet Mom has some soup or whatever, I'll get by."

We drove down Buckeye and out west on 3rd to Mom and Dad's house, parked in the driveway and then walked up the front door steps where Dad saw us first and yelled, "Molly, they're here." Dad never was much on hugging and all that since I was grown up but he put his arms around me saying, "Mick, I love you; I'm so glad you're in one piece." Mom rushed up, hugged me as well, in tears, and said, "Oh Mick thank God you are all right. The worst is we had no idea where you were and that you were involved in all this. We know you go down to the library sometimes but didn't know anything about today." Just then the phone rang, it was Caitlin saying Ron had talked to Sheriff Wiley (both Knights of Columbus at church and close friends) and got a quick version of what happened. Was I all right? I said "Yes, Cait, a little worse for wear but I was luckier than Wiley. I'll tell you all about it in a day or two." "No, we're driving in right now; we'll see you in a few minutes."

"Okay."

50

EXPLANATIONS

Mariah spoke up, "Mrs. O'Brien, Mick hasn't had anything to eat since noon. Can I help you rustle up something?" Mom said, "Sure. I guess toasted cheese sandwiches and tomato soup would be the quickest." We all sat around the dining room table, Ron and Caitlin walked in, Ron winking at me, "Wiley told me all about it. Let's see if your story holds water." And laughed.

After a bit of food fortification, Dad did something unusual. He keeps a pint bottle of Old Granddad in the hallway closet that he gets out maybe twice a year; he pulled it out of the closet and said, "Those that want, I'll join you." We did, Ron, Mariah and me, that is; Mom and Caitlin had a glass of Mom's stash, Mogen David cooking wine, I think. Everyone got quiet and Ron said, "Go ahead, we're all ears."

"First of all, we should all bow our heads and say a prayer to St. Christopher or maybe St. Michael for me just being okay right now. Before I get into it, I understand the entire issue of the "Reflector" tomorrow morning will be dealing with all this, and I suspect they will have information I don't have now. Here's the short version (I repeated most of what I've already written here):

"I was down at the Eisenhower Library working on my research, talking to Don Winston, and left at 6:00 to go to the car. I saw a green van parked close to the east end of the Eisenhower Center lot, checked to see if there were any flats, got an "We're okay" sign from the driver and was heading out of the lot home when a pickup pulled in, heading for the van. I noticed the license plate was smeared with mud, something clicked and I figured I better notify Sheriff Wiley.

"I did, and he said we'd better check on it, I could go along and identify the vehicles. Why he wanted me to have my 357 I don't know, but he did, asking me to get it from my car and put it on the floorboard of the patrol car, and take it out of its holster. We drove back to the parking lot and Joe Weston the night watchman was in the process of checking on the van and pickup. That's when the van driver decked him, got in the pickup, and they peeled out of the lot in front of us. Wiley took off after them, me hanging on for dear life, him in the process of radioing an "All Cars" to the parking lot to check on Joe and us in hot pursuit of the pickup. Just then we heard and felt the concussion of the explosion. Wiley said, "No time for that. I'll call it in." We then were tearing down old south 15, he on the radio for "All Cars" for any law enforcement in the area. Wiley pursued the pickup to a section intersection west of 15 and that's when all hell broke loose. He put on the speaker phone, told them to get out of the truck, hands up, no weapons. They shot at us, he gave another warning for them to drop their guns and stand in front of their truck, they got out of the truck, dropped a rifle, but then one of them pulled a pistol and shot Wiley in the arm he was holding his own shotgun.

"That's when something happened again, a lot like back in '57 when I was on the tractor and the bank robbers showed up. Adrenalin, I don't know what. I grabbed the 357 from the floorboard and stepped out (the open door blocked me from view) and shot it as many times as I could at the guy holding the pistol. That's when somebody, some saint or guardian angel must have stepped in. I hit the shooter in the shoulder, he dropped the gun and both men were on the ground. Wiley had his own revolver in his right hand, took over and asked me to keep them covered. Help arrived soon, we were put in the ambulance back to the hospital, but with Wiley wanting to stop to check the explosion scene. The deputy said it was all under control and packed us off to the hospital. They bandaged up Wiley, gave me a sedative and he insisted I go with him back to the explosion scene. That's when we got all the bad news, about Joe Weston, all the damage, and the KBI and feds from the ATF either on the scene or on their way. That's when I was driven to my car at the jail, called you and picked up Mariah and here we are."

Everyone was pretty quiet for a bit. I downed my slug of whiskey and probably had a weary look on my face. "Hey folks, I've got to get to bed. We've got classes tomorrow." Ron got up, motioned to Caitlin for them to leave and said, "I'll see you at the Turkey Shoot out at the river farm. Get your shooting iron on and this time we'll be betting to see who's better." He heehawed. Caitlin, old 'sis of mine, hugged me and said to Mariah, "Take care of this guy and see he gets home okay and gets some rest." Dad and Mom hugged me again, and hugged Mariah as well, "Mick, you're in good hands. I guess we'll talk again tomorrow, for sure after the paper comes out."

I did something different that night, bunking at Mariah's and sharing her bed (no sex but none requested, just comfort). She said, "Let the tongues wag. Truth wins out. I am so glad I am loved by such a brave and crazy guy." I thought of her parents (the news would be national, in all the papers and the morning TV news). She said she would give them a short call, fill them in, tell them we are all okay and would talk more tomorrow and for me to go to bed "like a good goy (or boy)" and she laughed. It must have been the accumulation of it all, including the sedatives because I conked out the minute my head hit the pillow.

The next morning it was routine as usual, or almost usual. At the juco Dr. Halderson and then colleagues all came up, asking if I was okay. They all had some version of what happened, but not necessarily accurate. I did not have the time or really the inclination to go into it all then, but assured them the real hero in all this was Joe Weston and then Sheriff Wiley. Anything I did was just pure luck. I said the same thing to all of them, that the "Reflector" would have more details that p.m.

It came out with a huge headline,

EISENHOWER CENTER BOMBED BY EXTREMISTS
JOE WESTON KILLED

There were vivid pictures of the explosion scene on the front page, an account by Sheriff Wiley of all that happened (including Mick O'Brien's role), and that it was being treated as a national crime scene with the ATF and now the FBI investigating. As soon as more information becomes available, Sheriff Wiley will let us know. He added the suspects (I love that legal term) were at present in the county jail under heavy guard and suicide watch pending arraignment. That would be complicated since it was now a federal case.

The "Republic" then raved and vented on the editorial page:

> *There is no need to rehash our past articles from the last six years regarding the vandalism and crime in Abilene by members of rugged individualist groups, white separatist groups or of the KKK. Nor is it necessary to repeat details of victims brought to trial and their punishment. Yesterday's event far surpasses any of that.*

> *The attack on the Eisenhower Museum, the explosion, the death of our dear hometown friend Joe Weston, the subsequent wounding of Sheriff Wiley and the heroic efforts of Mr. Wiley and local Juco Teacher Michael O'Brien are all on our minds today. We can only be grateful things were not worse. Good fortune was that no one else was in the near vicinity and no vehicles at that time were on Buckeye when the explosion took place. The KBI and ATF agents are still canvasing the crime scene. Museum officials state that once the "all clear" is given, immediate repair of the west wall of the Museum will begin and the Museum will re-open as soon as possible.*

> *Our concern is simple: What next?*

Speaking for the entire community we demand first of all information: Who did this? Why? Are we as a community safe? What is being done?

We assume all law enforcement groups, the Abilene Police Department, the Dickinson County Sheriff's Department, the Kansas Bureau of Investigation and now the Federal Alcohol-Tobacco-Firearm Task Force and the FBI will be forthcoming as soon as possible with information to quell our fears. Make that a capital FEARS.

The Editor and Editorial Staff

51

MORE DEVELOPMENTS

Because the bombing was at a Presidential Museum, part of the Presidential Library System, it came under the federal umbrella. Arraignment and trial would be in the Kansas District Court in Wichita. However, Dickinson County, the County Seat, Abilene, with local jurisdiction, would handle pre-trail investigation. It was anticipated the prisoners would be transferred at some point to federal facilities in Wichita. This time it would be the full works, court trial by jury. And with the national media present.

Information was slow in coming, I guess because the law enforcement agencies wanted to have all the facts in order, no leaks to the press that might damage the case. But it's a small town and gossip was rampant. I might as well go ahead and say it, my phone and of course Sheriff Wiley's were ringing off the hook with requests for interviews, the big papers in Topeka and Wichita and the "Kansas City Star." Later even the "New York Times" and reporters from the three major TV networks wanted statements. I was advised by Sheriff Wiley that he wanted to be present at all interviews, to let him take the lead, this because we had to be careful legally to not accidentally say anything to prejudice the case. This was not a "prima donna" move, just being intelligent based on years of experience. So that is what happened, interviews basically repeating what I've already said, the sequence of events from the discovery in the parking lot to the scene at the hospital.

Wiley, a good friend of the family and now as he joked with my joke, "a cohort in crime prevention," did have a couple of private conversations with me. He said we were right in smelling the fertilizer; "It's ammonium nitrate the same stuff farmers spread on their fields before planting. And it can be useful in making a bomb. The ATF is gathering all the information, anticipating the trial. I'm sure though that the planning took knowledge of making bombs in the military; we will only know more as the 'suspects' are questioned. The public will not be present for that, at least not until a trial."

There's no need to get into all the details, and I'm not sure I would either remember them or get them straight. The intricacies of the Law are not my forte. A different case for Mariah (still thinking about Pre - Law and Law School), she followed it all, was present with me when I was asked to give testimony at the local courthouse and then sitting in the audience in the actual trial in Wichita. The "suspects" pleaded "not guilty," the s.o.b.s. Lawyers for the prosecution and defense did their interviews, but no public statements and the ATF and KBI reported their findings only to the proper officials. It all culminated in the trial in late November in the district court in Wichita.

Like I say, I'm fuzzy on details. The courtroom was jammed however as the squeaky wheels of the Law turned. A million dollars bond had been set; the prisoners ensconced in the federal facility in Wichita. They were present at the arraignment, then the long process of jury selection took place, the lawyers having a hard time finding twelve people who had not read of the bombing, much less being neutral about it. Kansas being a high leaded religious state managed to produce twelve jurors the lawyers expected to be good citizens and honest. Reporters were not allowed in the courtroom with cameras or recorders, but some did sketches of the participants that appeared in the papers and even TV the next day (CBS, NBC and ABC all had crews present).

The prosecution brought in reams of items: enlarged photos of the damage at the bomb scene and just as important the findings of the forensic people (I'll talk about that in a minute). Many participants and witnesses were called, Sheriff Wiley, myself, other law officers and ambulance drivers and even hospital staff. When they called on the two suspects, both again (with instruction from their lawyers) pleaded "not guilty" and refused to answer the prosecuting attorney's questions. That left him to present his case with the photos, testimony and ATF report.

The reporters hungry for details reported it all. It was astounding to me all that the forensic people found and their conclusions. All was from bits and pieces, some up to a foot in size, some miniscule, but here is my understanding, flawed probably, of how the criminals put the bomb together (accurate reporting is in the newspapers). They would mix, solder, and go through many procedures I don't even begin to understand. The basics were several bags of ammonium sulphate, small amounts of liquid nitro methane, tubes and fuses, spools of shock tube, and finally blasting caps. The whole thing was packed into four barrels in the back of the van and set to go off with a timer (that was why they were in such a hurry to get out of the parking lot and why we heard the explosion just minutes later as we chased the pickup south out of town). Pieces of all this stuff were found.

More important to all of us was the motive. The prosecution had done their homework: both men were former U.S. Army soldiers, one of them with a dishonorable discharge for insubordination, the other out after serving his term, this just one year ago. They got to know each other in the Army, found they had similar interests, and moved up to Idaho, both doing construction jobs near Coeur d'Alene. What was key was that one of them had been trained in demolition. They were not KKK, at least not initially, but did meet individuals from the original KKK group once living west of Abilene and now living in a compound out in the country east of Coeur d'Alene. They came into contact with them when the group was building a big barn and granary with a tool shed attached and they were hired to help put it together. More would come out on that at the end of the trial. The law, amazing once more, traced the purchase of both the pickup and the van to a used vehicle lot in Boise, and the purchase of the fertilizer at a

Farm Coop in the same town. That would raise no questions; it was a small amount, just what you might use on a good-sized truck farm. The other bomb makings were a different deal, most stolen from a Martin Marietta Quarry outside of Ogden, Utah.

It only took three days to present all the evidence, call all the witnesses and take final statements from the two sides, prosecution and defense, the latter a weak statement from the suspects that they had been surprised by Sheriff Wiley, falsely accused of loitering, and when driving from the scene, were once again falsely stopped and defending themselves when the Sheriff pulled a gun. All a pack of lies and not believed by anyone seeing all the prosecution's evidence. The jury was out two hours and came back with a "guilty as charged" to the judge. Oh, the charges were malicious intent for property damage and destruction to a federal building, second degree murder of Joe Weston, and fleeing the scene of the crime. The fireworks came when the judge announced the sentencing.

You've got to remember this was a **federal** case and with the death of a federal employee. That amplified everything. Plus, the possibilities of what the bombing might have done under worse, unlucky circumstances (brought out by the prosecution, i.e. employees still on duty in the Museum and chance passersby in cars on Buckeye). The federal judge, not one to put up with any nonsense and correctly understanding the gravity of the act, asked for a final statement from the suspects before he pronounced sentencing. When they stood up and protested their innocence, but with no further details, the judge said, "Life Imprisonment at the United States Penitentiary at Leavenworth, Kansas. No bail or early dismissal or any other efforts to reduce the sentence. The prisoners will be immediately transferred to Leavenworth. Court closed and dismissed."

Suddenly one of the prisoners, shackled and in orange prison garb, stood up and shouted, "We won't forget this and we've got friends. This country's going to hell in a handbasket and we and people like us won't let you assholes in the government run all over us anymore." He and his buddy were escorted, that's a nice word, dragged from the room. There was all kinds of murmuring by the crowd, sighs of relief, words like "They got what was coming to them" and "Good riddance." But unsaid, and I'm sure on everyone's minds was "What friends? Who and where are the 'people like us?'" That would all be clarified, slowly but surely, in coming days.

It came in the form of an "Open Letter to the Citizens of Abilene and Dickinson County" printed in the "Reflector Chronicle" the week following the trial:

OPEN LETTER TO THE CITIZENS OF ABILENE AND DICKINSON COUNTY

This is a joint communiqué from the Kansas Bureau of Investigation, the Bureau of Alcohol, Tobacco, Firearms and Explosives of the United States Government, and the FBI. We are informing you that the criminals responsible for the recent bombing incident at the Eisenhower Complex are in the Federal Prison at Leavenworth in Kansas serving life sentences – no parole.

Secondly, the AFT has done extensive research in the State of Idaho, has identified the place of residence of the criminals while in Idaho, has contacted all possible connections to them in that State, and we are positive the two acted alone. In addition, we want you to know that the ATF and the FBI have been canvasing this area for some time, we have complete documented files on any possible separatists, individualists, survivalists or even KKK activity in the area. All are under constant surveillance and we can report with confidence that they are of no danger to other U.S. citizens. We send our condolences to all of you in Abilene but once again wish to assure you that all is well. And we commend your local law enforcement and legal authorities on the yeoman work they have done to protect Abilene and to cooperate with us in the investigation. Once again, you are safe, and it is safe for tourists to visit your wonderful town and the Eisenhower Complex. Thank you.

52

NOW WHAT?

It's a bit anti-climactic and a cliché, but life went on and returned to normal. That does not mean people forgot, certainly the Weston family, but mainly as far as I'm concerned, unspoken outside the family, the O'Briens and Caitlin and Ron's family. It would all be dredged up again a few weeks later before the Thanksgiving Holidays. School and classes had returned to normal; Mariah had done her visits to the big schools for her promising and interested English students; I had done the same for Spanish classes. We saw each other regularly outside of work, in fact were seldom without each other's company, both of us very comfortable with each other and may I say, in love. I guess it showed because Mom and Dad were getting used to the idea, more comfortable with Mariah and she with them, not quite yet a part of the family, but getting close. I need to talk about our visit to Overland Park during that time, shortly after the trial and the newspaper account and then the publicity gradually dying down.

First though, because it's not so involved, was a great day out at the Knights of Columbus Turkey Shoot that late October. It was unseasonably cold, even thought it should have been a bit frosty in Fall. It was not only a church event, but really local and regional, young men and old men, all used to shooting skeet and loving it, and a few feisty girl friends and wives, and the local St. Andrew's ladies handling the home cooked pies and cakes and making the coffee. In some senses it was a replay of the year before.

Lots of talking, laughing and wisecracking by the participants. When it came my turn, with a borrowed shotgun from Dad, I missed most of the skeets, and Sheriff Wiley standing nearby said in a low aside, "Mick, glad you did not have a shotgun in your hands awhile back!" Mariah took her turn and did a respectable job of hitting several skeets. As usual a flask or two was passed around and that swallow of bourbon whiskey burned all the way down. Many folks had not seen either Wiley or me since the bombing incident and were effusive in their congratulations. There was a lot of chatter and good feeling from the ole' church ladies for Mariah, and Mom and Caitlin introduced her to the few who had not met her the during the preceding months. She wasn't exactly quizzed about us but she told me later that that was definitely on some ladies' minds. Some were known to be notorious gossips. A great day.

I needed to tell the above before going on to bring you up to date on Ben and Ariel and family in Overland Park. We actually drove down to see them on a Saturday a week after the Eisenhower bombing. Mariah had called them the night of that day, after we got home from Dad and Mom's, giving them some information so they would not freak out when they saw TV news or the "K.C. Star." And more calls took place as they saw the news. They were a lot more "linked in" because of their visit to Abilene months earlier plus all our conversations, but this added a certain gravity to the conversation. When we drove up and were getting out of the car, they were both out the door and over to hug us, expressing their worry, then their relief. We had dinner, where else? The Stockyard Restaurant and the conversation began there, but ended up in the living room over a couple of scotch and waters.

We basically were asked to give a blow by blow account of it all which we did, me doing a lot of the talking, but Mariah filling in and giving more perspective. Ariel basically wanted to know one thing: were we safe in Abilene? Mariah got up from the divan where we were sitting, went over and gave her a big hug and said, "Yes Mamá. And if it helps you can be reassured by no less than the federal agents and their statement to all of us in Abilene (I noted the "all of us," maybe Mariah felt it was a little more like home). I had brought copies of the "Reflector" with all the stories and pictures, said "It's all here in the paper for you to read and keep." Ben said, "Mick, if it was not confirmed before, you are a true mensch!" And he laughed and laughed. They were both greatly relieved but after a bit the conversation turned to something really more difficult – the future!

I couldn't give a definitive answer because frankly there had been no time to think of it, and Mariah said the same. I did say we had not forgotten the views he had expressed a year ago, and mainly, that we were basically in agreement – Abilene Juco was a small place and maybe our future was larger. I said Mariah and I would talk very soon and let him and Ariel know. Meanwhile, things were the same at Ben's practice, in their lives, in Overland Park. The boys were doing well and were apprised of developments and send their best.

Now with Thanksgiving upon us and Christmas soon, one evening we sat down on the divan over at Mariah's, opened a bottle of wine and had a long talk. As much as we liked each other, make that love, there was the now important matter of the future. We decided, for now, to take it one day at a time. We were committed to the Juco through the end of Spring Term in May. After that, it was decision time. How did we, Mick and Mariah, see the future? After much discussion, swearing to each other our feelings about us, we had to look at the future, options, whatever. One obvious was to sign up for another year in Abilene. Another was that whole concept of a bigger, brighter (may I say) future with graduate school – me in a Ph.D. program of Spanish and Latin American Studies (including starting language study and area study of Brazil), Mariah finishing her Master's in English and then applying to Law School. If we chose the latter, we had to get hot and start the paperwork for entrance to programs, grant applications and all, a huge and time-consuming project. And it meant telling Mom and Dad, Caitlin, Ron and my two far away brothers. And cutting the umbilical in Abilene, that was the worst, I mean, most difficult. We were both well known in town, respected for our work up at the Juco, and in my case, a bit of a local hero. After the Eisenhower Center business and its aftermath, I probably could have run for Mayor (Mariah joked) and won it.

These are the things that change the entire course of your life! And what happens to us if we go the school route? A Ph.D. at best was a matter of three or four years, and so was Law School. We reluctantly concluded marriage was not the answer at the present, for a lot of reasons. So how do you keep the flame burning? The $64,000 question! Pretty sobering. It takes two to tango. Mariah as much as she felt welcome in Abilene, mainly by my family, and secondarily up at work and in the community, said, "We're still so young, only two years going on three out of college. Mick, I'm not ready to settle down, and not in a small country town, in spite of how I love Abilene. But, hey, I think I've found my man." After I recovered from that, I stammered "Me too Mariah." Some kissing and hugging went on. Then, for my part I said, "The study of Spanish, the time studying in Mexico City, our travel, they've all whetted my appetite and also made me think I've got the talent and desire to pursue all that and maybe teach at a university. I think it outdoes the feeling to stay here. I think we have job security and life as you've described, but I think we have to throw the dice."

Agreed. We began the paperwork in early November, applications to college with good programs, in both cases applications for scholarships or fellowships, getting the requests for letters of recommendation in place. That involved one sticky item: we had to tell Professor Halderson and hope he would give us each a fine letter of recommendation. I think he surmised the difficulty when we both made an appointment to see him jointly in his office. His response was great, "Mick and Mariah, the Juco will really be losing a significant part of our efforts and spirit if you go, but I have been in your position years ago, and do appreciate it. You will get the best of recommendations, and as long as I am here, an open door to returning. Two brilliant young professors with advanced degrees would be welcome. I guess it hinges on the outcome of your applications but more so on how you feel at this point being in Abilene. Let's let things stand until May, I'll write your letters right away however. Let's enjoy these next six months. I understand we are a Juco and a new one at that. But we do play an important role, and you have been a big part of that. We'll keep this matter and the letters in private." He shook our hands, said he would be touch.

As we walked out of his office that p.m. got into my car and drove to Mariah's place, we were both pretty quiet. The old cliché, "The Die is Cast." I said, "I can't allow myself to think about it, Mariah." She said, "Mick, that's all right for now, but the decisions won't go away. We love each other." I spent the night with Mariah and we both got down to the serious work toward the future.

53

NO SURPRISES

Thanksgiving and Christmas came and went, really a happy time both with my family in Abilene and Mariah's in Overland Park. She and I packed the car and did a road trip in those cold days, all the way to Destin in Florida with the amazing white sand beach, sea oats, swimming and snorkeling and eating tons of shrimp in all kinds of prepared ways and falling back on southern fried chicken. I can say I didn't eat any grits. On the way down we got a taste of Civil War Days in Jackson, Mississippi, crossed the big river, and spent a night in New Orleans and drank some draft beer in plastic cups on Bourbon Street and some chicory coffee at the Café du Monde on the main old plaza with the church. Oh yeah, and shrimp 'po boys.

There was the now usual stop at the Palafoxes on the way home, the drive to Abilene, checking in with Mom and Dad and getting ready for Spring Term. I think because we were anticipating the future but did not really want to talk about it, all those days with routine, all the social moments and mainly our time together were magnified in mind and memory.

January came, classes started, we all settled in, and then in March the Kansas college visits again. In the middle of March, we each got important letters, Mariah first. She was accepted into the Columbia Law School in New York and Harvard in Boston. I was accepted in the Spanish and Latin

American Studies at Georgetown and the same at Brown. She was offered financial aid, student loans and the like at Harvard (Ben would offer to supplement any help, it was a big order). I was offered a "full-ride" NDEA at Brown, maybe relatively modest but with great care it would cover most expenses. I wrote to Brown right away asking for details, what my eighteen hours of graduate Spanish at K.U. would be worth, and basically how long it might be to the degree. They told me it would cut the time to four years if all went well (three in the classrooms and or in-country experience, one for the dissertation). Part of my decision would be the fact Brown had a terrific Luso-Brazilian program as well, and I was really interested in Brazil. Correspondence back and forth went on, but by the end of April it was time (I hate to use the Kansas cliché again but I will) to "fish or cut bait." It is no accident or coincidence that we ended up choosing Harvard for Mariah, Brown for me. Even though Brown's Portuguese program had closer links to Portugal (the New England connection in Providence), it had fine coverage of Brazil and a couple of the best-known scholars dealing with Brazil. And Providence is just a bus ride from Boston; I joked to Mariah, "The road goes both ways."

We spent the end of that spring term basically saying our goodbyes to friends at the Juco, going to our favorite places to eat (that didn't take long), checking in with Wally Galatin at Frank's Friendly Tavern, Don Winston at the Eisenhower Library (he thanked me and said there would always be a desk in the research area open for me), and then mainly to Mom and Dad, Caitlin and Ron. I don't know if there was disappointment that no "formal" arrangements had been made (i.e. engagement), but we explained the whole rationale, how we were still so young, ambitious for advanced degrees and finally, would be just down the road from each other, an easy arrangement for weekends.

Pretty much the same routine went on in Overland Park. I could tell Ben and Ariel were happy with Mariah's decision, and yes, for me too. They said it would be a good excuse to get back to Boston (visited just once by both) and to see Brown and Newport. We talked of a tentative visit.

We in fact were making the move early, the first week of June, my Fellowship allowing me to start anytime at Brown, and Mariah taking advantage of the final three classes for her Master's in English before starting Law in the Fall. We loaded up both cars and drove together to Boston where she settled down in graduate school housing. We inaugurated the new life with a wonderful time downtown at the Irish Bar next to the famous Boston Oyster Place (we learned a favorite of JFK and his family), and a teary goodbye the next day when I drove on to Providence. Some time passed, it all seemed to be going well, according to plan, when Mariah saw a small item in the "Boston Globe," inside pages. I got an unexpected call from Sheriff Wiley the same day, all this before the stuff hit the fan in the national media the next day.

54

SPEAKING TOO SOON

Wiley's call and then the others were all based on this associated press release of June 11th, 1966:

COMBINED FBI AND ATF FORCES MOVE ON SEPARATIST COMPOUNDS IN IDAHO

(June 11, 1966, AP) Armed Contingents of FBI and ATF Officers surrounded two different compounds of known separatist — extremists and KKK supporters in the wilds of northern Idaho last night and this morning, a few miles east of Coeur d'Alene. The two attacks were synchronized to take place at the same time (to avoid communication and possible escape by the targets). The officers moved in utilizing stealth mode by horseback, foot and supply jeeps in the far rear. Using battery powered megaphones, officers called for the inhabitants living in log cabins and barns on the two sites to come forward with hands up, surrender and be taken to holding sites where they could be transported to jail in the area. The demands were met with shots from windows, doors and barn doors from high-powered rifles and AK 47s. Gunfire took place off and on during the night hours of yesterday and resumed at dawn this morning. Tear gas and smoke grenades were used to flush the separatists from their cabins and barns. Eleven men were killed, four more injured and three Federal Officers were wounded. The injured extremists were taken by

jeep to the Coeur d'Alene federal security prison and its hospital facilities. Officers report that no one escaped the perimeter of the actions. Families of the separatists lived in yet another large compound five miles east of the attack, and all are being held in isolation at present.

What led to the government attacks were several accounts of burglary in the area along with cattle rustling. Unusual sales and hoarding of arms and ammunition were also reported from stores, gun shows and the like as far away as Boise and Pocatello. Additional information was gleaned from neighbors following the bombing attack at the Eisenhower Complex in Abilene, Kansas last Fall.

Although the FBI and ATF had publicized earlier in a rare letter in the "Abilene Reflector Chronicle" addressed to the local citizenry that the "all safe" signal had been given in the town and area after the extremist bombing incident, the arrest, trial and conviction of its perpetrators, it is obvious the Agencies had more under their hats, and perhaps even used the article as a ploy putting associates of the criminals off guard and making them brazen enough to broaden their activities. This latter concept is conjecture at this point but unofficially given by a source in the Agencies.

What is on the mind of this reporter and of the Associated Press itself is this: Was this yet another isolated incident of a local malady or part of a larger "movement" and conspiracy in the United States of America. America is in the midst of a significant military buildup in faraway East Asia in Viet Nam and a battle to contain the Communist threat in that country emanating from Red China. Do we have a small war closer to home? We consider this a wake-up call to all good citizens to be vigilant, to report unusual and suspicious activity to your local law enforcement agencies. We do not know what is on the horizon in this our new "wild west" but it bears watching.

EPILOGUE

Telephone calls and the U.S. mail enabled the communication that ensued between the O'Brien household, the Palafox household, close friends in Abilene and colleagues from the Juco. Front page articles and editorials from "The Abilene Reflector Chronicle" were passed on to me and then to Mariah. The tone was similar to that of the original Associated Press release of the affair. What next? Abilene and the Nation were on alert and on edge. And so were we.

MICK O'BRIEN'S
GALLERY OF PHOTOS

The Farm House

The Eisenhower Museum

The Eisenhower Library

General Dwight D. Eisenhower

The Lebold Mansion

The Seelye Mansion

Another Victorian in Abilene

Yet another Victorian, Abilene

The Sunflower Hotel

The Abilene Public Library

Third Street and the Post Office

The Union Pacific Train Station

The Crucifix, Abilene Catholic Cemetery

The Brown Tombstone

The Seelye Tomb

The Duckwall Stone

The St. Joseph Orphanage Monument

St. Andrew's Stained Glass Window

Pryamid of the Sun, Teotihuacan

The Aztec Sun Calendar

Classic Maya Stela

The Cathedral, Mexico City

Diego Rivera, History of Mexico Mural

Palace, Tomb of Pacal, Palenque

The Palace, Palenque

The Castillo, Chichen-Itza

The Palace and Pryamid, Uxmal

La Giralda, Sevilla

Cathedral Entrance, Sevilla

Catafalque of Christopher Columbus, Seville

The Guadalquivir River, Roman Bridge, Cordoba

The Choir, Renaissance Chapel, the Mosque, Cordoba

The Hapsburg Double
Eagle, the Chapel

The Pulpit and the Bull,
the Chapel, Córdoba

The Statue of Maimonides, Córdoba

Interior Patio, the Alhambra

Salon of the Two Sisters, the Alhambra

Patio de los Leones, el Alhambra

Patio, Gardens, the Alhambra   Mick's Lladro
Piece, El Greco

Famous View of Toledo

The Cathedral of Toledo

The Transito Synagogue, Toledo

INTERNET SITES CONSULTED FOR "A RURAL ODYSSEY II – ABILENE - DIGGING DEEPER"

1. List of Religious Colleges in Kansas
2. List of the Junior Colleges in Kansas
3. Ku Klux Klan – Wikipedia
4. Ku Klux Klan in Kansas – Kansapedia – Kansas Historical Society
5. Kansas Ku Klux Klan - Home
6. The Ku Klux Klan in Kansas City, Kansas. Tim Rives
7. Dickinson County, Kansas, Wikipedia
8. Dickinson County, Kansapedia, Kansas Historical Society;
9. Abilene, Kansas, Wikipedia
10. History of Abilene - Kansas Cattle Towns
11. Major Figures in Abilene, Kansas Cemetery, Bing
12. Churches in Abilene, Kansas – Church Finder.Com
13. St. Andrew Parish in Abilene, Ks: About
14. The History of St. Joseph Home and Orphanage – St. Joseph Sisters of Concordia
15. National Register of Historic Places Listings in Dickinson County
16. David Andrew Brown (1879 -1895). Find a Grave.
17. Views of the Past: C.L. Brown and his Effect of Abilene
18. Jeffcoat Photography Studio Museum – Home
19. Jeffcoat Photography Studio Museum – Live Video
20. Kansas Jewish History

21. Sephardi Jews – Wikipedia
22. Religious Beliefs and Practices of Jewish Americans
23. Judaism 101: Jewish Names
24. Shabbat. Wikipedia
25. Jewish Diaspora. Wikipedia
26. Lebold Mansion – Wikipedia
27. Abilene – Queen of the Kansas Cow Towns – Legends of America
28. The Joseph McCoy Story – Abilene – R.C. Com
29. Timothy Fletcher Hershey (1827-1905) Find a Grave.
30. Chisholm Trail – Kansapedia – Kansas Historical Society
31. Museo Nacional de Historia y Antropología. Wikipedia
32. Diego Rivera. "Historia de México." Mural. Wikipedia
33. La Catedral, el Zócalo. México, D.F. Wikipedia
34. Teotihacán/ Palenque/ Chichén Itzá/ Uxmal. Wikipedia
35. Querétaro. Wikipedia
36. Emperor Maximilian, Wikipedia
37. San Miguel de Allende. Wikipedia
38. Guanajuato. Wikipedia
39. Guadalajara. Wikipedia
40. Acapulco. Wikipedia.
41. La Torre Latino Americana. D.F. Wikipedia
42. History – Abilene Public Library
43. National and State Registers of Historic Places – Kansas
44. Union Pacific Overland Depot – Abilene, KS – Train Station
45. Abilene Depot
46. Street Map of Abilene, Kansas – Bing
47. Views of the Past: the Kirby House Restaurant Destroyed in Fire (The Wichita Eagle)
48. Kansas Department of Transportation: History of Kansas Railroads
49. Union Pacific Railroad – Abandoned Rails
50. About Abilene
51. Barbara Ehrsam – Kansas Historical Society

52. Duckwall – ALCO Stores, Inc – Company History
53. Alva Duckwall Sr. – Kansaspedia – Kansas Historical Society
54. Alva Lease Duckwall – Wikipedia
55. Nicodemus, Kansas, Wikipedia
56. Kansas City Stockyards, Wikipedia
57. Union Stock Yards, Wikipedia
58. History of Antisemitism in the United States, Wikipedia
59. Jewish Sevilla, visit Sevilla from a Jewish perspective
60. Centro de Interpretación Judería de Sevilla,
61. Seville, Spain Jewish History Tour;
62. Parroquia Santa Maria la Blanca
63. Córdoba, Spain, Wikipedia
64. Córdoba synagogue, Wikipedia
65. Mesquita de Córdoba desde el aire
66. The Mosque, Cathedral of Córdoba. Wikipedia
67. The Jewish History of Granada, Spain
68. Maimonides, Wikipedia
69. Alhambra Decree, Wikipedia
70. Hall of Two Sisters, Nasrid Palaces, Alhambra
71. Federico García Lorca. Wikipedia.
72. Seville, Wikipedia
73. Seville Cathedral, Main Altar
74. Alcazar of Seville, Wikipedia
75. The Prado, Wikipedia
76. El entierro del señor de Orgaz, El Greco
77. Burning of the Heretics (Auto da Fe), Berruguete
78. Toledo Cathedral, Wikipedia
79. Toledo School of Translators
80. Sinagoga del Tránsito, Toledo
81. Oklahoma City Bombing

ABOUT THE AUTHOR

Mark Curran is a retired professor from Arizona State University where he worked from 1968 to 2011. He taught Spanish and Portuguese and their respective cultures. His research specialty was Brazil and its "popular poetry in verse" or the "Literatura de Cordel," and he has published many articles in research reviews and now some sixteen books related to the "Cordel" in Brazil, the United States and Spain. Other books done during retirement are of either an autobiographic nature – "The Farm" or "Coming of Age with the Jesuits" - or reflect classes taught at ASU on Luso-Brazilian Civilization, Latin American Civilization or Spanish Civilization. The latter are in the series "Stories I Told My Students:" books on Brazil, Colombia, Guatemala, Mexico, Portugal and Spain. "Letters from Brazil I, II, and III" is an experiment combining reporting and fiction. "A Professor Takes to the Sea I and II" is a chronicle of a retirement adventure with Lindblad Expeditions - National Geographic Explorer. "Rural Odyssey – Living Can Be Dangerous" is "The Farm" largely made fiction. Finally, "A Rural Odyssey – Abilene – Digging Deeper" is a continuation of "Rural Odyssey,"

Published Books

A Literatura de Cordel. Brasil. 1973

Jorge Amado e a Literatura de Cordel. Brasil. 1981

A Presença de Rodolfo Coelho Cavalcante na Moderna Literatura de Cordel. Brasil. 1987

La Literatura de Cordel – Antología Bilingüe – Español y Portugués. España. 1990

Cuíca de Santo Amaro Poeta-Repórter da Bahia. Brasil. 1991

História do Brasil em Cordel. Brasil. 1998

Cuíca de Santo Amaro – Controvérsia no Cordel. Brasil. 2000

Brazil's Folk-Popular Poetry – "a Literatura de Cordel" – a Bilingual Anthology in English and Portuguese. USA. 2010

The Farm – Growing Up in Abilene, Kansas, in the 1940s and the 1950s. USA. 2010

Retrato do Brasil em Cordel. Brasil. 2011

Coming of Age with the Jesuits. USA. 2012

Peripécias de um Pesquisador "Gringo" no Brasil nos Anos 1960 ou 'A Cata de Cordel" USA. 2012

Adventures of a 'Gringo' Researcher in Brazil in the 1960s or In Search of Cordel. USA. 2012

A Trip to Colombia – Highlights of Its Spanish Colonial Heritage. USA. 2013

Travel, Research and Teaching in Guatemala and Mexico – In Quest of the Pre-Columbian Heritage
Volume I – Guatemala. 2013
Volume II – Mexico. USA. 2013

A Portrait of Brazil in the Twentieth Century – The Universe of the "Literatura de Cordel." USA. 2013

Fifty Years of Research on Brazil – A Photographic Journey. USA. 2013

Relembrando - A Velha Literatura de Cordel e a Voz dos Poetas. USA. 2014

Aconteceu no Brasil – Crônicas de um Pesquisador Norte Americano no Brasil II, USA. 2015

It Happened in Brazil – Chronicles of a North American Researcher in Brazil II. USA, 2015

Diário de um Pesquisador Norte-Americano no Brasil III. USA, 2016

Diary of a North American Researcher in Brazil III. USA, 2016

Letters from Brazil. A Cultural-Historical Narrative Made Fiction. USA 2017.

A Professor Takes to the Sea – Learning the Ropes on the National Geographic Explorer.
Volume I, "Epic South America" 2013 USA, 2018.
Volume II, 2014 and "Atlantic Odyssey 108" 2016, USA, 2018

Letters from Brazil II – Research, Romance and Dark Days Ahead. USA, 2019.

A Rural Odyssey – Living Can Be Dangerous. USA, 2019.

Letters from Brazil III – From Glad Times to Sad Times. USA, 2019.

A Rural Odyssey II – Abilene – Digging Deeper. USA, 2020

Professor Curran lives in Mesa, Arizona, and spends part of the year in Colorado. He is married to Keah Runshang Curran and they have one daughter Kathleen who lives in Albuquerque, New Mexico, married to teacher Courtney Hinman in 2018. Her documentary film "Greening the Revolution" was presented most recently in the Sonoma Film Festival in California, this after other festivals in Milan, Italy and New York City. Katie was named best female director in the Oaxaca Film Festival in Mexico.

The author's e-mail address is: profmark@asu.edu
His website address is: www.currancordelconnection.com

Printed in the United States
By Bookmasters